I0568007

# Queens of the Apocalypse

Rob Rosen

Published in the United States by Fierce Publishing
Second Edition

ISBN-10: 0983767858
ISBN-13: 9780983767855

*For Kenny,*
*thank you for rocking my world.*

# PRAISE FOR ROB ROSEN'S NOVELS

*Queens of the Apocalypse*
"One part tongue-in-cheek humor, one part sweet romance, and one part paranormal free for all. The action in the novel is stunningly fast paced, the dialogue clever, and the characters simply hysterical! ... Rob Rosen is one of the most cleverly gifted m/m writers on the scene today."
– Joyfully Jay

*Vamp*
"This is a highly original twist on the whole vampire/werewolf genre. Snarky, saucy, witty. It will keep you howling."
– The San Francisco Examiner

*Queerwolf*
"You have to read this book. It is by far the funniest, best crafted novel I've read in a long time! It marches on without a pause, and sweeps you along in its action packed wake, leaving you gasping for breath and wiping the tears from your eyes from laughter!" – Reviews by Jessewave

*Southern Fried*
"Hands down, this is one of the funniest and oddest books I've ever read, and I mean that in a really good way!" – Rainbow Book Reviews

*Hot Lava*
"Hot Lava by Rob Rosen is, for this reader, another vastly entertaining and winning book. Actually, I'd go so far as to say that it is a winner for anyone who loves humor, mystery, adventure and, oh yes, men… lots of sexy men and some very steamy lovin'" – Dark Divas

*Divas Las Vegas*
"A rollicking, roller coaster of a read, sure to keep you smiling. Five stars out of five on your fun reading slot machine!" – Echo Magazine

*Sparkle: The Queerest Book You'll Ever Love*
"A gloriously, uproariously funny and immensely touching novel that's impossible to pigeonhole into a single genre. Part who-dunnit, part satire, part memoir, with a perfectly portioned serving of poignancy on the side, this story will surely touch your heart and tickle your funny bone."
– Top 2 Bottom Reviews

# FOREWORD
## BY SISTER ROMA

Two hours. That's the answer to the #1 question people ask me: "How long does it take you to do...*all that?*" Most people just nod and give an appreciative coo, while others are completely flabbergasted. "Two hours? Wow! That's a long time!" Though, there are many who reply with "Two hours? Is that all? Your makeup is so perfect/beautiful/amazing" which, by the way, is the correct and perfect response. You see, the first thing you must know about all drag queens is this: we love compliments, flattery, and adoration. We don't spend two hours in the mirror beating our mugs and agonizing over the perfect outfit and accessories to go unnoticed. I'm just going to admit it: I crave attention—and I get a lot of it. I mean, I'm not "The Most Photographed Nun In The World™" for nothing. I love interacting with people—it gives me life. I'll never understand the occasional queen who gets all dolled up and goes out, then acts like a complete bitch. If you don't like interacting with people, you're wearing the wrong shoes, lady.

The second thing you must know about drag queens is that it takes balls to wear a dress. True, our balls may be tucked up and put away for future use, but trust me, our balls are huge. We are fearless, brave, and tough as nails. I will boldly go where no drag queen has ever gone before. I've spoken at national press conferences, flown on airplanes, shopped at Safeway, stumbled drunkenly through the Tenderloin at 4 a.m., and marched proudly in the first ever Fresno Pride Parade—all in high drag. And if you've ever been to Fresno, I don't have to tell you which was scarier.

1

The Fresno chapter of the KKK was out in full force, complete with their "God Hates Fags" signs and six year old children flipping us the bird. They were almost as hateful and scary as the right-wing Christians protesting at the National March on Washington in 1994. Now there's the face of evil. But this is America, so both the KKK and the Fundamentalists have a right to their opinion; they have just as much right to protest as we do to celebrate. Don't worry, I know that most of those people are bat-shit crazy, but, to be completely honest, I admire their conviction. They believe they're right and I'm wrong just as much as I KNOW that I'm right and they're wrong. I take a great deal of satisfaction in knowing that I've enraged, shocked, and pissed off a group of close-minded, homophobic bigots. Those are the people who need to see me and hear what I have to say, goddammit. And, yes, in case you can't tell, I'm a bit of an activist, so having such huge balls comes in really handy.

Here's another thing you should know about drag queens: don't call us by our boy name when we're in drag. Don't call a drag queen or anyone who presents themselves as female 'him' or 'he' or 'sir' or 'man'. It's rude. In public, it's pretentious to attempt to show familiarity with a drag queen by letting others know that you know her 'real' name. To be honest, my given name is rarely used by me or anyone else. If you ask me my name, I'll tell you it's Roma; that's the name I chose and I'm proud of it. Everyone calls me Roma, especially my closest friends. Even friends from high school and some family members who knew me long before I did drag call me Roma, whether I'm in drag or not. It doesn't get any more real than that.

The fourth thing you should know about drag queens is very important: we don't hate women. In fact, quite the contrary. Drag is an homage—a tribute—to women and all things female and feminine. If drag queens didn't respect women, we'd dress like a member of the Texas Senate, not a smoking-hot member of the Pussy Cat Dolls.

Just for the record, I'm not making fun of nuns either. I am a nun. The Sisters of Perpetual Indulgence ARE nuns. We minister to our community, we educate, we protect, we fundraise, we feed the hungry, we care for the sick, and we provide spiritual enlightenment. Each of us takes a vow to "expiate stigmatic guilt and promulgate universal joy"—and we look fabulous doing it. The organization was founded on Easter Sunday in 1979 and remains one of the most controversial and iconic LGBT organizations ever devised. Among other things, the Sisters have always been on the front lines in the battle against HIV/AIDS, focusing on education and raising funds for organizations that provide practical care to the community. The Sisters were the first group ever to produce a safer-sex pamphlet called Playfair (which continues to be updated and reprinted today), and the first group ever to produce an AIDS fundraiser: a dog show at the Castro Theatre hosted by Shirley MacLaine. I'm very proud to be one of the longest standing, continuously active, and most recognizable members of the Order. That being said, if someone had told me that one day I'd be a drag queen who dressed like a nun, I would have thought they had certainly lost their damn mind. Who had ever heard of such a thing?

I discovered the Sisters and drag at the same time, and it was quite by accident. I moved to San Francisco to escape the oppression and banality of Grand Rapids, Michigan immediately upon graduation from college in 1985. (This brings us to the fifth thing you should know about drag queens: never ask us our age. Most of us will give you the age we hope to be perceived by others. I will give you the number of years I've been doing drag, which is 26. I'm dreading turning the "big 3-0," but I digress.) I was your atypical gay twenty-something living the dream in a new city. I had my own place, a decent job, and I believed the whole world revolved around me. I was out to get made, paid, and laid. I had a wonderful social circle of similarly self-centered but amicable upwardly mobile homos with whom I spent many a happy hour boozing it up in the Castro. One evening after work, I was standing in the middle of the Midnight Sun dressed in my pinstripe button-down shirt and power tie, swilling two-for-one cocktails, and laughing at a clip from *Designing Women*. Suddenly the front door flew open and in sashayed Sister Luscious Lashes—and my life changed forever. Now mind you, I had never heard of the Sisters of Perpetual Indulgence, I had never known a drag queen personally, and I certainly had never been in drag or even considered it. So you can imagine my utter shock when this queen walked right up to me and said "Hello, Michael" (oh-oh, I just told you my given name. Don't ever use it.) It turns out that Sister Luscious happened to be one of my best friends that, until that moment, I had only known as Norman Schrader. Norman was a bartender in the Fillmore (back when there used to be gay bars on Fillmore Street) and one of my best drinking buddies. Norman told me about the Sisters and persuaded me to volunteer at different events with the group, but I always remained in my civilian clothing. That is until one fateful Sunday afternoon when we were getting ready to go to root for the S.F. Eagle's gay softball team, and Norman casually suggested that I just "try the makeup." As it turned out, makeup was like my heroine. All it took was once, and I was 100% hooked.

Aside from discovering a deep, deep love for makeup and drag, the most earth-shattering change in me was on the inside. The Sisters awakened in me a deep sense of love for my community and mankind. They turned my focus from my hair to the injustices and hypocrisies of the world. I was impressed by the accomplishments of the Order, which at the time was just really about six or seven active members, and by the impact this handful of passionate people was having on society and the world. I realized that was passionate and even compassionate and that I wanted to be a part of it. I decided that I wanted to join the Order so that my life would not have been in vain. I want people to say that the world is a better place because I was in it.

There is a lot of power in drag. Drag has been my tool, and Sister Roma has been my vehicle to create change, to bring joy, to expand people's minds, to make a difference. My, that sounds terribly lofty. Don't get me wrong, I do it for a lot of other reasons too—like to get dick. Yes, there are guys who are into sex with drag queens. (This may be the sixth thing you should know—whether you want to or not.) I also do it so I don't have to pay for drinks, wait in line, or pay a cover charge. Actually, these are all perks (even the dick), but it doesn't hurt.

It might be important to realize that not all drag queens get the same treatment, though. I've achieved full-on rock-star status. Not gonna lie. People know me. But the newer queens, they don't have it so easy. Just like Joan Rivers playing a dive bar in Omaha, a drag queen must pay her dues.

This brings us to the seventh thing you must realize about drag queens: we wear many different hats. We are simultaneously the mothers, the sisters, the cheerleaders, the spokes models, and the scapegoats of the LGBT community—but above all else, we are entertainers. The first drag queen I ever saw perform was Odessa Brown at the Carousel bar in downtown Grand Rapids. She performed "And I Am Telling You," Jennifer Holiday's iconic showstopper from *Dreamgirls*. When that 400-pound black diva got on her knees and started pounding the stage screaming "and you, and you, and you, you're gonna LOVE ME," I did. I jumped to my feet and screamed and cried and threw dollar bills at her. She was a star, and I was starstruck in the truest sense of the word. Back in the day, that's what drag queens were, local stars headlining at local dive bars, pouring their hearts and souls out for their local fans. Today, thanks to social media and the phenomenon of RuPaul's Drag Race, drag queens are international superstars. Today's top drag queens are world-famous moguls with their own brands (RuPaul, ChiChi LaRue); comic geniuses (Jackie Beat, Lady Bunny, Varla Jean Merman, CoCo Peru); and hard-working Hollywood actors (Willam Belli, Shangela). Drag queens are taking over the world, appearing at Pride celebrations, in nightclubs, and on TV and radio around the globe, from Hollywood to Dubai. Today, the sky's the limit for a man in a dress!

So, c'mon, just "try the makeup." And then get some fierceness tips from the queens in the hilarious pages that follow.

*xoxo Roma*

# CHAPTER ONE
## THE LEAST OF OUR PROBLEMS

"That bitch!" shouted Blondella as a silver can whizzed by me.

"Which bitch?" I asked with a heavy sigh, Lee Press-ons held up for close inspection as the can rolled around the floor before coming to a rest against my fabulous Jimmy Choos. Knock-offs, yes, but the guy on the corner promised me that no one would know the difference. Or at least no one past the first few rows—when the lights were dimmed, of course. And who could possibly spot the glue that held the heels on anyway? From past the fourth row, I mean.

"Which bitch?" came her world-weary reply. "Kit. Bitch used up all my hairspray yet again."

I turned and glanced her way. Blondella Bombshell had her hair jacked up so high it was a wonder she didn't topple over. Then again, drag queens frequently wobble, but they never fall down. When they're sober, at any rate. Which, thankfully, we rarely were. "One errant match," I made note in reply, pointing at her platinum hive, "and *KAPOW!*" Then I turned back to the mirror and began my daily moisturizing routine.

She chuckled as she rummaged around for a second can. "Be that as it may, Destiny, it was mine, not hers, and she is, as I said, a bitch." The second can was promptly found, another coat applied to the towering, temporarily inferno-less mess that sprouted dangerously above her head like a garden desperately in need of a good pruning.

I nodded. "She's only a bitch when she's low on sugar."

The chuckle repeated as the heady aroma of jasmine-infused aerosol wafted my way, an ozone hole seemingly widening above our heads. "And exactly what year was Miss Kit Kat low on sugar? She practically owns half the *M* and most of the *&* with a lease on the second *M* as it is."

Blondella had a point. Still, who was I, Destiny St. James, to cast the first stone? Or in Kit's case, boulder, because one measly stone would barely leave a dent in all that girdle-encased rotundity. Yes, though far be it from me to say it—to her face, as opposed to behind her wide expanse of back—Kit looked like a cross between Aretha Franklin and Jennifer Hudson, pre-Weight Watchers. And by "cross" I mean take Aretha and take Jennifer and mash 'em together, and voila, you get Kit in size, color, and diva-demeanor. Seriously, she should've been counting her blessings that the music at the club was so blaringly loud, because otherwise, she'd be lip-synching to nothing but the squeaking floorboards beneath her size twelve feet all night long.

In any case, in she walked, or at least waddled, a few moments later, the steel door shutting behind her. And yes, I said steel. See, the dressing room had once been a meat locker back in the day, the club itself a converted restaurant located just outside The Castro. Pretty to look at, but, like my shoes, only in dim lighting and from a distance. Or if you weren't sober. Then again, like us, our patrons rarely were. Thankfully. Because tip ratio equates to drink ratio. In other words, the drunker they were, the better we looked and the more do re mi dough (hairspray, moisturizer, candy bars) for all of us.

"Bitches!" Kit shouted in cheery greeting, a Snickers bar waved like a wand above her head.

"Yes," said Blondella icily. "We already covered that." She gave Kit the onceover—twice. "Girl, you look like ten pounds of potato in a five-pound sack."

"Says the queen in her fifties wearing the fifteen-year-old's dress," came the snarky reply as Kit took her squeaking seat in front of her makeup mirror. "Was there a rummage sale down at the high school, hon?"

"Thirties," came the teeth-gritted reply. "*Not* fifties."

Kit turned and squinted at the ever-shellacked Blondella. "If you say so." Then she giggled and turned back to the mirror, lipstick tube momentarily replacing the Snickers bar.

In truth, none of us knew exactly how old Blondella was. None of us, after all, had ever seen her out of drag, out of makeup, or out of her monstrous expanse of wig. If she had a driver's license, it was about as well-hidden as the pores on her face. Best guess, though, I'd say forties. High-end. Low in the dim light. And yes, there wasn't anything above fifty watts within the club's walls. Mandatory. Drag queens' law. Enacted and brutally enforced by all ten of us girls. Well, boy-girls. Um, men-bitches, really.

In any case, terms of endearment at an end, we went back to work on our faces. With the club opening in a few hours, we barely had enough time to prepare. Especially once the other performers arrived and war promptly ensued. Because ten of us and six makeup mirrors made Vietnam look like a night at Disney.

So before all hell broke loose, we eagerly primped and preened and glossed and coated and sprayed and glued and—*groan*—tucked merrily away.

Though, of course, all hell did in fact break loose soon enough.

Seriously.

*SERIOUSLY!*

All hell and a good part of Oakland, for that matter. *BOOOOM!* we heard first, with a couple of extra vowels thrown in the middle for effect. Then the floors shook, the steel screeched within its brick encasing, and Kit's belly Jelloooed, again with a couple of extra vowels in the middle. And then the three of us shrieked, very unlady and certainly unmanly like.

"Earthquake!" shouted Blondella. "Duck and cover." She quickly ducked under Kit's broad cover.

Me, I dove under the table my mirror sat upon. "That didn't feel like any earthquake I've ever felt before," I managed, body trembling, manicured hands grasping the table legs, mouth in a pant. "That felt like an explosion. Like a friggin' bomb went off."

"Or a case of Blondella's hairspray," offered Kit, kicking the drag queen at her feet.

Blondella grunted. "Hammer-toed bitch. Stop it," she whined. "That was an earthquake, and you're the thing in here least likely to crumble under your own weight." She paused and reconsidered her remark. "Probably."

Then we all sat there and waited for the aftershocks. Because any earthquake that large had to have mighty-ass aftershocks. Loads of 'em. Only, all we heard was our collective breathing. The earth, it seemed, had raised a ruckus and then promptly piped down, which, all in all, was very unlike itself.

"Huh," huhed Blondella ten minutes later. "Guess that was it. Let's go survey the damage."

"Gin bottles better be in one piece," groused Kit.

"Amen," I agreed, hand resting over fake chest at the mere thought.

And so out we went, my heart racing as the steel door swung open and the three of us peeked outside. A trio of relieved sighs followed as we emerged, the club just as we'd left it. Then we rushed up to the bar, only to find that all was a-okay as well. Deathly silent, yes, but in one glorious piece, gin bottles included. *Phew.*

"Guess we eluded catastrophe this time," said Kit, kissing the side of a clear bottle of booze, lipstick smudge left in her hefty wake.

Still, something didn't seem right, didn't *feel* right. "Sure is quiet, though," I made note. "No one milling about, no cars driving by, no sirens or honks or shouts. Nothing."

The other two craned their necks up, ears pointed to the front door. "She's right," said Blondella. "Nada."

"Weird," agreed Kit, a lemon-sized lump gliding down her less-than-slender throat.

We each moved forward, side by side by side as we headed for the door, my heart beating in my chest, the padding doing little to hide the obvious *lub-dub* pounding in double time. Slowly, I opened the door, the sun so bright that we were instantly blinded, hands quickly raised to block the rays as a tear streaked down my face, my mouth going all Saharan on me.

Sunlight: the bane of a drag queen's existence.

Too bad that turned out to be so literally true, though.

"Look," croaked out Blondella, finger pointing left, right, left again, up and down the block, her mouth gaping open, eyes wide, sweat smearing through all that caked-on makeup.

"What the…" I barely managed.

"Fuck?" Kit finished my train of thought.

"They're not moving," whispered Blondella, finger still outstretched as we took in one lifeless body after the next, all of them flat on the sidewalks, in the street, hunched over steering wheels, crumpled against buildings, the absolute silence of the grisly scene completely unnerving. "Are they…"

"Dead?" It was Kit again.

I moved away from the door, tentatively stepping a few feet up the sidewalk to the nearest body, a woman on her back, eyes staring up into nothingness, chest still. Dry heaving, I bent down, two fingers held out just above her jugular. I pressed down only to retract them a fraction of a second later.

"What's wrong?" shouted Blondella, gripping the club's door.

I jumped up and turned. "She's searing hot," I yelled back. "Burned my fingers." Blondella scratched at her wide expanse of wig, while Kit just scratched at her wide expanse. I, in turn, hurried back their way, terrified that whatever happened to these people was soon to happen to us as well. "She certainly looked…"

"Dead?"

I punched Kit in her arm. "Stop doing that," I told her. "And yes, dead. Hot and dead. Baked where she stood, by the looks of her, and of… of them." And now it was my turn to point.

"But how?" croaked out Blondella. "Some sort of weapon? Kills everyone but leaves the buildings intact?"

"Everyone but *us*," amended Kit as she wiped the sweat off her furrowed brow.

"We were in the meat locker," I reminded them. "That must've protected us; the steel, I mean. Blocked whatever it was that baked them." And still my finger kept pointing. "But how many of *them* are there exactly?"

Blondella reached into her front pocket and removed her cell phone. She looked something up and then dialed. "Police," she mouthed as we waited. And waited. And waited some more. "Fuck," she soon cursed, then dialed 911, only to repeat the curse a minute later. "No one's answering. What if they're all…"

I turned to Kit. "Don't say it."

"But what if they are?" she replied, tears welling up in her chocolate-brown eyes. "What if everyone is… is…"

"Impossible," I said. "It has to be localized. If it's a weapon of some sort, it can't go beyond a few miles, right?"

We all took our cell phones out, all of us dialing. And dialing. And dialing, until my fingers began to cramp and sheer panic ran up and down my back like a runaway freight car.

"No one is answering," said Kit, voice cracking. "No one anywhere. And I called friends in Europe, too. All I got were messages, answering machines."

"Same here," coughed Blondella.

"Same here," said I, head low as I imagined all my friends and family, all of them looking like the bodies scattered around us. "But it just can't be. What if the phones aren't working properly? What if the satellites are down?"

Kit shook her head, jowls jiggling. "Then we wouldn't have gotten rings on their ends and bars on ours."

And then, when all seemed lost, Blondella nearly dropped her phone. "I have a message," she informed, almost breathless now. "From Johnny. And it came not five minutes ago."

Johnny was Blondella's supposed boyfriend. Supposed because, like her age and boy-face and body, he was a mystery, never seen or heard of except in passing by Blondella herself. "What's it say?" I asked, panting again, a sea of sweat pouring down my face, my makeup thankfully waterproof and surprisingly holding up much better than I was.

She pressed a button and held the phone to her bejeweled ear. It didn't stay there long, but a smile quivered on her face just the same. "Are you okay?" she said.

Kit chuckled. "Girl, I've been a hell of a lot better."

"No," said Blondella. "That's what the message said: *are you okay?*" Again she stared down at the phone screen. "It came just after the blast. My phone was on vibrate. I probably didn't feel it since the room itself was already vibrating. But it definitely came after the blast; I'm sure of it."

I grabbed the phone and also stared down. It was impossible to tell when the blast hit, but it was certainly around the time of the call. Plus, there was the message itself: *are you okay?* Meaning, was she okay after what had happened. "Johnny's in New York, isn't he?"

She nodded, gulped, clearly understanding the question's implication. "His business is there."

Kit was also now looking at the phone. "What kind of business is he in?"

She looked at each of us in turn. "Shipwrecks."

"What, is he some sort of pirate?" asked Kit, always eager to make a dig, even at the worst times. And, clearly, *this* was the worst of times. Ever. Wait, let's go bigger with that. *EVER!*

Blondella shook her head. "Salvages them. Up and down the Eastern coast."

And then my own smile quivered, as did Blondella's. Kit, suffice it to say, remained lost. Perhaps her sugar had indeed run low; that always seemed to do the trick. "I don't get it," she freely admitted, reaching into her other pocket for a Milky Way bar. Eagerly, she bit down on it, her eyelids fluttering upon contact. When they opened up again, she too was finally smiling. "Wait, don't those salvage boats have mini-subs?"

Blondella's smile returned as well, brighter this time. "Now she's getting it."

"So he could've survived whatever it was that blast was," I said. "If he was in a metal boat beneath the water's surface, I mean. Right?"

She didn't answer. In fact, she was already turning and heading back inside the club, the two of us running after her. Or at least, me running. Kit, well, she was just barely managing a rapid waddle, the remnants of her Milky Way getting sucked off her fingers.

Still, we followed Blondella back inside the dressing room. Seconds later, she was flinging gowns and makeup into every bag she could find, just like a whirling drag Dervish.

Kit grunted as she sat down and watched. "'Bout time you got rid of that crap."

Blondella turned and glared. "I'm not getting rid of it, you fat fuck. I'm packing it up."

"Um, and why is that?" I hazarded to ask.

She paused momentarily and wiped the sweat from her forehead before she pushed her tits back in place. "I'm going to New York. Johnny is alive. I know it. And I have to get to him. Fast."

"Call him then," said Kit, saying it more out of a dare than anything else, knowing full well that Johnny was likely more dead than alive, that there might've been a delay before the message went to voicemail. I knew it too, but didn't especially feel good about rubbing salt in the gaping wound.

Blondella stood there, staring at us. "I… I already did. He was the first person I dialed."

"And?"

Her lips went reedy thin. "He didn't answer."

"And?" Kit crossed her thick arms over her ample bosom—no padding needed, just some cinching to create the effect of real girly boobs. It was oddly effective if not a tad bit disconcerting.

Blondella closed the gap between them. "*And* I'm going to New York. *And* I know he might be dead, but I don't care, because he could just as easily be alive, like we're somehow still alive. *And* for all we know, maybe lots more of us are alive and it'll just take us leaving San Francisco to find out. *And* if you want to come, then come, but, for the love of God, please shut the fuck up already and start packing."

I nodded and walked toward her, my hand on her shoulder, a comforting squeeze administered. "Blondella, you saw the bodies out there, the cars. The roads will be blocked, even if the devastation is simply localized. There's no way we can drive out of here."

It was then that Kit snapped her fingers. Or at least tried to. Because that was like snapping two sausages together and hoping for a popping sound. "The TV up at the bar," she said. "Let's see about that localization."

"Good idea," I said, already heading out of the dressing room, the others behind me. The TV flicked on a moment later as Kit poured us all a round of tequila shots. "Or, um, maybe not such a good idea," I added as I pressed the channel button on the remote, each station with their emergency messages flashing and not one with a live person staring back our way.

"Doesn't prove anything," said Kit, downing her glass in one fell swoop, eyes squinting as the alcohol burned down her throat. "The blast. It might've just knocked everything out, everything, it seems, but the electricity."

"She has a point," I allowed.

Blondella grimaced. "No points," she said, finger aimed Kit's way. "All rounded edges. In any case, yes, the blast might've knocked out the TV." She turned on the nearby stereo, static crackling through the speakers, the grimace widening. "And the radio." Then she held up her phone, only to find that there was nothing new on Yahoo News past the blast time. "And the Internet." She sighed and slammed her shot glass on the bar. "But I'm still going to New York. Sitting here and waiting is *not* an option. Johnny needs me. I can feel it."

"Girl," said Kit. "What you're feeling is that too-tight wig of yours cutting off the oxygen to your pea-sized brain." Then she held up her hand before the verbal sparring could pick up again. "But I agree with you on one thing: waiting here doesn't seem like such a hot idea,

13

despite the ample quantities of booze at our general disposal."

I groaned and downed my shot. "But that doesn't solve our problem," I told them. "*How* do we get out of here?"

It was then that the door burst open, a thick shaft of light pouring in as we three, um, *girls* screeched like a record album with about fifty scratches running across it. "Least of your problems," he said, standing there in jeans and boots and a tight denim jacket and not the least bit dead and scorching like all the others. Though he was awfully *hot* just the same.

"What's that supposed to mean?" I asked. "And why aren't you dead?"

He chuckled, the sound riding shotgun down my spine before swirling around my midsection, prick pulsing upon impact. Then he raced to the bar and also poured himself a shot from our tequila bottle, a double, gulping it down in a heartbeat. And speaking of which, mine went into overdrive when he reached into his jacket and pulled out a gun before setting it down on the bar. "Funny thing that," he replied, with a satisfied belch.

"Funny *ha-ha?*" asked Kit. "Because that gun of yours looks anything but."

He shrugged. "Okay, nix funny and go with lucky." He grinned and downed a second shot, also a double. "Lucky for me, anyway." Then he jumped up and locked the door behind him. With us inside. And suddenly that midsection of mine was knotted up so tight that it could just about dock the Queen Mary. The boat that is. Not the performer who went on just after my act. If I even still had one, that is. If any of us did.

"Um, not exactly good timing to rob the place," I told him, voice trembling just about as much as my legs were by that point. "The register is empty, and the world seems to have gone to pot."

"Speaking of which," he said, reaching into his other pocket, a joint held up like a beacon in the night. It was promptly lit, promptly toked, and then, thank goodness, promptly passed around. "Now, as to the lucky thing," he continued, inhaling all the while before letting out an acrid blast of smoke that wafted in swirls as the light from the darkened window hit it. "I was down the street in my bank when that weird sonic boom shit happened."

"But, again, how come you're still alive?" asked Kit, a second blast of smoke blown up, the joint held out to me next.

He nodded. "That lucky thing." He took another shot, another toke. "I was inside the safe deposit vault when…"

"*BOOM!*" blasted Kit.

We all jumped, the stranger included. "Sorry," I said. "She does that a lot. Too much sugar."

He nodded as he stared her way. "I can see that. In any case, I went outside to see what was up, and everyone was dead. Everyone in the bank, everyone in the street, everyone in their cars. All dead. Which meant that I needed a drink more than a fistful of cash all of a sudden. Hence my entry into your fine establishment. And the gun I grabbed off the guard, just in case."

I too nodded, eyes still fixed to said gun. "You were, it appears, safe in the vault. Same for us in our dressing room. Must be all the metal, blocks whatever it was that happened. But, uh, if you don't mind me asking, uh…"

"Max," he informed, hand held out, contact made, heart *lub-dubbing* all over again.

"Yes, Max, a pleasure," I said. "And I'm Destiny, and this is Blondella, and this is Kit." I pointed to each of us in turn. "But if you don't mind me asking, what did you mean when you came in here and said *least of our problems*?"

He snapped his fingers and hopped off the stool, motioning with his upheld digit that we should follow him, which we did, to the window to the right of the now-locked door. "Ah, right. Nearly forgot. Geez, that's some strong weed."

"Got that right," agreed Kit, teetering at his side.

"Anyway," he continued, with a stoned grin. "See, the dead were scattered everywhere, just like I said." He paused. "At first, that is to say."

And no, I didn't like the sound of that. Especially when he stared out the window and pointed outside. And then I knew what he meant by *at first* and *the least of our problems*. The dead, you see, were even more of a problem for us now that they were no longer quite dead. Or at least not the prone or crumpled or leaning-against-buildings kind of dead.

"Holy crap," I managed, a lump the size of Cleveland lodged in my throat.

"Ain't nothing holy about *that*," said Kit, pointing at the throng that had amassed outside, all of them very much erect. And not the good kind of erect either. No sir, no how. Not by a long shot.

"But how?" squeaked out Blondella.

Max shrugged and again turned our way. "Beats the hell out of me," he said, turning to go sit on his stool again. "One minute they were dead, the next, well, undead. Sort of. Like, uh, mostly dead but with privileges. And by the looks of things, they know we're in here, and they look kinda hungry, if you ask me."

Blondella pointed at Kit. "Buffet."

"Funny, tired queen," she said, slapping Blondella's hand away. "And fuck you very much."

Max suddenly squinted at each of us in turn. "Wait a minute. *Tired queen?*" Then he looked around. "What kind of bar is this?"

I grinned. "Drag bar. Couldn't you tell?"

He shook his head. "Place is fucking dark as night in here."

The three of us smiled knowingly and nodded in sync. "We know, sugar," said Blondella. "We know."

# CHAPTER TWO
# WALKING THE PLANK

"Is there a back door to this place?" asked Max.

Kit snickered. "I got your back door right—"

"Stop it, Kit," I cautioned. "Not now. Please." Then I turned to Max and replied, "Sadly, no; just the front one. The back one got closed in when they built a condo behind us."

To which Blondella added, "But there is a roof exit and a fire escape."

I nodded, having forgotten that route. "She's right."

"She?" he asked, with a tilt of his head and a grin on his stubbled face.

"Sorry. Pronoun rules sort of fly out the window around this place." And since a pronoun is merely used in place of a noun, we long ago decided to use she and her in place of our names, which, granted, was kind of redefinition of she and her—as if anyone could define us to begin with. Besides, we knew that deep down (like Marianas Trench deep), we were all men. Well, mostly all.

"Plus," said Kit, pointing at Blondella, "if she's a he, we ain't never seen the proof of it."

Blondella pushed past us and headed for a side door. "*She* is most definitely a he, whore," she replied over her shoulder. "And, trust me, my *proof* trumps yours eight to one." She turned and glared. "In inches, I mean."

Kit adjusted her girdle and ignored the comment, mainly because it was most likely true. Or at least from what I could tell in the changing room. Not that I looked. Usually. And then we were all following Blondella through the door and up the stairs to that aforementioned roof.

Again the sun hit, wilting us upon impact. "Fuck, it's hot," groused Kit. "And it ain't ever hot in San Francisco, at least not this time of year."

I nodded as I made my way to the side of the building, uneager to look over and down to the street but doing so just the same. There were more of them now, and many more slowly approaching, dragging their bodies as if on impulse alone, heads lolling to the side, hands limp, jaws the same. They looked like rag dolls that had somehow been wound up and set in motion.

Kit and Blondella were suddenly standing to my left, Max to my right, all of us staring down as a hot breeze whipped past us. "Maybe they're just here to see the show," offered Kit.

Blondella snickered. "They didn't make it when they were alive, so why bother now?"

I nodded, stomach turning like so much rancid milk. "If we're the only things alive"—I pointed to the sky, not even a pigeon flitting about—"and they're all down there"—my finger moved skyward to groundward—"then they must be able to smell us or hear us or, well, just know we're here. But why act on that?"

It was then that we heard the telltale click, which echoed out in all directions. I turned and stared as Max held the gun in front of him, aiming it down to the sidewalk below. "Better question, what are we going to do about it?"

I sighed and wiped the river of perspiration off my forehead, the pot-high evaporating right along with it. "Unless that gun of yours is a fifty shooter, Max, I'd say we should go back to the why and skip the what for now."

He shook his head and fired, the sound ringing in my ears as we watched the bullet slice through a man in the crowd before coming out his back and ricocheting off the street. It lodged in a Mini Cooper. As for the man, he reeled left, but then just as quickly reeled back right, apparently no worse the wear, apart from already being dead and all.

"Know thine enemy, Destiny," said Max, another shot fired, this time taking off half the dead guy's face, a third slamming into his chest, but still he remained upright if not at a slight tilt. The dead, it seemed, couldn't get any deader. Go figure.

"And what do we now *know*?" moaned Kit.

Max pocketed the gun and turned her way. "That we're screwed."

She touched fingertip to nose. "Bingo, hon. B-I-N-G-the fuck-O. Anything else?"

He shrugged. "Nope. That about covers it." He turned and stared at the fire escape this time, the one leading right down into the thick of things—and undead things at that. "That the only escape?"

Kit nodded, Blondella nodded, and I made it frightfully unanimous. "Afraid so, hon," lamented Blondella.

I tapped him on his shoulder. "Think they'll just give up and go away? I mean, we have enough booze and pretzels and nuts to last us for weeks and weeks. Why not just hunker down and wait them out, then hightail it out of here once the coast is clear?"

But it was Kit that answered. "There's not a Snickers or a Mounds or even a lowly Hershey's Kiss, Destiny, that's why," she said ever so sadly. "And besides, why would they give up? They have all the time in the world. Doubtful they need food or water or shelter, doubtful even that they have thoughts anymore, so maybe that coast of yours will remain forever fog-enshrouded."

"She's probably right," said Max.

"First time for everything," Blondella chimed in with. "But what choice do we have?"

We four stood there on the roof, all of profusely sweating as the silence enveloped us. Strange that the world is usually so loud and it takes the end of it for you to realize that. Still, we weren't quite out of hope just yet.

"The condo," said Max, with a snap of his fingers, the sound jolting me out of my stupor.

I looked from our building to the one behind it. There was a gap between them, and a pretty wide one at that. "Not in these shoes, dude," I groaned.

"Not in any shoes," tossed in Kit. "Not unless they got some with wings on them."

"And are jet-fueled," added Blondella, pointing at the mass that was Kit.

"Ladies," said Max, hands up all referee-like. "Please, it's our only chance to make it out of here alive." He walked to the rear ledge, gauged the distance, and then returned. "Watch," he said, taking off at a gallop before all of a sudden jumping in the air, legs pedalling as he majestically soared and came in for a perfect landing on the other side. "Easy."

"Blondella is easy," Kit snapped. "*That* was anything but."

"*Hardy har har*," faux-chuckled our mega-wigged friend as she slipped off her heels and also took off, rhinestone-studded mini-dress shimmering in the sunlight as she dove across the great divide, rolling on the other side with a loud *hrmph* before popping back up. "Easy *and* alive! Top that, you fat cow!"

Kit now looked worried and turned my way. "I'm scared, Destiny," she managed, voice uncharacteristically trembling. "Help."

I nodded and walked to the edge of the building. "Anything over there to make this a little easier? A board, a plank, something sturdy, besides Blondella's hair?"

The two across the way nodded and started looking around, the seconds ticking by like they were steeped in molasses, the sun hot enough to fry an egg, or perhaps a drag queen or three.

"Found one!" shouted Blondella, Max running to her side as the two lifted up a board, which was about ten feet long and a foot wide.

Again Kit looked my way. "She's kidding, right?"

"How thick is it?" I shouted to them.

Blondella grunted. "Thicker than your head, bitch. Take it or leave it."

I looked at Kit. "It's our only shot, Kit. You have to try." Max lifted the board and slowly pushed it across to us until one end was resting on our building, the other on theirs. It looked sturdy if not frightfully narrow. Emphasis on the narrow. Though looking at Kit, maybe the emphasis should've gone to the frightfully. "I'll hold it over here, sugar. You just take it slow, and you'll be fine."

"Says the skinny-ass bitch," she grumbled as she suspiciously eyed the board. "You, um, you think it'll hold?"

*Fuck if I know*, I thought, but said instead, "For sure, Kit. For sure. Just go really slowly and don't look down."

She nodded, gulped, and kicked off her heels before hiking up her skirt. "Slowly. Don't look down." She moved to the edge of the building. "Slowly. Don't look down." I held her hand as she managed her way atop the board, Blondella and Max already holding the other end as they stared anxiously our way. "Slowly. Don't look down." Then she looked at me. "Hold it steady, girl."

"I will, Kit," I told her, keeping my voice as soothing as possible.

"And you do the same."

She turned her head and stared across the chasm. She'd have to walk barely six feet or so, but it might as well have been the Nile River, with Kit being the barge that crossed it. "You holding your end, sugar?" she asked Blondella, hands held out to her ample sides.

Blondella didn't tease this time. "I'm holding it, Kit. Just be careful; we'll be here for you on the other side. Take your time."

Kit nodded, exhaled sharply, and took her first tentative step across. The board creaked a bit but otherwise held strong, as did the three of us on either end. "You're doing great, Kit," I told her.

Again she nodded, another half-step forward, then another, head up, eyes staring dead ahead, right foot moving, then left, right, then left, snail-slow, but that was fine by us. "Halfway there," said Max, holding her gaze and smiling bravely for her.

I held my breath as she continued sidling across, sweat stinging my eyes, dress sopping wet by that point, but still I held on tightly to the beam. Again it creaked, louder this time, slightly giving by a quarter of an inch. "A little faster, Kit," I told her. "Just a little."

Again she nodded, well aware that her luck was just barely holding out as it was. It and that board. Still, even though her legs were now quaking, she continued moving, half an inch by a half an inch, slow and steady. Then, all of a sudden, *creak, groan, CRACK!*

"Kit!" I hollered, watching in desperate fear as her body lunged forward, the wood now split in two before it fell to the ground below.

"*Oomph,*" I heard next. "Get off. *Off!*"

"What happened?" I shouted across the void.

Kit popped her head up and smiled. "I'm okay."

And then I heard Blondella. "Which makes one of you. Now I know what the witch felt like when that house landed on her."

I laughed, more out of relief than anything else, though now it was my turn to leap for my life. In other words, the laughter abruptly stopped. I stared down at my soaking dress and at my shoes, at the glue oozing between the wooden heel and the leather. "Not my day," I groaned, tossing the pair over the edge before shimmying out of my dress and also tossing it, leaving me in my panties, stockings, and padded bra, chest rapidly expanding and contracting all the while.

"It's not as far as it looks," shouted Blondella, at last freed from the fallen house, her wig miraculously still in place.

"Looks far," I coughed out.

She nodded and shrugged. "Okay, so maybe it is as far as it looks, but I did it in my dress, and I'm fine."

"Matter of opinion," I mumbled as I moved ten feet in reverse and revved up my engines. "Here goes nothing," I added a second later, running for dear life, quite literally, and then leaping as high as I'd ever leaped before, landing, thank goodness, in their waiting arms.

We three stood there, huffing and puffing, arms wrapped tightly around one another. "Those shoes were nasty anyway, girl," said Kit, a kiss placed on my cheek.

"Dress, too," added Blondella, a welcomed kiss on the other side.

I sighed and fought to stand on buckling legs. "Gee, with friends like you, who needs enemas?" I winked and returned their kisses in kind. "Thanks," I whispered.

"Same here," said Kit.

"Ditto," said Blondella. "Now what?"

"Now," said Max, who was standing off to the side watching our veritable lovefest, "we climb down the fire escape to safety." He looked to the left and then to the right. "Um, where's the fire escape?"

The three of us broke from our huddle and scattered, with Kit shouting a moment later, "You've got to fucking be kidding me."

I looked over the side of the building: no zombies, but no escape either. "No kidding," I shouted. "Fucking or otherwise."

Then we rushed to the roof door. "Phew," added Blondella, the knob giving way and the door opening, the stairwell gratefully cool and empty of any undead. So down we went.

"Um," I said, at about the middle floor. "Not that I'm usually all that modest, but…" And I pointed to my state of undress, then pointed to their state of disarray. "I think we could all use a change of clothes. It's hot as hell out there and we're not exactly dressed for it."

"Speak for yourself," said Blondella. "This dress cost me an arm and a leg."

Kit chuckled. "And if those zombies out there catch you in it, I'm guessing that's exactly what it'll cost you. Better to change into something less, um…"

"Expensive?" tried Blondella.

"I was going with tacky, but fine, have it your way."

Max looked at his boots and jeans and denim jacket, and then nodded. "Agreed." Then he went from door to door to door to door, each time blowing the knobs off, the sound nearly deafening, though also the last we'd be hearing it, seeing as at the last door all we heard was *click*. He tossed the gun to the carpeted floor. "Not like it was going to do us much good anyway." Then he stared down the hallway as we stared back at him. "Shopping time, ladies."

I raised my hand. "Um, what if someone's home? And undead? And, uh, *hungry*?"

He shrugged. "Doubtful. It's the middle of the day. Plus, these zombies seem to be pretty slow. Just turn and run and close the door behind you."

We nodded, each of us going to a door, but since there were only three blown open, Max joined me at mine. "Ready?" he whispered, slowly pushing it open, the sound of silence all we heard from within.

"As I'll ever be," I managed, heart racing at what might be lying in wait. And, of course, at being alone with him. Mostly the latter. Okay, entirely the latter. "Be careful," I turned and shouted to my friends.

"You too, girl," said Kit, pushing her door in.

"Don't do anything I wouldn't do," replied Blondella, also pushing her door in.

"Short list," said Kit.

And then Max and I were slowly walking inside, my head craned left, his right, the apartment, it seemed, dead as its thankfully not there occupant: a male, late twenties, our build, if the pictures scattered about meant anything.

"Nice-looking guy," I made note, a sadness creeping into my voice as I lifted a framed candid shot of him off an end table.

Max stood by my side and also looked down. "*Mhm*. Very."

I turned and locked eyes with him, his a startling blue, especially from that close up, sparkling in the light that came through the parted curtains. "You mean that in a purely academic sense, right?"

He shrugged. "Nope. Dude's hot. *Was*, um, hot, I mean."

I gulped. "Wait a minute. You're... you're..."

He smiled and patted my exposed shoulder. "As a three-dollar bill, Destiny."

"But you said... you acted like..."

His hand remained on my shoulder, burning a path down to my crotch, which gleefully pulsed to life. "I said that I didn't know that you worked in a drag bar. But, duh, I knew it was a gay one, what with the flags hanging outside and all. Hence the fact that I beelined my way inside and not to the Irish pub down the street."

"Oh," I managed, gulp suddenly lemon-sized.

The silence grew until it became practically unbearable. Plus, my panties wouldn't exactly help much should my woodie untuck, *ouch*, so I quickly changed the subject. "You go, uh, *shop*, and I'll go de-Destiny myself in the bathroom. Find me something fashionably seasonal, please."

He bowed. "My honor, Madame."

I groaned. "Soon to be *Monsieur*, but thanks just the same."

I raced to the bathroom, shut the door behind me, and finally exhaled. Figures I'd find a nice, normal, cute guy and it's the end of the friggin' world: Murphy's Law run amok. In any case, the wig came off, then the lashes, then the padded bra before I found some expensive night cream and moisturizer—which meant that the previous owner was more than likely also gay, God rest his soul—then I scrubbed the layers of makeup off my face with it all.

I sighed as I watched it all colorfully swirl down the drain before I gazed back up at my wet boy face and combed my hair back into place. "Ready?" I hollered through the door. There was no answer. "Ready?" I tried again, though more urgently this time. "Max!" I shouted as I ran from the bathroom, heart suddenly racing.

"What? What?" he said, slamming into me in the bedroom. "You okay?"

He was standing there in his boxers, two inches from me, his hands on my elbows, concern etched across his adorable face. "You didn't answer. I was worried."

He laughed. "I was in the closet. Literally speaking, of course." Then he paused and stared at me, my belly, and certain other body parts. "You, uh, you clean up nicely, Destiny."

"Dennis," I informed, trying—and failing miserably—not to stare down at his wide expanse of hairy chest.

His smile amped up, fifty watts to a blazing two hundred. "Nah. You look more like a Destiny."

I grinned. "It's the panties, right?"

He stared down and nodded. "Yeah, that must be it." Then he looked back up, and his face suddenly closed the barely there gap between us. His lips were soft, like a cotton ball on a cloud tipped with feathers, his tongue deftly swirling around my own as a moan pushed its way up his lungs and down into mine.

"Ow," I managed, a minute later.

His face inched in reverse. "Ow?" He laughed. "That hurt? Not from my end of things, it didn't. Can I have a second chance then?"

I shook my head. "No," I rasped, eyelids fluttering, brain in a horny daze. "I mean, yes, you can have seconds, thirds even." *Tenths.* Then I pointed down to my crotch. "Still tucked, Max. So, like, *ow.* Big time."

He tilted his head and scratched his dimpled chin. "How big?"

My grin echoed his. "Big, Max. *Really* big." Then I motioned for him to turn around because there was no way I was gonna let a complete stranger, albeit more than likely the last one on Earth, watch me untuck. Call me old-fashioned, but still.

In any case, he winked and turned, and I promptly slid out of my panties and freed the beast. "*Aah*," I soon said, swaying it left and then right, to and a wildly happy fro.

Max turned and his jaw promptly dropped. "Yikes," he uttered, eyes on the prize.

"Careful, it senses fear," I cautioned, swaying it in reverse, a mild breeze forming in its wake.

The gap was again closed, his hand held out for a squeeze and a stroke. "Trust me, Destiny, *fear* didn't even make the list."

The kiss was repeated, again and again and, *mmm*, again, same for the heavenly squeeze and stroke. Still, I knew we had little time, and it wasn't like standing in a dead stranger's apartment was the ideal setting for all this, so I halted his progress, sad as I was to do so. Halted, that is to say, after I pulled on the elastic to his boxers and had a peek inside. "Yikes right back at you, Max." Then I ran my hands through all that soft, black down. "But the girls will be waiting. Or worse, will be storming in here at any moment. And, trust me, you don't want to see Kit storming. They've named tropical depressions after her, you know."

He cringed and shivered in place. "Not a pretty picture." Then he chuckled. "Rain check, then?"

I glanced outside. "Sun check is more like it, but yes, I'll hold you to it."

And then he held me to him. *Mmm* yet again. "Count on it."

Which I already was doing, suffice it to say. Counting on it as we made our way back to the closet, counting on it as we dressed in a dead man's wardrobe, and counting on it as we exited the apartment.

Kit was in the hallway waiting. "Oh my God, Max is gay!"

Max scratched his head. "Guess I'm butcher than I realized," he said.

"That ain't it, sugar," she said, waving a 3 Musketeers bar at us. "Sugar depletion must've put the old gaydar on the fritz. Plus, those shorts and tank top and boots are screaming Castro clone." She squinted and grinned. "*Pretty* clone, yes, but clone just the same."

"And me?" I hazarded.

She stood, arms akimbo, and replied, "Tired old queen. But don't worry, I'm used to it."

I couldn't help but laugh, not because she'd just dissed me, but because she herself, now he, was wearing jogging shorts and a T-shirt, the material stretched to its absolute limits—perhaps beyond. Plus, though she'd removed her makeup, she'd left her wig on, so she now looked like Richard Simmons on an eating binge.

"How are you breathing in that get-up?"

She pulled down on the shirt and up on the shorts, creating a caravan of camel toes. "Not fucking easy, but at least I won't suffocate in the heat." She turned and looked at the apartment next door. "But where's Blondella?" She smiled. "Think she'll finally be dressed like a boy?"

"Not likely," replied the drag queen in question, emerging in a lavender tennis outfit and matching Espadrilles. Not her usual attire, but it would do in a pinch, which we were certainly in at that very moment.

Kit coughed. "Don't tell me you found a wig, too."

Blondella grinned. "Isn't it to die for?"

"Bad choice of words," replied I. "But, yes, it's lovely." Then I turned to Max. "Okay, so, now we're all dressed appropriately." I gazed at Kit. "More or less. But how do we get to New York?"

Then it was his turn to cough. "New York? Why, the bagels here aren't good enough for you?"

And so we filled him in on the whole Johnny angle. "You don't have to go, you know," I told him, thinking the exact opposite, which I was sure my face was showing, too.

But his grin said it all. "I've always wanted to see New York," he said, without even giving it a moment's thought. "Plus, someone's gotta keep this group in line."

To which Blondella, Kit, and I all said in unison, "That's my job."

He nodded as he walked past us. "Point proven, ladies. Point proven."

# CHAPTER THREE
## A FLARE FOR THE DRAMATIC

Down the stairs we walked, slowly, heads turning from left to right, eyes scanning for any errant zombies, but like Max had said, it was the middle of the day; most likely everyone was trapped at work or wandering the streets.

We made it to the building's entrance and stared outside. "Coast seems clear," I hazarded. There were a few zombies walking in the opposite direction and a slew locked in their cars, pawing at the glass, unable to reason their way out, which was equal parts heartbreaking and relief, though mostly the latter, so out we went.

The street was silent, deathly still, not a car in motion or a pigeon pecking or a soaring plane to be heard, nothing but the sound of our breathing and the distant groan of a zombie or two. Plus, the sun was hotter than hell, which was about the most apt description for it, all things considered.

"*That*," said Max, pointing at the fiery orb above us, "must be the reason for *this*." He then pointed down the street, at the undead horde suddenly heading our way. Obviously, we gave off some sort of scent that attracted them to us, pulled them to us like magnets, moths to a flame. Or flamers. Again apt, all things considered. "Any idea why?"

Kit shook her head, as did Blondella, new blonde bob swaying in time. Me, I was wiping the torrent from my face. "*Hmm*," I hummed, moving our group away from the roving band that was now headed our way. "Seems I recall something sun related in the news as of late, but what was it?"

Max pointed across the street to a magazine store, a lone zombie scratching at the glass inside, a pile of newspapers stacked neatly on the sidewalk, waiting forever to be put away. "Let's go have a read, shall we?"

"Quickly," added Blondella, pointing in the opposite direction, the collective moan reaching our ears a split second later, the sound like a dirge mixed with nails raking across a chalkboard. Like a Yoko Ono album played too slowly. Or too fast. Or just like a Yoko Ono album playing. Meaning, it wasn't a pretty sound to hear.

We rushed to the stack and yanked a paper free from its binding. Thankfully, the headline said it all. Or maybe not so thankfully, considering that the horde had doubled in size in that brief time, the communal moan reaching its gut-wrenching crescendo.

"Solar flares," I read, pointing to the top of the page. "Largest in a decade."

Blondella grimaced. "Or ever, by the looks of things."

Kit grabbed the paper and read as her lips moved silently along. When she was through, she informed us, "Radiation. The article cautioned that the radiation would be minimal and not to worry. But, just guessing, if the solar flares were bigger than they expected, so must've been the radiation."

Max gulped and wiped the sweat off his brow. "It had to happen in a flash," he said. "I was only in the bank for a minute before the sonic boom. So the flare, or at least the heat of it, must've killed everyone, and then the sudden blast of radiation must've kick-started them back to... back to... *that*." He pointed to the hundred or so undead who were now barely fifty feet away, hands outstretched, mouths gaping, moaning and groaning up a cacophonous storm.

"Which was why that woman I touched was so hot," I made note. "Fried by the solar flare."

"Which gives me an idea," said Kit, snapping her thick fingers together, or at least trying to.

I stared from her to the KFC across the street. "Now, girl? Really?"

She smacked my arm and then stared hungrily at the KFC in question. "No, not that. Though I seriously wish you hadn't mentioned it." Then she turned back our way. "Just head down the side street, okay?"

Blondella patted Kit's broad expanse of back. "Way to take one for the team, girlfriend," she said. "They can snack on you while we get away." Then she patted Kit's barely encased ass below. "Though I'd say you're more of a nice-sized lunch than a snack for that bunch."

Kit pushed Blondella's hand away and sighed heavily. "It's a wonder you make any tips at all with that tired routine of yours, hon," she fairly spat. "In any case, just get them to follow you that way." She pointed to the street that ran off the one we were standing on.

I nervously turned from her to the moaning mob and back again. "You sure about this, Kit?"

She nodded and smiled. "Just go. Head down and around and come back and get me." Then she pointed her thumb at Blondella. "I'd say sacrifice the virgin while you're at it, but, well…"

I grabbed Blondella before another verbal parley ensued. "Be careful," I told Kit, our trio then quickly heading directly for the loudly groaning throng, which had somehow grown yet again, nearly filling the width of the street as they poured in between the cars and headed our way. When we were barely ten feet from them, we zigged, zagged, and went down the side street. Miraculously, they followed.

I turned one final time and spied Kit heading into a toy store. "What the fuck?" I said.

Blondella turned and shrugged. "Must be a candy machine in there. Figures."

Though right about then that was the least of our worries, mainly because the side street was narrow and blocked with cars, and the zombies were both behind us and up ahead, not to mention pawing from behind every steering wheel, which was unnerving as all get out—or all get in, as it were, as in inside a still-revving car, the door open, its occupant unaccounted for.

"Frying pan, meet fire," groused Blondella, slamming the door behind her after we all piled in front.

Max released the brake and inched the car forward. "If they're not smart enough to get out of these cars, then they're hopefully not smart enough to get inside of one either. Or, start praying, not smart enough to get inside this one in particular."

"Hopefully," I echoed, though my hope meter had plummeted to zero about the same time that solar flare had hit.

In any case, we scraped past the other cars, pushing them and crunching them and grinding them out of the way as we crept along. By then, the rear horde had reached us and was now rocking the car, desperate, it seemed, to pry us out. "Fuckers!" I screamed, terror-stricken at suddenly being surrounded by them on three sides, the fourth one just barely up ahead.

The zombies shoved their way against the car, a dense throng of flesh, all of them unblinking, mouths agape, moaning and groaning as their fingers reached for us and smacked into glass and metal. It was impossible to stare at them and just as impossible to look away, a train wreck to the $n^{\text{th}}$ degree.

"Faster, Max," I pled, my hand on his wrist.

"Amen," said Blondella from my right as she pushed as close to me and as far from them as she could get. "I mean, I'm all for a clamoring audience, but this is ridiculous."

Max continued to inch forward, knocking the dead and the cars away as best he could, bone and metal crunching all the while, nearly drowning out the moaning that was making my flesh crawl.

"Almost there," he whispered, one last car to get around before he could gun it, taking out as many zombies as he could, because, after all, the dead were already just that, whether they knew it or not.

Then *whoosh* the car went, the three of us getting knocked back into the seat as Max sped off, veering left and right until the mob could only be seen in the rearview mirror and then not even that as we turned eastward.

"Back for Kit," I said.

Blondella chuckled. "We're already headed in the right direction; I vote for New York instead."

"Then who would you insult?" I couldn't help but ask.

She looked from me to Max and frowned. "Good point. But let's make it quick. One close encounter with the gross kind per day is enough for me, thank you kindly."

I put my hand on her knee. "Um, hate to break it to you, but we have a whole countryful of them between here and Johnny to contend with, or so I'm guessing."

She groaned and tilted her head back against the seat. "Any way to sugarcoat that?"

I closed my eyes and nodded thoughtfully. "Free booze from here to New York."

Her groan ceased and desisted. "Well, that silver lining is a bit tarnished, but I'll take it."

"Thatta girl," said Max, again turning the car, finally heading back toward whence we'd started.

"There!" I shouted, finger aimed ahead. "There she is!" I squinted into the distance. "What's she holding?"

"A gun," replied Max, also squinting. "And it's pink."

Blondella squinted as well. "And a bucket of fried chicken. Old habits seem to die harder than those fucking zombies do."

We got nearer and noticed the zombies coming back her way. Surprisingly, she was standing her ground. Not as surprising, she was munching on a drumstick at the time.

"She's got more guns at her feet," I noticed, now that we were barely a quarter of a block away, zombies coming in at all directions again. "Orange and green and blue guns."

"Water guns!" shouted Max, his fist pounding the steering wheel. "Genius!"

Blondella snickered. "Let's not go overboard here, hon. Obese, yes. Genius, not even after a whole box of Snickers washed down with a liter of Mountain Dew."

Kit saw us coming and motioned with her free hand for us to hurry, which we did, slamming into a dozen undead as we did so, all of us pouring out of the car as she tossed us each a water gun, big suckers too, high powered and filled to the brim.

"Squirt!" she hollered, original recipe bits flinging out of her overstuffed mouth.

"Gladly!" shouted Blondella, letting it rip, water shooting out and hitting the closest zombie, a man whose body began to sizzle and steam upon contact, his head thrown back in apparent agony as liquid doused radiated flesh. "Die, undead scum!"

Which sounded like an oxymoron, like jumbo shrimp or compassionate Republican, but still we all screamed it, eager to be rid of them, even if only temporarily. And then, one by one, they went down, buckling at the knees before toppling over, melting like the Wicked Witch, post kick-ass-Dorothy. Yes, it was nasty to behold, but invigorating just the same. Like we'd finally done something to help our cause, good versus evil and all that rot. And who would've guessed that we'd be the good guys. Um, guys-ish, really, Max excluded, because, *yum*, he was all man.

The truly dead now formed a wall against the almost dead, who either tripped over the corpses or stood motionless behind them. They stared at us as we stared at them. I recognized a couple of the bar's regulars.

"Joe and Pete," I said, pointing as I nudged Blondella.

She sighed as her water gun again got lifted. "Rest in peace, boys." A tear streaked down her face as Kit and I both stroked her back. They were better off that way. I knew it and my friends did as well, but that didn't make it any easier, nor did I think it would ever get any easier for that matter, but at least we now had a fighting chance. "Damn it," she added, lowering the gun.

"I know, girl. I know," said Kit.

"And they were our best tippers, too."

"I know, girl. I know," repeated Kit. "But we gotta go now, before there's more of them or we run out of water."

"Or both," I groaned, already heading for the car, the others quick to follow. Max got in the front seat, Kit and Blondella in the back. "Now what?" I asked. "Anyone got a plan?" Naturally, we all turned to Max as he looked from me to them.

"Really? You don't even know me," he replied.

Kit chuckled from the back seat. "But we know *us*," she said. "And I vote for you."

"I second that!" said I, more exuberantly than intentioned.

Blondella patted the back of his headrest. "She always was sloppy seconds, but I'll make it unanimous. Not like you could do worse than any of us, anyway."

Max turned her way. "Your confidence is truly inspiring."

She pointed to the pile of still-sizzling corpses in the street, at the lifeless cars turned this way and that, at the zombies standing on the other side of it all, and she replied, "Under the circumstances, best I can do."

He grinned, which put a *boing* in my shorts. "Granted, and I do have a plan of sorts."

"Of sorts?" asked Kit.

"Well, the start of one, at any rate. Enough to get us out of San Francisco and headed to New York, I'd imagine."

She nodded, as did Blondella and I. "Sorts it is then. Lead on, my good man. And if it involves a drink or six, then by all means."

"I second that one, too," said I, hand held up.

"Unanimous again," said Blondella. "And hurry."

* * * *

After we drove away from the carnage, we headed through The Castro, past the Mission, and, from the looks of things, to South of Market. It was slow going the entire way as we swerved in and out of traffic, trying our best to avoid the zombies. Though in a city now full of them, that was, of course, impossible. Still, they were fairly ineffectual while we were in our car, which rose and fell as it ran over pigeons and other assorted birds. It seemed by the looks of things that only the humans came back to, um, *life*, all other wildlife dead and sizzling on the street and sidewalks.

"So what's the plan?" I eventually asked, pit still lodged in my stomach.

"Ditch the car," he replied, thereby bursting my fairly ineffectual bubble.

"Come again?" said I, blushing at the unintended—though probably subconsciously intended—double-entendre.

"Yeah," said Kit from the back seat. "We're safe and sound in here." She cleared her throat. "Well, safe at any rate."

He pulled the car over and sighed. "It took us nearly an hour to get this far, which was barely a few miles. Yes, like you said, we're safe in here, but we can't easily get anyplace. And what's going to happen when we reach a highway or a busy intersection? We'll be trapped, boxed in, forever backtracking."

Blondella tapped his shoulder. "Well, unless you're a pilot with access to a plane, what choice do we have?"

"You don't happen to have a plane, do you?" I thought to ask, just in case.

"Nope," he replied, putting the car back on the road. "But we do have another option."

That option presented itself about fifteen minutes later, and I couldn't help but laugh at what he had in mind as we parked in front of the bike shop. "I've heard of dykes on bikes, but drag queens on motorcycles? Sounds like a fifties schlock movie. Besides, I don't even know how to ride one."

"Don't need to," said he. "You'll be on the back of mine." That, of course, I liked the sound of. "After all, someone has to shoot the water guns should we get attacked." That, of course, I *didn't* like the sound of. He then turned to the other two. "Either of you know how to ride a motorcycle?"

Kit shook her head while Blondella nodded hers. "I was much butcher back in the day."

"When, 1912?" asked Kit with a laugh, and then all of a sudden stopped. "Wait, I'm not riding on the back of hers, am I?"

"As if," replied Blondella. "Not unless we can attach a trailer-pull and I drag you, no pun intended, to New York."

Max raised his hand, palm out. Clearly, though he'd only known us a very short while, he knew where these conversations led. "Don't worry, Kit; that's also part of my plan."

"Oh goody," sniped Kit as we all hopped out of the car, water guns held up high, though by then they were dangerously low on liquid ammo.

There were two customers and two workers in the shop, all of them eager to see us. Or smell us. Or tear us limb from limb. Hard to tell which exactly, especially since they were smoldering gobs of flesh in mere moments, the stench making all of us wretch before we grabbed for nearby bandanas and covered our faces up.

"Next?" asked Blondella, her voice muffled behind the cotton.

Max smiled and motioned with his index finger for us to follow him, and follow we did, to a side door that led to the showroom. Obviously, this was not the kind of showroom we were accustomed to, but we knew what he had in mind for the rest of his plan as he pointed from one motorcycle to the next, the keys already in their ignitions.

Ours—mine and his—was a snazzy black and chrome number with a seat big enough for two. My heart raced at the sight of it. And at him, too, especially once he straddled it and smiled up at me. "Hop on, Destiny." Again the double-entendre made me blush—hop on, indeed; yes, please. In any case, I hopped on, my legs vise-tight against his, hands resting on his belly. Oh joy, three thousand-plus miles like this. "Blondella, now you pick one," he soon added.

She crisscrossed the showroom, eyeing each one as if it were a designer gown, and, exactly like one of those, she picked the showiest one: pink with flaming roses painted along the sides.

Kit chuckled. "I though you said you were butch, girl?"

Blondella hopped on her, uh, *hog* and replied, "It's more of an internal thing, hon. Buried deep, deep down. Like that shriveled-up heart of yours."

Kit kept right on chuckling. "I think you're confusing butch with bitch, sugar." She then turned to Max. "And me?"

Max pointed to a cycle with a sidecar attached, a four-wheeler, for all intents and purposes, and one she couldn't easily topple with her wide expanse of belly. "Sidecar is for supplies." He pointed to the water guns. "And weapons."

Blondella rubbed her hands together as she revved the engine. "Shopping time," she practically sung. "Goody!"

Kit grinned and also turned her ignition on. "No credit cards. No cash. No waiting. Like stealing candy from a baby."

Blondella drove by the two of us, shouting over her shoulder, "Thank goodness you already have experience with that, girl; should make it even easier then."

"Funny," said Kit as she took up the middle, with us right behind in the rear. "Lucky for us you do *easy* so well!"

I tapped Max on the shoulder as we zoomed out of the lot. "What about helmets?"

He shrugged. "No one enforcing that law anymore, Destiny." He then pointed ahead. "Besides, those *fat heads* up there are already amply protected."

"They mean well," I replied, mostly believing it.

"I think that's what they said about Bush."

"Which one?"

He laughed and gunned the motor, passing my friends in a cloud of dust. "Take your pick."

I wrapped my arms tighter around his waist. "No picking needed, Max," I said in his ear. "They're all gone now anyway, every Bush and Reagan and the like, every last rotten one of them, and even more brain-dead than before."

Gosh, we should've been so lucky.

But life, or death, or all points in between, is never that simple.

\* \* \* \*

We drove through town, the only sound that of the hot air whipping past our ears. Max had been right about the bikes; they were great in terms of getting around all the stopped cars and milling zombies, who were never quite fast enough to make a grab for us.

36

Instead, they stared hungrily our way as we zipped by, hundreds of them aimlessly plodding about, thousands beyond them, millions, all moaning, as was their apparent custom.

Lord only knew how many were trapped in stores, in houses, in apartment buildings and offices. Then again, that might just have been our salvation. For now, all we had to deal with were the dead tourists, the bums, and those people off work.

And that was plenty, let me tell you.

"Where are we headed?" I asked, staring straight ahead, avoiding eye contact with the zombies as best I could, my hand beneath his shirt, tracing the muscles with my fingertips. Flesh on flesh. Suffice it to say, it was a much-needed distraction.

"Grocery store," he replied, over his shoulder. "Stock up and ship out." Then he giggled. "That tickles."

I leaned up and blew in his ear. "Want me to stop?"

"Nah," he quickly replied, the motorcycle speeding up at an unblocked stretch of road. "It's either laugh or cry, I think; might as well go with the former."

I nodded. *Might as well indeed.*

And then we were pulling into the grocery store. And that was problematic, to be sure. During the day, that was the one place where there were lots of people. Inside and out. Every-fucking-where.

"Damn," I hissed as we stopped cold, Blondella pulling to our right side, Kit to our left.

"Plan B?" asked Kit as she wiped the sweat away with the back of her hand.

"All we need is essentials, right?" asked Blondella.

"Right," said Max. "Food, water, for us and the guns, toilet paper, and anything that can easily fit inside the side car for the trip out east."

"Chocolate," Kit piped up with. "Let's not forget that."

Blondella sighed. "Try as we might. In any case, how about… *there.*" She was pointing down the street at a small deli beneath an apartment building. There were few zombies outside and certainly ample essentials within.

In any case, right about then I would've settled for a simple blast of cold air. And to think, just that morning I was complaining about the fog. Guess you don't miss something until it's gone. Talk about your gross understatements.

"Park around back," I suggested. "So the zombies don't see us or try to follow us." Which they were already doing. In droves, no less. Hordes of them, in fact, were filing out of the parking lot as we sat there idling.

"Good idea," said Max, quickly speeding away before circling around the block and driving down an alleyway behind the store. We zapped a lone zombie with one of our guns. He went down in a hazy mist that stunk of death and decay. "Maybe we should make this a quick one, huh?"

"Amen," agreed Kit as she hopped off her bike and gave the back door a tentative push, Blondella at her rear, water gun pointed dead ahead. Emphasis on the dead, who came out charging. Or at least trudging. "Fire, bitch!"

Well, there wasn't much left, water-wise, in our guns, but there was just enough in Blondella's to take out the clerk and a couple of customers, all of whom went down in a sizzling clump at the edge of the door.

"Yuck," I said with a grimace, as I stepped over them, flesh squishing beneath my sneakers. I held my nose and averted my eyes.

"Tuh huh," grunted Kit, following my path, Max and Blondella in the rear, shutting the door, lest any zombies decided to join the party.

The deli's front door was already closed, and even though they could probably see us if they walked by, it seemed that they pretty much operated on smell alone when it came to the living, namely us. Evidence to this fact was that several walked by right at that very moment and didn't stop to, well, window shop, again namely for us, prime grade-A meat. I shivered at the thought.

"At least it's cool in here," stated Kit, immediately heading for the candy section.

"Yep," agreed Max as the two of us each grabbed a basket and opted for the nonperishables. "Still, let's make it fast, just in case."

So we divided and conquered. The deli was a corner store, too, and there were ample essentials to be had: water, toilet paper, soap, toothpaste and toothbrushes, canned food, can opener, candy, of course (mostly of the chocolate variety), *InStyle, US, People*, nail polish (mostly of the red variety), lipstick (ditto), nail files, moisturizing cream (sadly on the cheap side), hairbrushes and hairspray. Like I said, the essentials.

"You're joking," said Max.

We all looked at him, confused. Then Blondella put the *People* back on the shelf. "Better?"

He chuckled and shrugged, heading for the back to fill up the water guns and to make us all sandwiches. To go.

Or at least so we thought.

So close. But that only counts in horseshoes and hand grenades. Too bad we had neither at that very moment.

# CHAPTER FOUR
## CRY ME A RIVER

With baskets full, we again headed for the back door. "Wait," whispered Blondella. "Do you hear that?"

We froze and tilted our ears up. "Moaning," I lamented, the frown sagging on my face.

"And lots of it," added Kit, who then moved to a window a few feet from the door. She lifted the shade and threw a moan in herself. "I, um, think we were followed."

We all moved to the window and glumly stared outside. "The alleyway is full of them," I made note, heart racing like it was suddenly competing at the Indy 500. Which meant our bikes were no longer an option. And without them, we were back to square one. Heck, we weren't even on the playing board anymore. "Suggestions?"

Kit reached into her basket and pulled out a 3 Musketeers. It was halfway done before I could even manage to blink. "It's getting late," she said. "And I'm tired and dusty and sweat-soaked. I vote for calling it a day and praying they're gone by morning. Anybody else?"

Blondella raised her hand, as did I. Max shrugged, stared around, and replied, "Not exactly the Four Seasons."

"Fuck it," said Kit, disappearing down an aisle before returning with a hammer. "I say we do some breaking and entering; this girl needs a shower." She turned to Blondella. "Don't say it." She waited as our bewigged friend scratched her chin. "Don't even think it."

Blondella nodded. "Fine. For once, I agree with Kit here. Plenty of beds and showers upstairs."

"But the upstairs means going outside first," I reminded them, sweating again despite the cold air blowing over us.

Max moved to the front door. "There's only a few of them in the front. We just have to break in before they can get to us. Easy as pie."

Kit grimaced. "You ever try to bake a pie, sweetie? From scratch, I mean?" She stood there, arms akimbo. Or at least as akimbo as her frame allowed—so, more akimb*ish*. "It ain't so easy, let me tell you. And neither is breaking into a locked apartment building."

"Um," ummed Max. "It was your idea, remember."

She sighed and finished her candy bar. "Oh, right." Then she opened the door. "Cover me." She turned to Blondella. "Don't say it, bitch." And before we knew it, she was pounding on the door to the apartments overhead with the hammer, which, suffice it to say, drew quite a bit of unwanted and undead attention. "Mother fucker!" she hollered as the hammer flew and we stood guard. "Mother fucking! Thick-ass! Fucking! Door!"

Well, it might've been thick, but not much could stand up to Kit when she put her weight behind it. In other words, it gave way just as a few dozen zombies were about ten feet from us. "Nice, girl," said Blondella. "But now the door is broken, and though we can get in, so can they." We rushed through the deli door and into the apartment door and slammed said door as best we could, all of us holding it in place as the zombies poured onto the stoop, all of them pressing their lifeless bodies together like a giant festering battering ram.

"Ideas?" I asked, fighting to keep the door against the frame. Fighting, that is to say, and quickly losing, as their hands reached inside, scratching the air and trying for a piece of us, their united moans rattling my bones to the quick.

Max looked around and then barked, "Fire extinguisher!"

But diving for that meant that one of us needed to release their hold on the door. And all in all, that didn't seem like such a swell plan of action.

"I have an idea," said Kit.

"You just ate a candy bar, right?" asked Blondella, pushing the door with all her apparent strength.

"Uh huh."

She glanced Kit's way. "I'm listening, then."

Kit nodded. "On the count of three, everyone fall back."

Blondella grunted. "You sure that wasn't one of those sugar-free bars, girl?"

Kit chuckled. "As if. Now, ready?" We all nodded as sweat poured off our faces. "One." She was still pushing against the wood. "Two." Still pushing. "Three!" We all quickly released and fell back. The door gave at once, and the entire front line of undead instantly toppled in and over and fell on one another, thereby creating, at least temporarily, one disgustingly undead blockade.

"I can't believe that worked," I commented as I wiped the sweat off my forehead.

"Believe it," said Kit as she yanked the fire extinguisher off the wall, bolts and all. "Eat it, bitches!" she hollered, the hose at once spraying, the small lobby filling with the extinguisher's contents.

Now then, I've heard some awful noises before—babies crying in tandem, Republican convention speeches, Celine Dion—but this, well now, this was by far the worst. Because when that fire extinguisher sprayed, dozens upon dozens of undead went all screeching crazy on us before they all promptly died. Well, died again. One minute they were writhing on the floor, the next they were nothing more than a rather large pile of simmering flesh.

"Voila," said Kit, dropping the metal canister to the ground before wiping her hands on her hips. "Door blocked. Shower time."

She turned and headed up the stairs, tightly encased mammoth ass swaying as we watched in astonishment. "Unbelievable," said Blondella.

"What, that her idea worked?"

She turned and shook her head. "No, that the door gave, but those shorts she's wearing are still in one piece."

Exhausted, I barely had the energy to laugh. Mostly. In any case, the zombies were in fact blocked from getting in, and us out, for the time being, so we did the only logical thing and followed Kit up the stairs. And, yes, if that was the only logical thing then, okay, we were royally screwed.

The hallway was empty, and Kit had little trouble hammering the locks off and busting her way inside. Poor doors didn't know what hit them.

Five minutes later, she turned to each of us and said, "Good fucking night."

She went inside the first apartment, Blondella the one next to it, me the one across the hall, and Max the one next to mine. "Holler if there's a zombie inside."

"Duh," replied Blondella.

Though we did each have our water guns with us, so we were, potentially, safe. Still, I eased my way inside the apartment. "Yoohoo, anyone home?" There was no answer. Or moan. So I closed the door behind me and, since it was fairly busted, propped it closed with a folded chair, planning, just the same, to lock myself in the bedroom.

I turned to head for the bathroom just as I heard a light rapping on the door. I tiptoed up to it and peeked through the keyhole. No undead, but my heart rate quickened just the same.

"Max," I whispered, cock pulsing inside my shorts. I removed the chair and quietly opened the door. "Everything all right?"

He grinned, which just about entirely lit up the darkened hallway. "Apart from the end of the world as we know it? Sure, right as rain, Destiny." He moved another inch forward, his head poking through. "And speaking of getting all wet. You, uh, need a shower, and I, uh, need a shower, so why not conserve water and, uh…"

"Shower together?" I gulped.

"It's the green thing to do."

I nodded and opened the door for him. "Anything for Mother Earth," I said. "Besides, the old girl's been through a hell of a time lately."

"Amen," he said, closing the door behind him before sliding the chair back beneath the knob, great minds obviously thinking alike. Testament to this was the fact that he was leaning in to kiss me at the exact same moment that I was leaning in to kiss him, and he was grabbing my tenting shorts as I was grabbing for his. Like I said, great minds—or horny ones, at any rate—and ones that had also been through the wringer lately and that desperately needed a little R&R.

I pulled an inch away. "So how about that shower then?"

He grinned and stroked my cheek. "Sounds dirty."

I nodded and grabbed his hand before leading us down the hallway in search of the bathroom. "Then thank goodness we'll have some soap nearby."

And ample quantities of it too. The woman who lived there, sadly past tense, was stocked to the rafters with shampoos, soaps, conditioners, scrubs, exfoliants, moisturizers, oils, creams, and anything else you could think of to apply to your skin. This wasn't just Bed, Bath & Body; this was Bed, Bath & Body & Body. Namely ours: his and mine.

Max looked awesome naked, too. Nah, scratch that. Max looked AWESOME NAKED!!! With a couple of extra exclamation points thrown in for good measure. He was lean and hairy, naturally muscled, like a runner or a swimmer, and quickly had a thick dick aimed my way, cocked and ready, as it were. Max was, to say the least, divine. And, yes, I couldn't believe my luck that the last man on earth wasn't straight, fat, or ugly. Or a combination of any of the three.

"Damn, you look good," he said, taking the words right out of my mouth as we both stood there, hard, naked, and filthy, in more ways than one.

"Weird," I said, taking him in.

"What?" he replied with a mischievous grin that made my knees fairly buckle.

I shrugged. "All of this, Max. Me, you, *this*." I pointed around, my aim stretching far beyond the porcelain confines of that bathroom.

He closed the gap between us and wrapped his arms tightly around me, his cheek on my shoulder. "Granted," he whispered. "But fate does seem to be having a field day with us…"

"So why tempt it?"

He chuckled and kissed my neck. "Exactly."

He had a point. And right about then, it was poking me in the thigh. So I stopped thinking about the circumstances that had brought us together and simply concentrated on the together part.

In the shower we went, hot water pouring over us as a dusty river of brown began washing down the drain, one bar of soap in my hand, one in his, our mouths again united, tongues thrashing. I lathered his chest while he did the same to my ass, paying particular attention to my hole. He moved to my back, massaging the soap into all my sore spots, while I moved below, his cock in one hand, hefty balls in the other.

"*Mmm*," he groaned, exhaling up his lungs and down into mine.

Slowly, I jacked his prick, hot flesh pulsing in my grip. He moved his hands from my back to my front, quickly aping my maneuver. "*Mmm*," I echoed, my mouth moving away from his, wet forehead pressed to wet forehead as I stared down at his soapy cock. "Nice," I purred.

"Ditto," he cooed back. "But how on earth do you drag-tuck all, well, *this*?" He gave my *this* a tug.

I laughed. "Ain't easy." I glanced up, eyes locking, his bluer than the sky on a beautiful summer's day. "Doesn't bother you what I do, um, *did*, for a living?"

He smiled and kissed my nose. "Destiny, I'm just glad that you're still living." Him and me both. "Besides, you seem to have enjoyed it and, I assume, were good at what you did, so why judge?"

I sighed, sad and contented at the same time. I'd waited ages to hear a man say that to me, even longer for my family, which was now never to happen, my heart breaking at the thought, and here he was saying it to me as the world was coming to an end. Then again, he was saying it as I too was coming, lips again on his as my cock suddenly spewed, aromatic spunk hitting his belly and bush and thigh before running down his legs. His back arched as he moaned, his cock erupting a split second later, so thick in my hand that it was difficult to hold on to. But hold on I did, to it, to him, to the moment, as our loads combined and washed down the drain together.

"Sorry," I said. "Guess I got overexcited."

The smile rose on his face, eyes sparkling like sapphires beneath the bathroom lighting. "Makes two of us." He pointed down to the gobs of come that were still making their way through the drain. "*Made* two of us. And thanks. Nice compliment." He put his hand on my chest. "Nice, um, well, everything."

"Minus the hordes of undead and the searing heat."

He nodded. "Yep. Minus those. But at least there's a plus in that column, namely you." He tickled my belly.

My chuckle returned. "You always this upbeat, dude?"

"Must be all the doom and gloom. Always brings it out of me."

I tilted my head. "Always?" I asked. "How often are you around doom and gloom?"

He started running the soap through the come that had lingered on my skin. "Pretty often, Destiny." He stopped mid-scrub. "I'm a funeral director. Or at least was. I mean, doesn't look like anyone's dying anymore. Or dying and in need of a burial. You okay with that?"

I grinned. "Were you good at what you did? Happy with your work?" He nodded. "Then that's all that counts, Max."

He went back to scrubbing. And smiling. "You're the first man to ever say that to me."

My bar of soap was making its way across his taut stomach. "Girly-man, you mean."

With his soapy fist, he again grabbed my still-semi prick. "All man, Destiny, the way I see it." And he was the first man that had ever said that to me.

Weird, just like I'd said.

Weird, but, okay, nice.

As for his timing… well, not so great. But then again, like they say, better late than never.

\* \* \* \*

The next morning, we awoke to a loud knocking on the door. We, that is, as in me and Max, who'd spent the night curled up in my arms.

"Do zombies knock?" he asked with a yawn and a stretch of his arms.

"Doubtful," I replied with a yawn and stretch of my own, a kiss happily thrown into my repertoire. "But drag queens do. Though generally not before noon." I wrapped a towel around my waist and headed for the door as the knocking continued. "Keep your shirt on, I'm coming."

I removed the chair and opened the door. Kit was standing there looking none too happy, but at least she'd found some clothes that mostly fit her. And a Heath Bar: breakfast of champions.

"Morning," she said.

"You left out the standard adjective: good."

She shook her head and frowned. "Wish I could, sugar." Max was suddenly at my side, a matching towel wrapped around him. Kit looked past me to him. "No fucking way."

"Way," said I with a grin.

"Big time way," tossed in Max, also with a grin and a pat on my bare shoulder.

I nodded. "Emphasis on the big."

Hearing the commotion, Blondella's door flung open. Shockingly, she was resplendent in rhinestone-studded shorts, rhinestone-studded shoes, a rhinestone-studded blouse, and, suffice it to say, rhinestone-studded sunglasses.

"What's the hubbub, bub?" Then she noticed Max, who was awfully hard not to notice, towel and all. "No fucking way."

Kit sighed. "Please, not again. Too early." Then she turned to Blondella. "Have you looked out your window yet, or were you too busy with the Bedazzler you obviously uncovered?"

She twirled around in a circle, ambient light bouncing off of her like a disco ball. "Isn't it fabulous?"

"It's *something* all right," answered Max, scratching his glorious right pec. Then he turned to Kit. "But what, exactly, is outside your window?"

She motioned with her finger for us to follow, which we did. Their side of the building overlooked the back alleyway, the place where our motorcycles were sitting, the place also where the zombies had been and still very much sadly were. Them and a few hundred of their closest friends, all of whom were staring up at all of us, moaning up a veritable storm. And I doubted it was because they spotted Max in his towel, moan-worthy a sight as that might've been.

"We're fucked," I said.

Kit looked from me to Max. "Yeah, sugar, I can see that." Her grin faltered. "But aside from that, we need those bikes. And let's not forgot the provisions still in the store downstairs." She rubbed her now-gurgling belly. "And breakfast."

I pointed to the remnants of the candy bar still smudged on her chin. "Um…"

She wiped the chocolate off. "I needed something. Previous tenant was apparently on a diet: soy milk and leafy greens and diet pills for days. *Blech.*"

"One problem at a time," said Blondella, pointing down below, the crowd at a fevered pitch now. "Because you're not the only one who seems to be hungry."

I turned to Kit. "That candy bar still in full-force, hon?"

She smiled and stroked her chin with her index finger, the smile growing even wider within moments. "Way ahead of you, sis," she said. "Get dressed and meet me downstairs in ten minutes." She turned to Max. "Or, hey, just go with the towel; your call."

I grabbed Max's elbow. "We'll see you in ten."

"Spoilsport," chided Kit. Then she glanced at Blondella. "And bring the Bedazzler. Gotta have some bit of fabulousness in this new world of ours."

We all matched her smile with ones of our own before heading back to our temporary abodes.

"Think she can do it?" asked Max once newly dressed, his arms again wrapped around me.

I nodded. "She keeps a dozen drag queens in line five nights a week," I told him, staring into those dazzling pools of blue. "A few hundred zombies ain't nothing for Jabba the Slut back there to handle."

He took my word for it and followed me downstairs, where my friends were waiting for us behind the pile of sizzled dead undead. We all had our water guns with us, all newly filled, all held up high. "Just get us back inside the store," Kit told us. "I'll take it from there."

I looked from her to the stack of flesh and then to the milling zombies outside, and promptly frowned. "Gee, is that all?"

She sighed. "It's two feet from this door to the one we need to be in. Just aim, shoot, fire, and run." She then waved her thick index finger in the general direction of the blocked door in front of us. "After we, uh, climb over, um, *that*."

My belly started to churn fast enough to make butter. Still, there was no other way. It was either climb over the pile of flesh or wait it out upstairs. Alone with Max. Without the towel. So, okay, maybe there was another way. Sadly, I didn't have time to voice my opinion, seeing as Blondella had already covered her nose with a rhinestone-studded hanky and was rapidly climbing, mashing into grayish purple flesh all the while.

"It's not too bad," she told us, her voice muffled. "Rigor mortis has made them a bit, shall we say, *sturdy*." She aimed the gun to the street outside, the zombies already headed our way, slow and steady. "Hurry!" she hollered. "Before they reach us!"

I groaned and ran, hand over nose, imagining a field filled with poppies, that the hill was nothing more than a pile of moss-covered rocks, minus the hair, pus, blood, and oozing flesh. Max was a step behind me, Kit three behind us, Blondella already shooting a stream of water out front, the zombies falling and creating yet another demarcation line.

After we helped Kit to the undead apex, we hopped down and rushed inside the store.

"Gross, gross, gross!" I shouted, trying and miserably failing to erase the sound of crunching bones and the stench of decaying flesh out of my already fucked-up-enough head. Then I shivered uncontrollably for the next five minutes and balled up into the fetal position on the floor, possibly peeing my pants a bit. Possibly. Probably. Definitely.

Blondella stood over me, arms crossed over fake chest. "Is the drama queen finished yet?"

I stared up at her and nodded. "Almost." Then I added a final "Gross!" and hopped back up before turning to Kit. "Now what?"

In the five minutes I'd been hyperventilating, my friend had been amassing her arsenal. On the floor by the window sat every bag of ice the store had carried, perhaps about seventy in all. "The water guns will only reach so far, and there are way too many of them out there," she informed. "We need to widen our net, so to speak."

"You lost me," admitted Blondella.

"Shock," chided Kit. "Look, we don't have a hose or a way to spray the ones standing on the other side of our bikes, and we need to be able to get to said bikes, hop on, and ride them back in here."

"In here?" I dared ask.

She pointed out the window and down the alley. "Well, there's no way we're riding through *them*, plus we need to load the supplies," she ever so calmly/bitchily explained. "In here is the only way. The double front doors should be just wide enough for us to drive back through, and the street out front is only sparsely populated with zombies."

"And the ice?" Max asked.

"Cry me a river, hon," she sang. "Cry me a fucking river."

Max grinned. "Genius."

"So I've been told," she agreed, with a knowing smile. "Now help me dump this shit out the window."

Blondella unlatched the window and pushed the levered glass outward. Instantly, we were overcome by the sound of them, the smell of them. It filled the store, filled my very soul even. Yes, drama queeny yet again, but true. Then we flung the ice in the general direction of our bikes, bag after bag of them, until the street was littered with cubes, a large pile of ice just beneath the window.

"Now what?" I asked, which seemed to be the question of the day.

Kit pointed to the rear of the store. "Sink, pots, hot water, go!"

And it was then that I fully understood her plan. "Ah, cry me a river! Genius!"

She smiled. "Never gets old. But hurry, please; we ain't got all day."

And so the drag queen bucket brigade sprang into action. Max filled the pots and handed them to me, who handed them to Blondella, who handed them to Kit, who promptly dumped them on the ice pile outside before handing the pots back our way, over and over and over again, until the ice had melted, flowing in all directions and thereby melting the ice we'd already flung. Then we waited, oh, about thirty minutes, for the water to soak through everyone's shoes, all while we continued to pour water out the window and spray the zombies closest to us.

After that, all hell literally broke loose. I mean, I'd heard of hot-footing it, but this was ridiculous. Because their wet feet seemed to start a sort of chain reaction in them, a spark that ran from bottom to top, one zombie after the next moaning, then yelping, then crumbling to the ground in smoking piles.

"Now run!" shouted Kit. "Get your bikes and drive them in here before the outer field of zombies can work their way past the sizzlers."

Hopping over the dead-again corpses, we raced to the motorcycles, the outer field of zombies heading our way all the while. But with all the sizzlers—our apparent new word for those we rekilled—the outer field was, thank goodness, fairly blocked. Because, no, zombies don't hop or jump or skip; they trudge. And when blocked, they stand and moan even louder, petulant zombies that they are.

In other words, we were home-free. The bikes revved, and we slowly drove, because motorcycles don't do a great job of hopping, skipping, and jumping either, at least not at two miles an hour. Though they do make fairly disgusting noises when they crunch flesh and bone beneath their tires. Suffice it to say, that butter I'd churned in my belly was souring awfully quick.

A few minutes later, we were all inside the shop again, bikes standing between the aisles, Kit's sidecar filling up with all our essentials, water guns newly filled and on top.

"Ready?" I asked, trying to catch my breath.

We all looked at one another, but Kit was shaking her head. "Not yet," she replied. "Prayer time."

"As if this day couldn't get any odder," said Blondella. "Really, girl?"

Kit's shake turned to a nod. "I, for one, am all about taking whatever help we can get. Besides, *He* kept us alive for a reason." She pointed to the ceiling, but we knew that her aim went a lot higher.

"Fine," sighed Max. "But perhaps we should make it a short one, before the ones out back decide to change course and head up front."

Kit nodded and amassed us mid-store in a circle, or at least a square, since there were four of us, and then had us all hold hands. She closed her eyes; we followed suit.

"Dear Lord," she began. "Thank you first and foremost for not turning us into zombies." I giggled, and she admonished me by squeezing my hand even tighter. "We know you have a reason for keeping us alive, Lord, and we ask your help in showing us the light and keeping us safe from harm on our long journey ahead."

"And for keeping Johnny safe, too," added Blondella.

Kit continued. "And for keeping Johnny safe, too. Yes. In your name, we pray."

"Amen," we all said in unison.

Now all we had to pray for was that *He* was in fact listening.

# CHAPTER FIVE
## CREATURE COMFORT

We were on the road soon after that, avoiding congested streets and opting for routes that would usually have the least amount of foot traffic and, therefore, fewer zombies to contend with.

The sun again was broiling down upon us, sweat soon stinging my eyes as I held on tight to Max. There were no clouds, no fog, no noises except for the sound of our bikes as they sped east, heading for the Bay Bridge and I-80, then ultimately New York.

"Stop!" I suddenly heard, barely a mile from the city limit.

Our bikes came to screeching halts as we turned to find Kit pointing to the sidewalk. I squinted and realized in an instant what she was pointing at, my stomach lurching at the pitiful sight.

"Creature," I whispered, voice very nearly catching in my parched throat.

"I don't get it?" said Max, also staring. "It's just a zombie, like all the others. Why are you calling it a creature? There a difference I'm missing?"

I shook my head and forced back a sob. "No, Max. Creature with a capital C. That's her name."

"His name," he said, clearly confused.

"Her name," I reiterated. "Creature Comfort." We stared at her, and she stared at us, her legs now moving in our direction. I'd rarely seen her out of drag, but it was definitely Creature.

I turned around and looked at Kit and Blondella. "What do we do? Put her out of her misery?" If in fact she was even in that. If in fact she felt anything anymore besides the need to extinguish life, presumably our own.

Kit hopped off her bike and rummaged around in the sidecar, while Blondella pulled her bike alongside. "What are you looking for in there? Another candy bar?" Kit merely glanced our way and then lifted up a large canister of salt. "Why did you bring that?" added Blondella. "Because if you got a margarita machine in there, we'll be good to go."

Kit shook her head and motioned for us to join her.

When we were again huddled together and Creature was but twenty feet away, though closing in just the same, she replied, "My father was a nuclear physicist."

"He must've been *insanely* proud of your choice of occupations then," said Blondella. "And?"

Kit sighed. "And that's why I know that radiation pills are comprised primarily of potassium iodide, and that's why I brought this canister. Now I can test my theory."

"Okay," said I, wiping the sweat away. "I'll bite. Theory?"

She pointed to Creature, now barely fifteen feet away, her desperate moans filling our ears. "Yes, theory. As in, what if there's a cure?"

I stared at the canister of salt. "With that? But that's not potassium iodide; it's sodium chloride, right?" And that was the extent of my memory of chemistry class. To be fair, had they taught us about mixing chemicals to make, say, a fabulous blush, then perhaps there might've been a plus at the tail end of that C.

Kit shook the canister. "It's iodized salt, Destiny, the next best thing, at least for us. And maybe it can cut through the radiation." Again she pointed to our undead friend. "In her, I mean."

Now it was my turn to sigh, my hand atop of Kit's. "She died before the radiation kick-started her. So, even if that, as you say, can cut through the radiation, she'll still be dead." It pained my heart to say the words, to even think them, but it was the truth and needed to be said before we put ourselves in harm's way.

"But we don't know any of that for certain," came her reply. "And if we don't at least try, then we'll never know."

Max raised his hand. "Um, *how*, exactly, do we try? Need I remind you that your friend is more than likely approaching us in order to kill us?"

Blondella turned and glanced at Creature. "She always looks like she'd like to kill us. We tend to piss her off quite a lot."

Max snickered. "*Shock*, to use your wording. In any case, I'm all for trying, but how do you intend on administering the dose? Certainly not in water, which would kill her even more."

Kit turned and moved to the sidecar and then retrieved a Hershey Bar with almonds. We waited for her to down it. It was, not surprisingly, a short wait. Then she grinned and backed up a few feet, legs wide as she hunched over.

"If you didn't eat so fast," shouted Blondella, "you wouldn't feel the need to hurl."

"And if you didn't wear that shade of lipstick and eye shadow, I wouldn't feel the need either," came the standard-issue reply. "In any case, watch and learn, children."

And then, to our utter amazement, she took off running, very linebacker-like and rather spry, all things considered. Even more startling, though, was that she was headed directly for Creature.

"Hey!" I tried, but was way too late to stop her. In any case, it was over in a flash. One minute Creature was plodding our way; the next she was down on the ground, moaning up a storm as Kit stood over her. "Huh," I then added, all of us moving toward them.

"It's that rigor mortis we discovered when climbing that pile of them back in the apartment building," she explained. "They can walk, but they can't do much of anything else, least of all stand up once they're down." She again stared at the horizontal and moaning zombie at our feet. "Sorry, girl."

We stood on either side of Creature as she thrashed on the ground, eyes staring lifelessly at us, the moan ever-present as her jaw hung loose from her face. Not a pretty sight. Then again, she wasn't all that pretty to begin with.

"Hold her down," said Blondella.

"Yuck," said I. "She's dead. Bad enough to climb one, now you want me to hold one down?"

"She's your friend," countered Blondella.

I shrugged. "We were never all that close."

Blondella sneered my way. "Bitch, just hold her down on one side, Max on the other. Avoid her teeth, just in case she's trying to eat our brains."

"Light snack," snickered Kit, crouching behind Creature's head as she grabbed hold of the back of it, the zombie hissing as she moaned.

"Fine," I relented, grabbing an arm, the heat rising through her shirt, but not enough to burn me. Max then did the same on the other side until she was fairly immobilized.

Then Blondella grabbed the canister of salt and opened the silver spout on top. With Creature's mouth already opened, all Blondella had to do was dump the contents, which is exactly what she did, the fine grains disappearing down my undead friend's throat until said throat appeared way full.

"Think that'll do it?" I asked, looking at Kit.

"Either that," came the reply, "or she's gonna be hella thirsty."

Though, all of a sudden, she wasn't hella anything. She just lay there, staring up into the oblivion, arms unmoving beneath our hands, legs locked, jaw slack.

"We killed her," I whispered.

"Technically," said Kit, "she was already dead; we merely finished the job. So much for curing her. Prayer time again?"

I started to complain, but then Creature coughed. Not moaned, not hissed, but coughed. "*Kuuuh*," it sounded like, her left eye suddenly blinking, which was odd looking to say the least.

"Creature," I managed. "Are you... are you, um, *okay*?"

"*Kuuuh*," she coughed yet again, right eye now blinking.

Kit continued to hold her head. "I think she's trying to say *okay*."

"Or *cunt*," offered Blondella. "She never really liked you all that much either, Destiny."

Max grimaced. "I think she's just choking on that pound of salt you dumped into her," he said. "Turn her head sideways, Kit."

Kit nodded and did as he said. This time when Creature coughed, a cloud of salt got expelled, then another. She blinked again, both eyes in sync this time, but she was still hot beneath my grip, her skin still gray. Then again, she wasn't moaning or thrashing anymore, so the salt did have some sort of effect. Perhaps the radiation got diminished just enough to make her not so fucking testy.

"Creature," I said, slightly releasing my grip. "Can you hear me?" There was no reply, just another cough, another salty cloud. "Blink once if you can hear me, Creature."

"She blinked!" shouted Kit.

"She was already blinking," griped Blondella. "So that doesn't prove anything."

I looked up at Blondella and nodded, then back down to Creature.

"Blink twice, then pause, then once."

Blondella harrumphed. "Why not have her do a Goddamn tap dance while you're at it?"

I started to reply that Creature could barely dance when she was alive, when she blinked twice, paused, then blinked again. "She understands!" I shouted instead. "Let her go, Max, slowly, and then back away. Same for you, Kit."

The three of us released our grips and backed away, but still Creature lay there. "Help her up, Blondella," said Kit.

"Nice try," came the reply. "I'm not touching *that* with a ten-foot pole."

"More like a three-inch one."

"Pot, kettle, black, bitch."

I held up my hand. "Truce, please. We need to get her upright and see if she still wants us dead. Or at least one of you two, Lord willing."

Max nodded, looked around, and returned with a balled-up piece of newspaper, which he then unceremoniously shoved into Creature's mouth. "At least she can't bite us," he explained, grabbing our friend by his/her/its T-shirt before yanking him/her/it up off the ground in one mighty heave-ho—or just ho, because Creature was sort of an easy lay in life. Then he yanked the paper out and again we all backed up.

"She's not going for us," I said. "Or moaning."

Kit moved in closer. "Do you know who we are?" she asked. There was no answer. "Blink once for yes, twice for no." She blinked once. "Do you know who *you* are?" Another blink.

Blondella tried next. "Do you know *what* you are?" Creature's arm rose just slightly, a finger pointing Blondella's way. "A drag queen?" Yet another blink ensued. "Yes, we know that. But do you know what happened to you, what you are *now*?" There was a long pause. Clearly, she didn't understand the question. "Okay," tried Blondella. "Better question. Do you want to kill us?" No pause, just a blink. Blondella sighed. "Any more than usual, I mean?" Two blinks. *Phew.*

I pulled my friends away and whispered, "We can't tell her just yet what happened. She's been through enough, what with being dead and all."

Kit bobbed her head. "Plus, there's not enough makeup in the world to adequately cover that gray complexion up with." She nodded Blondella's way. "Case in point."

"Wait," said Max, stopping the volley before it started. "So what do you suggest we do with her, Destiny? She can't ride on one of the bikes; she's not bendy enough. Ditto for the sidecar, which is full enough as it is anyway."

"But we can't leave her here either," I replied. "We brought her back, mostly... somewhat... um, *ish*; so she's our responsibility."

The silence returned as we all looked around, trying to think of a solution to our latest dilemma. It was Max who finally found the answer. "Rigor mortis," he said, snapping his fingers as he started jogging down the street. We watched him go, ass shaking in his teeny-tiny shorts.

"Nice," whispered Blondella.

"Fuck yeah," agreed Kit.

"Amen, sister," said I.

Creature moaned, but it was hard to tell if that's just what she did now.

In any case, he quickly returned with a skateboard in hand before rummaging around the sidecar for some rope. Then he tied the rope to the sidecar and tentatively approached Creature. She stood there rigid—and not in the good sort of way—and stared from it to him, the moan repeating as her eyes went wide. Well, as wide as they could, all things considered. Then she shook her head. Again, as much as she could.

"There's no room for you on our bikes," he explained as comfortingly as possible, just as we spotted zombies approaching from the end of the street. "It's either this"—he pointed the other way—"or them."

Her hand slowly lifted up, fingers locked in place. He moved in closer to her and looped the rope around her digits, then squeezed her hand in his to lock said digits tightly around the rope. He gave a pull, and the rope stayed put, while I in turn placed the skateboard in front of her. Again Max acted, lifting her up and setting her down on top of it.

Blondella coughed. "X Games, here we come."

I turned and glared. "Not helping." Then I looked back to Max. "Think it'll work?"

He shrugged as he began tying the rope to the sidecar. "Think, yes. Know, guess we'll find out."

We all mounted our bikes, the zombies drawing ever nearer, their moans drowned out by our roaring engines. Then we took off, Max and me in the lead, Blondella next, then Kit and the sidecar. I turned around to make sure that Max's plan was working and that Creature wasn't being dragged through the streets of San Francisco.

"Well?" shouted Max over his shoulder.

I patted his arm. "Rope's holding. Zombie's holding. Skateboard's holding." I smiled and turned back around. "Triple-check, boss."

"Now all we have to hope for is that she doesn't eat our brains while we're asleep."

My smile flat-lined. "Um, gross, for one, and not nearly all we have to hope for, for two. Besides, I think she's a vegan."

He put the pedal to the metal and zoomed toward the bridge. "Things have changed, Destiny. Things have changed."

* * * *

Too bad about that, too. Because things most definitely had changed. And none for the better. Oh, sure, the ride across the bridge went fine. That part of our journey was easy enough, seeing as the zombies were locked in their idling cars, lifelessly staring at us as we weaved between them, skating zombie in the rear, her hair flying in the breeze. Tony Hawk, eat your heart out—or brains, I suppose. But the bay beneath us, as I was quick to notice, wasn't as it had been before the sun decided to go all bad-ass on us. You could easily see that the water was lapping at places it had never reached before.

I pointed to my right. "Water's rising, Max."

He nodded as he quickly looked over. "Fuck," he cursed. "Mountain snow must've melted and fed the tributaries overnight. Bay must be four, five feet higher than normal. This heat keeps up, gonna be *Waterworld II* for us."

I groaned. "Goodie for Kevin Costner's career, not so goodie for ours. Don't we cross a bunch of rivers on our way to New York?"

Again he nodded. "And mountains, all of them full of snow. Possibly past-tense. *Definitely* if this heat doesn't let up soon."

We made it across the bridge, and Max pulled over, the others following suit. "Potty break so soon?" asked Blondella as we all cut our engines.

"'Fraid not," replied Max. "Change of course." He pointed to the bay. "Water is rising and might keep on rising. We stay on course, I-80's gonna run on through Tahoe soon enough and then do the same for the mountains in Utah and then the ones in Colorado, all of them full of snow this time of year. That means one swollen river after the next for us."

Kit frowned. "And I do so like swollen appendages, but…"

Blondella finished her train of thought. "But we're headed in the wrong direction. So what does that mean for us? Head for Oakland airport and see if we can tie a rope to a plane for Creature?"

Even though she was a good ten feet away, I could still hear her moan. "Please," I whispered. "She must be confused enough as it is."

"Join the crowd," griped Blondella. "But I-80 is the quickest route to Johnny."

"And the most dangerous," added Max. "We could easily get trapped or, worse, flooded out. A few more days like today and we'll be swimming to Johnny. And flying is out, unless you want to see about tying that rope to a kite."

Again I heard the moan. "So what do we do?" I asked.

"Head south," Max replied. "Skirt the California mountains and take a left at Bakersfield, then aim for the deserts and a more southerly route. Rivers might be swollen down there, but not nearly as bad as up north. Also, the deserts will have fewer cars and fewer zombies to contend with."

"But will add to our time," griped Blondella, looking none too pleased at the latest turn of events.

"Not if we get trapped by a flash flood up here," said Max. "And with less traffic and fewer cities to go through, we might even make it faster that way."

I tapped Max on the shoulder. "But the desert, Max? It's already hot enough now."

The others nodded. Not Creature, of course, but at least she stopped moaning. "I'm not saying it's an ideal solution," he replied, "but for now, or until the sun takes a bit of a break up there, it's our only one." He paused and solemnly looked to the three of us in turn. "Unless we just want to end the trip before it begins, set up camp on a mountaintop and see what happens next. I mean, there's certainly adequate shelter and food for the taking."

Blondella grimaced and cranked her ignition. "Fuck that shit. Johnny is alive. I know he is."

"You *think* it," replied Max. "Hope it, as do we all, but do you want to risk your life to find out for certain? And how will you even locate him if we make it to New York? And, don't forget, that's the one city that's chock full of zombies, millions of them in every direction."

Her grimace tightened on her sweat-soaked face. "I'll cross that bridge when I come to it."

I sighed and stared at the concrete. "But what if there aren't any more bridges to cross, Blondella?"

She released her hands from the handlebars. "What would you do if the man who you loved was even possibly alive? Or even your mother, your father? Anyone that you love who's not a zombie?"

My heart ached at what she said, because, more than likely, everyone I loved was indeed now a zombie. Everyone I ever loved, ever knew, except for her and Max and Kit and Cr... well, not Creature, but still.

And so I turned to Max and said, "I think we have enough *camp*, mountaintop or not, right here already."

He grinned. "More than enough, from what I've seen. And heard." Creature moaned, but I bet she was thinking something bitchy in reply. "In any case, there's one thing we overlooked."

"Gee, just the one?" asked Kit.

"As of late," replied Max. "And that is, what if there's life beyond California? What if there's more like us between here and New York." His grin amped up as he looked at our rag-tag-drag-team. "Well, maybe not like *us*, but you get my point."

Blondella again grabbed her handlebars. "Great. Anyone else in for some cross-country, cross-dressing adventure?"

I raised my hand, as did Kit, reluctantly. Creature seemed to try, and that was good enough for us.

As to anyone else like us out there, wait, just wait. They're a comin' alright.

Though, sad to say, not in a good way.

# CHAPTER SIX
## ALL THE CONVENIENCES OF HOMO

And so we headed south down Interstate 5. There were no rivers to contend with, no zombies, save for the occasional migrant farm worker along the side of the road, and certainly no sounds except for the growl of our bikes and the equally standard growl of Kit's belly. We stopped only to eat from our private stash and to pee behind the occasional bush. As to traffic, the road was littered with stalled zombie-driven cars and trucks, but not enough to cause us any problems; we merely weaved between them, ignoring the vacant stares of the undead as best we could.

Once we hit Bakersfield, we skirted around the town and headed east, the mountain chains that bisected Northern California no longer in our path. Still, it was getting dark, and we were dust-covered and exhausted; Barstow and then the Mojave could wait until morning.

"So what are our options?" asked Max, once we were all sitting together on a picnic bench out in the middle of friggin' nowhere.

"Hotel?" eagerly replied Kit.

"What if the zombies find us and we get trapped on an upper floor?" replied Max. "Doubtful we can find one with a fire escape from one of the rooms."

"Motel?" Kit offered, less-eagerly.

Max sighed. "Same problem. They smell us and trap us in our rooms."

I tapped him on the shoulder. "Well, unless we find a castle with a moat, the zombies are always going to be a problem, Max."

"Something remote then," offered Blondella. "Maybe a cabin,

someplace the zombies won't be able to locate us at."

Max scratched his chin and eventually nodded before pointing to some nearby green hills. "Good idea. Let's look up there before the sun goes down."

The hills, as it turned out, were pastureland, the cows all deceased and belly-up, not a *moo* to be heard. Still, there was one lone farmhouse atop the tallest hill, Ma and Pa farmer quickly dispatched with our water guns, a few farmhands the same. *Splish, splash*, undead bath. Then once we circled the property a few times, just to be safe, we settled in for the evening, leaving Creature outside to keep watch.

"Yell if you hear or see anything, girl," said Blondella with a yawn.

Creature groaned in reply.

"Okay," I added. *"Groan* if you hear or see anything. And loudly, please."

Then we locked the front door behind us, rounded up some food, and ate with gusto. Because, by then, even Kit was over our chocolate and pretzel and Pop-Tart rations. After that, we found our rooms and wished each other our goodnights.

"Now I lay me down to sleep," yawned Blondella over her shoulder.

"Emphasis on the lay," cracked Kit our way as, one by one, the bedroom doors got shut behind us.

And then I was once again alone with Max.

"Hi," he said, his arms quickly around me, pulling me in good and tight.

"Hi," I repeated, our lips pressed together as I fairly melted into him. "Pretty fucked-up day, huh?"

He rested his chin on my shoulder and stroked my back. "I have a feeling it's only going to get worse."

"Sugarcoating, please?"

He chuckled. "Tomorrow's another day, Destiny. Maybe all the zombies will be taking dirt naps by then, and we'll be the kings and queens of the grand old U. S. of A."

Now that I liked the sound of. "Make that king and three queens." I paused and sighed. "And their rather gray-tinged watch guard." Then I pulled an inch away and gazed into his stunning eyes of blue. "But that's not going to happen, is it, Max?"

He shrugged. "The living became the walking undead, Destiny. So anything's possible."

"Ronald Reagan and George Bush both got elected to two terms of office. Snooki wrote a book. And Larry King found seven women to marry him."

His chuckle repeated, which sent a spark of something nicely tingly down my spine. "Like I said, so anything's possible."

I kissed him again and then again after that. "And I found you through all this," I whispered. "Gray clouds, silver lining."

"See," he whispered back. "There's always a bright side to everything." His smile widened. "Wanna see another bright one?"

His smile turned devilish, which meant that the thought of zombies, at least for the time being, could simmer on the backburner. "Do I get to pick the side?"

He nodded, while I patted his rump, picking the side so bright that it could put the sun to shame. "Yes, your highness," he agreed, with a low bow.

And with that, he was shucking off his dusty clothes and hopping on the quilt-covered bed. In a heartbeat—which, all things considered, thank goodness, we still had—he was on the bed, on all-fours, legs wide, cheeks parted, hole winking out at me all come-hither-like.

Naturally, I came hither.

I knelt on the floor and prayed to the holy trinity: cock, balls, and hole. It was a beautiful sight to see, too. Bright side indeed. A perfect alabaster ass, soft down along the crack, heavy balls swaying, thick prick hovering. Hell, even his feet were pretty. And so that's where I started from. After I got undressed first, I mean.

I pressed my thumbs into the sole of his left foot, kneading the tender area, all while he giggled. "Ticklish much?"

He nodded. "Feels good, though."

"I aim to please."

He shook his stellar ass, balls swaying in the opposite direction. "You might want to aim a little higher, then."

I spanked said ass. "Getting there."

I had my hands resume their upward course. From his feet I moved to his well-defined calves. Clearly, Max jogged or ran or did something sporty, because it was like massaging a rock.

"Jogger?"

He shook his head. "Nope. Line dancer."

I stopped massaging. "Huh?"

"Country line dancing."

I grimaced. "Nobody's perfect."

He turned his head my way and grinned. "Not a Reba or a Dolly or a Shania fan?"

I moved my hands to his hairy thighs, rubbing the tightness out as best I could. "Shanoa. Not even to lip-sync to for money." I continued, left hand on left cheek, right hand on right cheek, digging my fingers in as I spread them apart, gazing longingly at the crinkled center of his universe. "More of an eighties pop fan. Madonna, Cyndi Lauper, Bjork."

Again he turned his head my way. "Bjuck. Nobody's perfect, or so I've been told."

Once more I slapped his ass, red quickly rising to the surface. "They were my saviors, Max," I told him, now stroking his pole with one hand as I caressed his hole with the other. "Alone, in my room, back in high school, I would listen to them, music cranked up, divas before I even knew what the word meant. They were different when different wasn't cool. They were who and what they wanted to be. They were, like this ass of yours, *fabulous*."

He rolled over on his back and gazed up at me as I again grabbed his prick. His eyelids fluttered, but then he looked at me knowingly. "Ah," he said. "Gay was not okay in the day?"

"Gay wasn't even close to okay. Gay was leprosy in vivid pink. But in my room, with the music pounding away on my eardrums, I could…"

"Disappear?" he finished my train of thought. "Got it. Been there and sadly done that. Funny, I think I became a funeral director for the same reason you became a drag queen."

I stopped stroking. Clearly, he lost me on that one. "The dead buy you free drinks, Max?"

His smile returned. "You became what you most loved: a diva. Someone spectacular. Your differences became what other people admired, not ridiculed you for."

In truth, I'd never thought about it quite like that. Basically, I got to talk trash, drink at work, and wear a lot of sparkly rhinestones. For cash! Okay, small fish in a small pond, but at least I was still swimming—in a dress and tucked, but still. I leaned over him and planted a warm, wet one on his thick lips. "Makes sense, but how did you become a funeral director while I became"—I pushed my cock between my legs: instant vjayjay—"*this*."

He stared down and frowned. "Doesn't that hurt?"

I shrugged. "You get used to it." Sad but true. Though those free drinks are generally strong, so I'm fairly anesthetized by the end of the night anyway. In any case, I set my prick free and again grabbed onto his, while he, in turn, took hold of mine. "But how does that explain why you work with the dead and I work with the merely inebriated?"

He smiled as he picked up the pace on my ever-growing tool. "You disappeared behind the makeup, the kitsch, the dresses; I disappeared behind my own sort of mask. We both console people in our own special way. But, at the same time, few people ever get to see the real us."

My smile faltered at that. "Sounds sad, Max."

He leaned up and kissed me. "I suppose everything in life comes with a price, Destiny. We love what we do, but not everyone appreciates us for it. Still, we can be who we want to be and still remain anonymous, to a certain degree. As teenagers, that's probably what we wanted most: anonymity. And voila, that's exactly what we got."

"What? Single?" Sucked to say it, but it was true.

He reached up and stroked my cheek. "Takes a special kind of man to love a funeral director."

I nodded, ignoring for now the love part. "Takes a special kind of man to love a drag queen. Out of a dress, I mean. And while they're sober."

"Stone-cold here," he informed, the smile wide on his handsome, scruffy face.

My pace picked up on his prick. "And stone-hard, too." I laughed. "Now that is *special*."

Again he stroked my cheek. "As are you, Destiny," he rasped, just before his cock exploded, all Vesuvius-like. "As are you."

My cock shot a split-second later, heavy load raining down on him as his spewed out at me, both of them quickly pooling on his hairy belly before dripping onto the quilt below. He huffed while I puffed, and then I fell down on top of him and eagerly swapped some heavy spit.

"You always this philosophical during sex, Max?" I asked.

"Only when the rest of the world goes to pot, Destiny. Or when

I'm high on pot. Ironic, huh?"

Exhausted, I shut my eyes and rested my head on his shoulder. "If you say so, Max. If you say so."

* * * *

The next morning, we awoke to the alarming sound of groans. We jumped up and dressed and ran into my friends in the hallway. Blondella lifted her index finger to her mouth and quietly said, "*Shh.*"

We all shushed and followed her to the front of the house, four bodies ducking, four heads poking up to stare outside. Fortunately, it was just Creature doing the groaning. I cracked the window. "Zombies?"

She blinked twice.

"Just hungry?" tried Kit.

She blinked once, then twice. Which I took to mean that, yes, she was hungry, but, no, that wasn't why she was groaning. She also didn't wait for another question from us; instead, she managed to slightly raise her arm and point. And since we couldn't see what was agitating her so, we quietly tiptoed to the door, quietly unlocked and opened said door, and then quietly, mostly because we were suddenly in shock, stared at what she was trying to point at.

"Army trucks," I whispered, staring down the hill to the road below. "Is there a base nearby?"

We all shrugged in sync. Apart from occasionally playing the Andrews Sisters on stage, the military wasn't exactly our forté. Still, it didn't much matter; they were here now, and maybe they could save us. I started to shout, but Max quickly covered my mouth.

"Wait," he said.

"Why?" I replied, the word muffled behind his hand.

It was Blondella who answered, though. "How can so many of them still be alive?"

"Exactly," said Max. "We were all fatefully in steel rooms when the blast hit; no way could they have been so lucky, not unless…"

He released his hand from my mouth. "Unless they knew about the blast beforehand," I said, finishing his train of thought.

"Fuckers," spat Kit.

"Mmm," groaned Creature in apparent agreement.

"But that doesn't mean they can't or won't help us now," I tried.

And it was then we saw a zombie horde heading their way from the opposite direction, at least a hundred of them, their collective moan reaching our ears a moment later. The sound was there briefly, however, because the guns appeared right at that same time, *rat-a-tat-tatting* until every last one of the undead was now fully dead within seconds, heads and brains splattered for yards around, the trucks not even bothering to stop; they just ran over the bodies. I looked at Creature and frowned. "Or maybe not."

In any case, the trucks rode past, a cloud of dust in their wake. "Their flaps are down," said Kit, pointing to the convoy below. "What do you think they're carrying?"

"Weapons, food, more military," replied Max. "Could be anything."

"Probably weapons," said Blondella. "They're the military." We all nodded. "So maybe let's follow them. From a distance. God forbid we need future help, at least they won't be too far away then. If they're heading east, I mean."

"Couldn't hurt, I suppose," said Max. "All in favor?"

We all raised our hands. Creature blinked. I still wasn't sure if she knew exactly what she was, and wasn't about to tell her just yet. Especially after the massacre we'd just witnessed. Still, it would have to happen soon, and before we got anywhere near those trucks and those guns.

In any case, we gathered our meager belongings, loaded some more nonperishables into the sidecar, and headed out, Creature getting towed in the rear once again.

It was easy enough to safely follow them, too, from a distance, as agreed. No, not because they left a dust cloud, which they didn't, or because we could hear them, which we couldn't, and with the road being flat, we couldn't even see them, but we had a secret weapon that they didn't have. I mean, who needed radar or obviously nonworking satellites when you had Creature, who could smell a human from a mile away. After all, she was still a zombie at heart, non-beating though it was.

We'd just look back, and if she blinked once, we were still heading in the same general direction they were. Twice meant that they'd taken a turn; though that hadn't seemed to happen yet.

So to Barstow we headed next.

"What if they can help us?" asked Max over his shoulder, a few miles into our journey for the day.

"You saw what they do to zombies, Max," I said into his ear.

He nodded and paused: one of the pregnant variety, where you're clearly eager to push, but afraid of the consequences. "She's... she's already dead, Destiny."

I nodded and paused as well. "They're the military. They must've known about the blast beforehand. They didn't help us then, so why would they now?"

His nod turned to a side-to-side shake. "Even if they knew, what could they have done? It's the sun. It affected the entire planet. All they would've done is caused pandemonium, with the same general outcome."

"I still don't like it."

"What's to like?" he replied. "It's a lose/lose situation."

I gripped my arms tighter around him. "Still, they're headed somewhere; they must have a plan. Maybe they even had one before the blast. What if it doesn't include civilians like us? I didn't see any nonmilitary folks when they opened fire. What if they always shoot first and forget to ask questions later? What if it's us their shooting at next?"

"Point taken," he allowed. "In any case, following, for now, still seems like the best bet. And they are heading east, like us, so no harm, no foul."

"Point taken," I echoed, turning back to Creature, her single blink every few minutes appearing like a beacon. Was she dead, like Max had said? She certainly looked it. But she was blinking and groaning and protecting us, and the dead, zombies especially, didn't do those sorts of things.

So for the time being, we were done racking up points and simply following.

Barstow came and went, and with it a new trail of splattered undead. We veered around them, but it was impossible to ignore the sight, the stench of them. These were humans, after all. They'd all been alive a mere few days prior, unaware of what lay ahead. Which, of course, couldn't be said for the guys that had gunned them down. And no matter how we justified it, I couldn't get beyond that. Because they clearly had been aware.

An hour and a half later, the sun was fairly high overhead, and that far into the desert, which was unbearable most days anyway, we all felt much like a snowman in July: melting.

Blondella pulled up to us and fanned her face. "We have to get out of this soon," she said, loud enough for us to hear over the engines.

But it was then we all noticed Creature, who was double-blinking up a storm. We pulled to a stop along the side of the road and turned to her. "Did they go off on a side road?" Max asked, and got one blink in return. "Did they stop?" Another single blink. Then another. "You lost me, Creature. Did they stop or not?" Single blink. Pause. Single blink. And then Max snapped his fingers. "Two stops, Creature? Two caravans, Creature?"

Single blink.

"Fuck," cursed Kit.

"They're amassing," added Blondella. "But why? And where?"

"Why," said Max, "I haven't a clue, but where can only be one place, if they're ahead of us in the distance." He turned to us and informed, "The Mojave Desert."

"Why there?" I asked.

We all shrugged. "Only one way to find out," I said.

"At night," said Kit. "It's too fucking hot now. And if they're amassing, then hopefully they're staying for a while. If not, Creature will let us know, right?"

"Mmm," Creature moaned.

"See," Kit said, pointing at our still-tied-to-a-skateboard friend. "Let's find some air-conditioning and a few Cokes and a chair or two, maybe even a Snickers Bar—dear God in heaven, please—and wait until it's cooler outside before we see what these guys are up to."

"All those in favor?" Max asked, and all those in favor, namely all of us, raised our hands or moaned/blinked in reply. "Snickers it is then."

"Praise Jesus," said Kit, hands in prayer, face tilted skyward. "And there was a gas station/convenience store a few miles back, probably the last one this far out in the desert."

So back we went, the station appearing like a mirage in the distance, hot air causing that whole wobbly effect on it. We drove faster, all of us eager to escape the heat. When we arrived, we parked around back, cocked our guns and had Max open the door. The lone zombie charged out and was just as quickly mowed down. Or at least watered down. After that, we ran inside.

"*Aah*," came our collective sighs as the blast of frigid air hit our hot flesh.

"Look!" shouted Kit. I turned, ready to fire again, when I noticed what she was pointing at, my eyes landing not on a zombie but on a freezer case. "Frozen Snickers ice cream bars!" Again her head tilted skyward, or at least ceilingward. "Thank you, Jesus!"

Better yet, we were still fairly far from the generally dry state of Utah, so there were frozen malt beverages in that same freezer. And strawberry flavored to boot! "Amen!" I hollered, a foot behind her.

So on the cold floor we all sat, eating and/or drinking, though mostly drinking, equally cold food items and booze. "Any plans?" asked Max, chomping on some jerky that he downed with a Miller Lite.

"First the Snickers ice cream bar," said Kit, already halfway through with said bar, her second thus far, "and then another margarita."

Max shook his head. "I meant about the military."

Kit shrugged and scarfed down bar number two. "They can get their own."

I patted his knee. "Wait for the sugar to kick in, Max," I told him, watching her chew as I waited for the desired effect.

Thankfully, we got it a moment later.

She gulped, belched, and replied, "Best guess, they have some kind of camp up ahead. And if they really are shooting first and asking questions later, us strolling up to said camp isn't going to be such a swell idea." She chugged the margarita straight from the silvery pouch. "We need a diversion then. Something that will allow us to get a lay of the land without them knowing we're laying." She wagged a cautionary finger at Blondella and continued. "If we find that they're just innocent bystanders to the whole sun thing, then we ask for help. If not, we skedaddle, hopefully unnoticed." She unwrapped a third bar and took a chomp. "Or we say fuck it and head to New York right now, leave them to their own devices. We've made it this far without their help, I mean; what's another few thousand miles?"

"And a couple of hundred million zombies," I reminded her.

She shrugged, bar number three nothing but a distant memory. "They're slow, and we have ample water to defend ourselves with." Then she pointed at Creature, who was standing at the door, staring out. "Plus, we have her," Kit whispered. "If she can smell the living, maybe she can smell the dead, too, and warn us of impending hordes."

As if on cue, Creature moaned, all of us dropping our food. Though not our drinks. Those we carried to the door.

We lined up along the window and searched for zombies or the military or anything else that was apt to do us harm. But all we saw was what she had seen, namely an approaching silver bus coming from the south.

"Now what?" groused Blondella.

"Guess we wait and find out," replied Max. "No sense trying to run now; they'll certainly see us pulling out of here. Besides, it's not a military vehicle and there aren't any zombies chasing after it, so maybe this glass will be half-full."

Blondella downed her margarita pouch. "Glass, as it were, is empty." She ran and got another one. Peach, this time. "Just in case," she informed, tearing it open before sucking the slushy liquid out.

And then we waited.

And not for all that long, either.

Barely a minute later, up pulled the bus, squealing as it came to a stop just outside the door and alongside our bikes. My heart raced as we stared at it, eyes wide as it opened up and a heeled foot poked out. Wider still when we saw who emerged.

"It… it can't be," managed Blondella, again sucking on her pouch.

"Sure looks like her," whispered Kit.

"Easy enough to do," I replied. "Seen lots of queens look like her before."

"Not *that* good," said Blondella, as the *her* in question drew nearer, black hair blowing in the hot breeze.

"It's…" said I, voice suddenly catching in my throat as the convenience store door flung open.

"*Cher*," said Blondella, falling to her knees and nearly dropping her drink.

Nearly, suffice it to say, but not quite.

71

# CHAPTER SEVEN
## AFTER A NUCLEAR ATTACK

"But how?" I squeaked out.

She smiled and, yes, flicked her hair and licked her lips, just like Cher! Mainly because she was Cher! CHER!!! "You know what they say," she replied, standing there, arms akimbo.

"Never mix liquor and beer," replied Kit, one hand lifting the margarita, the other a Heineken. "Too late."

Cher shook her head, but I knew full well what she was getting at and said, "After a nuclear attack, the only things left will be cockroaches and Cher."

Fingertip got touched to nose. "Bingo," she said. "And I'm Cher, bitches." Then she pointed outside and up to the sun. "Nuclear-fucking-attack." Then she again turned our way. "Ergo…"

"We should watch out for cockroaches?" quipped Blondella.

"Makes sense," said Cher, grabbing the Heineken from Kit's hand before chugging much of it down.

"Wait," said Max. "Your bus."

She turned and looked at it. "Used to belong to Nixon. Campaign bus. I couldn't resist."

Max nodded. "Meaning, it's steel. Bulletproof, no doubt."

"Ah," I ahed. "Were you in that thing when the sun went all haywire?"

She nodded. "Heading from L.A. to my home outside of Vegas. Have a show there in a few days." She frowned. "*Had*, I mean. But L.A. is a nightmare right now, even more so than usual, as you can imagine, so I'm continuing on to Vegas rather than going back."

Then she noticed Creature. "Um, are we safe from…?"

Then it was my turn to nod. "Long story, but yes."

"And how come the rest of you are still so, well, pretty and pink?" She winked at Max.

"Drag queens don't die so easily either," replied Blondella.

Cher smiled and finished Kit's beer. "No shock there. So where you headed?"

"New York City," informed Blondella.

Cher frowned and looked at each of us in turn. "I wouldn't if I was you. If New York is anything like Los Angeles, it's overrunning with, well"—she pointed at Creature—"barely made it out of there myself, to tell you the truth. Luckily, we were already off the main highway when the sun thing happened. Been slowly weaving between cars all the way here. Fortunately, that bus is like a tank; pushes cars out of the way like they were made of tin."

I raised my hand. "Um, Miss… uh, *Cher*, one small problem."

She laughed, flicked her hair, and licked her lips. Just like Cher! Sorry, it bears repeating. CHER!!! "I survived Sonny, Studio 54, and Lady Gaga's meat purse. Small problems I can handle. Unless there's suddenly a Republican running what's left of the country. Then I'm gonna be mighty pissed."

"Just as bad," I told her. "Military's up ahead. And that bus of yours won't get by unnoticed. And, far as I can recall, this road is the only one that leads to Vegas."

She shrugged. "I'm Cher. What's the worst they can do to me?"

I cleared my throat. "Did you happen to pass a pile of newly-dead undead back near Barstow? With their brains scattered to Kingdom Come?" She nodded. "Well then, *that's* the worst."

She tapped her foot and sighed. "So what were you planning on doing then? Backtrack and go around them?"

I too sighed. "More belly of the beast option. See what they're up to first, then maybe ask for help in getting to New York."

"Uh huh," she said, clearly thinking something through in her head. "So, if they're up to no good—and the military being what it is, that's probably a given—then I'm probably going to get stopped in my bus and, Cher though that I am, get detained or worse, even though I'm barely a couple of hours from home—well, mansion, really, because, like I said, I'm Cher—while you all are planning on driving those motorcycles of yours cross-country, in this awful heat, for days and days on end, with no protection other than—"

"A few water guns," I interrupted her.

"Uh huh, right, a few water guns," she repeated, looking at us like we were crazy. "So why not trade then? I take a bike; you take the bus. I ride over the hills and avoid the military; you take your chances with them, which is what you were going to do anyway, and then, God willing, you'll be more comfortable for the rest of your long journey, while I'll already be inside my secure, gated mansion, stocked with enough provisions to keep me for quite some time."

"Your bus?" said Blondella. "You want us to take Cher's bus? *Cher's?*"

"Well, technically Nixon's, but yeah," she replied. "Besides, I got a Bentley and a Ferrari in Vegas."

"And you know how to ride a motorcycle?" Kit asked.

Cher grinned. "Of course. I'm Cher," she replied, looking at us with a *duh* expression on her face. "Anyway, don't have to ride it; my driver can drive us." She opened the door to the store, put her fingers in her mouth, and whistled. "Best driver money can buy."

The driver emerged, a Viking in jeans and a dress shirt, hair the color of wheat, muscles the size of melons (and ripe ones at that), and a smile that got some orthodontist a trophy sitting somewhere. In other words, *best* was an understatement of the gross variety.

"I vote we go with Cher," said Kit, mouth agape.

"We're going to New York," groaned Blondella. "And deal, Cher. You take the bike with the sidecar; we'll take the bus."

Which is how we came to be in Nixon's campaign bus, formerly owned by Cher, who was now driving across the hills, away from the military, in a sidecar next to the dreamiest driver this side of Jeff Gordon. And the other side to boot.

Since she had such a short drive, all she had with her were a few small water pistols from off one of the store's shelves and some bottles of water and snacks. We, on the other hand, had, as Kit exclaimed once we were on the bus, "Hit the motherfucking jackpot!"

"Tell me those aren't what I think they are," said Blondella, fairly hyperventilating as she collapsed on the leopard-print sofa, hand to padded chest.

I walked over, reverently, and searched for a tag. "Bob... Bob... Bob..."

"Mackie!" shouted Kit. "Bob *FUCKING* Mackie! A whole rack of them!"

By then, Blondella was drooling. "With matching shoes and wigs!" Even Creature, who we managed to lift onto the bus, along with her skateboard, just in case, was salivating. Then again, considering her current state, that might've just been real spit as opposed to the oh-my-God-those-are-Bob-Mackie-dresses kind, but she was moaning, so we took it to mean the latter.

"Who?" asked Max, scratching his head.

We all turned and stared at him in stunned silence. "You sure you're gay, sugar?" asked Kit.

"Oh, he's gay, all right," said I, knowingly. "Card carrying. But he's also into country line dancing, and Bob Mackie didn't exactly design for the hoedown."

"Hey!" objected Max.

"No offense," said I, mostly meaning it. "In any case, don't you think we have bigger fish to fry right about now?"

Kit nodded. "Like seeing what the military is up to without them seeing what we're up to, while in a giant steel bus?"

Since it was good enough for Cher, I touched fingertip to nose and said, "Bingo." Then I started rummaging through the dresses, my hands trembling as I touched one after the other, imagining all the tiny Chinese women and their arthritic fingers as they stitched each and every bead in place just so Cher could shimmer on stage. Glancing over my shoulder, I added, "Any ideas?"

I caught Kit's glimmer of a smile, the three Snickers ice cream bars obviously working their magic inside her twisted brain. "Well, back to our options. We either also find a way around the military, which seems even more difficult now, or we create a diversion and figure out what they're up to, praying that it's nothing and then asking for help. Does that about sum it up?"

I nodded. "Just so long as none of these dresses get hurt in the fray."

Kit frowned. "I don't suppose there are any in my size, are there?"

Blondella snorted. "Circus tents by Mackie? I doubt it. Maybe we can stop at a Lane Bryant along the way and check out the Oprah line."

A wayward heel struck our blonde friend before she even saw it coming. "Bitch," said Kit. "In any case, no dresses will be harmed."

Her grin returned. "The zombies, on the other hand, won't be so lucky."

"What zombies?" Max asked. "We're the only ones out here."

"Exactly," said Kit. "Why do you think the military is camping out in the Mojave?"

The light bulb above my head went from dim to blisteringly bright. "No people. Or zombies."

"Exactly," Kit repeated. "No zombies *yet*, that is."

I gulped. "I don't like the sound of that, girl."

"Well, at least *you'll* know what's coming, though."

\* \* \* \*

It was still early yet, plenty of time until nightfall. And plenty of time is just what we needed. Thankfully, though, we were going in reverse, following the same path the bus and the military had taken, so said path was already cleared, cars pushed to the side of the road, allowing us free rein along the highway all the way back to Barstow.

Max drove the bus through town this time as opposed to around, while me and Blondella, dressed in multicolored gowns—in other words, *pied*—hooted and hollered out the side door. As for Kit, she glumly sat in the passenger seat, window open, shooting zombies that got in our way with the water guns, while those that followed in the rear got *pipered*, as it were, trailing in our slow-moving wake, mouths agape, moaning up a combined storm.

By the time we circled through town, there must have been easily a few hundred of them following us, stiff legs creaking, arms rigid, eyes dead. They looked nasty and smelled even worse, but at least they were following us, our human scent slowly leading the way—and I do mean at-a-snails-pace slowly.

"This keeps up, we won't make it back until the middle of the night," said Max, foot barely on the gas pedal.

"Perfect," said Kit, window closed now that we were back on the road. Blondella and I sat on the couch, door still open. As for Creature, she was staring out, gazing at the undead masses that followed.

"Think she knows?" whispered Blondella in my ear.

I shrugged. "Impossible to say what she knows," I whispered back. "She thinks she's one of us, but as to those, those *things* out there, it's anybody's guess."

"You okay, Creature?" Blondella asked. Creature paused, but blinked once. "Guess we stay the course, then," came the next whisper.

I nodded, gut wrenching as I watched my friend stand there, nearly lifeless and gray. Which did, at the very least, give me an idea, seeing as we had hours and hours to, pardon the expression, *kill*.

"Creature?" I said, standing up, which wasn't all that easy, seeing as those dresses were made more to look good in than feel good in. "Have you ever worn a Bob Mackie gown before?"

Kit grumbled from the front seat. "Oh hell to the no," she said, turning our way. "*She* gets one, and I'm still wearing *this*?" She pointed at her recently borrowed and still too-tight shorts. Truth be, if she had lips down there, I would've been able to read them.

In any case, I replied, "A Bob Mackie dress is a terrible thing to waste."

"Amen," said Blondella, hand raised to the sky in praise.

Max chuckled as he crept along. "She's got you there, Kit."

Kit sighed. "Fine. But I'm doing the makeup." She stood. "Gray is *so* not your color, girl."

Creature blinked, and I could almost detect a smile on her face, her lips quivering, if only for a moment.

So to work we went, a makeshift dressing room set up in the middle of the bus. And since Creature couldn't move any of her limbs more than a few inches, it was our job to do it for her, arms, legs, head, all twisted this way and that, until her old, dusty clothes were off and a shimmering gown bedecked in reds and oranges replaced them, all while Kit expertly set the foundation, lots of it (lots and lots) for the makeup to sit on, until not a pore was breathing on her face. Then again, since Creature herself wasn't breathing, what did that really matter?

An hour later, auburn wig crowing it all, plus some jewelry we'd found—and definitely not our usual costume variety—we placed her in her heels and shined a spotlight on her (flashlight, but why quibble?) and then struck up the band (Kit was an awesome beat-boxer).

"Ladies and gentlemen… er, *man*… please welcome to the stage… er, *bus*… the incomparable (or at least undead)… Creature Comfort!" I shouted, with great aplomb.

Max stared at the spectacle through the rearview mirror. "No way," he managed.

"Oh, big fucking way," said Kit proudly. "Big fucking mega-shellacked way."

I rushed to the bathroom and found a gilded hand mirror. If it was really made of gold, I didn't want to know. Fucking Cher. Then I rushed back and held it in front of her face. Eyes wide and unblinking, she stared, taking herself in. "Mmm," she said, the moan all-telling. But then it extended, her face straining as the "Mmm" turned to "Mmm*eee*."

Because, apart from the unbeating heart and stiff limbs, Creature was exactly like us. Drag queen defined her. It was who she was, who we all were, and more so in a gown and flowing wig. Even more so in *that* wig and gown, the best money could buy. Again, fucking Cher, God love her.

"You," I replied, wiping the tear from my cheek. "Definitely you."

\* \* \* \*

It was hours and hours later, well past midnight, before we made it to deep within the Mojave. By then, there were no more cars on the road, no more obstacles, nothing but sand and scrub. The zombies hadn't slowed down all the while or sped up, hence the droning hours later, but they were all there, several hundred of them moaning as they trudged down the highway behind the bus.

And then, in the distance, we saw lights.

"Turn off your beams," said Kit. "We don't want them to spot us now."

Max did as she'd said, the road pitch-black save for the moonlight, the only sound that of the engine and the constant moans, which seemed to get louder the closer we got to the lights up ahead, to the scent of humans.

The camp was slightly off the road, fenced in, barbed wire atop, armed guards posted. That late, there were maybe three of them on watch. But what, exactly, were they watching? And if they knew about the solar flares before they actually flared, then what else did they know that we didn't?

"Pull up parallel to the camp, Max," said Kit. "I think that will be the tipping point, which should be followed by the diversion we're looking for. Then drive around to the rear of the camp. It's dark enough that they shouldn't be able to see us, and even if they do, they're going to be really busy all too soon."

Max nodded and sped up, leaving the zombies in a cloud of dust. As to them, with our scent no longer nearby, they aimed for the next best thing, namely a camp full of live military men and women, almost all of them presumably asleep.

We pulled the bus a safe distance away and watched. And listened.

We heard the gunfire first, but they were shooting in the dark. Plus, surprised by the attack, the guards were in disarray. It didn't take long for the zombies to reach the fence, where they were sitting dead ducks. But that's where the guards made their first mistake.

Seeing the first line of zombies, they fired at them, blowing their heads to bits, but that left them standing there, leaning on the fence and blocking the path of the bullets to the second line of zombies, the third, the fourth.

Which is when the second mistake was made. Because, with the gunfire having no effect apart from slamming into dead undead corpses, the guards opted for a more direct approach, namely opening up the gate and driving through with their Jeeps to get a better shot at the remaining zombies. Only, with it being so dark out, they had no idea what they were contending with.

"Not good," said Max, watching the scene unfold from down the road. "They can only see at most a hundred of them by way of the camp lights."

We all stood at the bus' windows now, watching as two Jeeps sped through the gate and into the throng, where they were quickly trapped by so many slow-moving bodies. The guards fired, but there were just too many of them.

And that's when we finally found out what the zombies did when they caught a still-living human.

And, Lord have mercy, it wasn't pretty. In fact, it might've been where the term gross understatement got its adjective: *gross.*

See, the Jeeps got caught in the dense throng of undead, the drivers, the gunmen, quickly gripped by hands that yanked and pulled as best they could. Which was, as it turned out, good enough.

We heard the terror-filled screams next as they echoed out into the desert, the men torn from their vehicles and then torn apart soon thereafter. The camp lights illuminated it all, the grisly dismembering that followed, the undead devouring what they seemed to miss most, namely the living.

"Go," whispered Kit. "Drive around back while the camp figures out what to do next with what's going on out front."

Max sped off into the desert, parallel to the side fence but out of sight of the light. Again we heard noises, shouts, as the camp awoke to find that they'd been set upon, the front gate now open, zombies pouring in, eager, we now knew, for flesh and blood and bone and gristle, for anything alive and breathing. Yes, there was bodily water mixed in, but clearly not enough to do any apparent harm. We guessed the radiation boiled it off, or something along those lines.

In any case, as it turned out, it wasn't just the military that was still alive.

We noticed the trucks we'd seen earlier were parked in the rear of the camp, abutting a fenced-in area within the compound.

"*That's* what they were carrying?" said Blondella, confused as all of us.

"Why are those people being held captive?" added Kit.

There were about twenty of them, men and women, all of them locked inside, all of them pressed up to the gate, watching, as we were, the zombies attack the groggy military folks as they emerged from their tents.

I turned to Kit. "Do you need a candy bar or do you already have an idea of what's going on?"

She shrugged. "Not a clue. Except that, if I had to make a guess, I'd say that the non-military people are being held captive, which is odd to say the least. I mean, how many people can still be alive now? Why keep the remaining few captive? Protective custody?"

Blondella didn't wait for an answer. Instead, she hopped off the bus and ran to the camp's outer fence. "Why are you all prisoners in there?" she shouted.

All at once, said prisoners turned and ran to the rear of the containment area, faces pressed to the chain-link. They all began to shout, the words varying, but the meaning the same: "Help us!"

Blondella turned our way and cocked her head.

"Ram it!" said Kit. "Now's our only chance."

She was right about that. The captors might've been groggy, but they were armed and well-trained. So while they were, for the time being, outnumbered, they could, in time, easily take the undead enemy down.

"Do it," I said to Max, my hand on his shoulder.

He gunned the engine a second later, the bus zooming as Kit and I held on to the seats, faces scrunched as we waited for the inevitable crash. Then *BOOM!*, steel met steel, our bus the clear victor as the outer fence gave way, then the inner one, the prisoners pressed to the front fence as the rear one ripped in two.

To the bus they quickly ran, hopping up the steps, huffing and puffing, clearly shocked at their rescue, and equally shocked that their rescuers were mostly all dressed in designer gowns before they put two and two together and realized that four of us were drag queens. Though they certainly didn't complain when Max put the bus in reverse and sped away.

"Why were you all being held in there like that?" I asked, still clutching the back of Max's seat.

There was silence as they fought to catch their breaths. "Are those Bob Mackies?" asked one of them, a man from the center of the throng, nice looking, well-coiffed, semi-buffed. In other words, most definitely gay, hence the question.

"Who?" asked another man by his side, clearly straight, or a country line dancer, maybe both, hence the plaid shirt.

I turned to the first man, the gay one. "Cher's Bob Mackies, in fact."

"No," he exhaled reverently, hand held out to touch the exquisite fabric.

"Please," said Kit, interrupting my newly formed fan club of one. "They're going to be following us soon enough. Tell us if we need to run and hide or stop and let you all off."

"Hide!" immediately shouted almost all of them.

"Quickly," added the gay dude, now by my side. "You're Destiny St. James, aren't you?"

I grinned, hand over padded chest as I fluttered my fake eyelashes his way. "You, um, you recognize me?"

Blondella sputtered. "Yeah, you recognize *her?*"

The man nodded as Max sped through the desert. Then he pointed to each of us in turn, "Blondella Bombshell, Destiny St. James, Creature Comfort…" He squinted at Kit. "And Kit Kat. The driver I don't recognize."

"Shucks," said Max sarcastically.

"Anyway," said Kit, "it's great that you have seemingly excellent taste in drag queens, but why, again, were you all being held like that? And how did you survive the blast?"

A woman made her way to the front of the bus. "We didn't, exactly. *They* survived it for us." She pointed to the camp, which was now fading in the distance, the trucks and Jeeps yet to follow.

"You lost me," I admitted, which seemed par for the course as of late.

The gay dude again spoke up. "We were rounded up just before the blast. We're all non-military personnel from a base outside of San Diego. Oh, and I saw your show once when you guys were guests at a local drag bar."

"Frocks," I said, remembering said bar. "Nice place. Strong drinks. Bad sound system."

"Exactly," he said. "Anyway, just before the blast, they gathered us all together in a room below ground. We felt the blast, and when we came back out, well…"

"Zombies," grunted Max, veering off the main road and onto a barely there dirt path.

"Zombies, right," said the man in plaid with a grimace. "Next thing we knew, we were loaded onto trucks and driven out here."

"But why?" asked Blondella. "And why were you locked up like that?"

For that, there didn't seem to be an answer. "They wouldn't tell us," said the woman. "They drove us out to the desert and were joined by a few other trucks a short while later, the camp already built and waiting for us."

"Circle back," said Kit. "Quickly."

"Back?" I asked. "Why back?"

"They must've known about the blast beforehand, even if only by a short while," she replied. "There's some sort of reason why they took prisoners, and I doubt they're going to let them go without a fight. So *back*, at least westward, would be the smartest way to go for now, because *east* is the direction they'll be heading. And this late and this dark they probably—hopefully—won't know we took that dirt road back there, so east is the direction they'll continue to drive in search of us."

"Probably, hopefully," repeated Blondella. "But west is not the direction *we're* headed."

Kit paused and seemed to measure her words, figuring, I guessed, that bitchy, for a change, wasn't going to cut it right about then. "*Temporarily* west," she eventually replied. "Just until we can lose them."

Though it was then that the gay guy again piped in. Too bad for us. "Um, hate to rain on your pride parade, but there are more prisoners coming."

I groaned. "And you know this how?"

The woman replied, "They were widening our enclosure just this afternoon, with us held at gunpoint in a corner. Stands to reason they needed more room for more prisoners."

Max sighed as he jerked the bus onto another dirt road, heading west, just as Kit had ordered. "Reason flew out the window when the sun decided to go all nutso on us." He dimmed his headlights, just in case, but still had the pedal to the metal. "So do we continue on or rescue more people? And FYI, where would we put them even if we could rescue them? Cher's bus is standing room only."

"*This* is Cher's bus?" asked the gay guy. *Figures.*

"Why is Nixon's picture on the wall?" asked the guy in plaid. *Figures.*

"And why is your silent friend over there salivating like that?" asked the woman.

*Figures, figures, figures.*

# CHAPTER EIGHT
## AN ADDITION TO THE FAMILY

At that very moment, Creature leapt at the nearest person to her, groaning loudly as she sunk her teeth into flesh, blood spurting when the jugular got ripped to shreds, as teeth chomped and stomped and tore on through.

Things seemed to go in slow motion after that. The bus veered; people screamed. Creature sank to the floor with her victim; people screamed. Someone knocked Creature off her victim, two of them holding her down, the bus veering again just as the victim went from recently alive to newly dead; and yeah, people screamed. In slow motion, all of this was doubly as terrifying.

So now, to recap, we had a bloody zombie, three drag queens, two of them in Bob Mackie gowns, one handsome undertaker driver, and just over a dozen and a half screaming people veering through the desert with the military maybe or maybe not following them—in Cher's bus, with Nixon overseeing it all.

Not exactly how I figured the end of the world to be, global warming excepted.

Though things did cool down some once the angered throng of survivors overthrew the bus and tossed us, plus the rack of dresses, out into the desert. Three drag queens, one handsome undertaker, and one blood-dripping zombie were all rolling around in the dust and sand a moment later. The bus then sped away, but not before the cute gay guy jumped out and also rolled in the sand and dust, joining our ragtag group on the desert floor.

"They kicked you off, too?" asked Max, standing up as he brushed himself off, spitting sand out of his mouth as he did so.

The guy grinned and shrugged. "Seemed more fun with you guys."

Kit snickered. "Fun? Bet you dig a good root canal too, huh, sugar?"

His shrug amped up a notch. "A busload of straight people and one bathroom versus you guys in the desert?" The grin repeated. "Seemed like the lesser of two evils." He pointed at Creature. "I never would've guessed, by the way." The point continued. "We, uh, safe out here?"

I turned to my bloody friend. "Full now, girl?" She nodded and blinked one time. I looked back at the stranger. "You're good, um…"

"Steve," he informed, hand held out.

"You're good, *Steve*," I told him, shaking his hand as I turned my head from side to side, checking out our latest surroundings. "Unless we die out here from dehydration or zombie attack."

Max shook Steve's hand next and introduced himself. "On the bright side," he added, "the banter is delightful." Then he turned to Kit. "Now what?"

"We need some sort of transportation," she said.

"Hate to say it," said Blondella, "but duh. And?"

"And the nearest transportation, seeing as we haven't seen any other cars out in this God-awful desert, is back at the camp," she replied. "Military truck."

Blondella sighed. "Military truck comes with military, need I remind you, plus whatever zombies are still around."

"I'm guessing that a great deal of said military are out searching for us," she replied. "Plus, they're still in disarray, probably repairing the damage done by the zombies and Cher's bus. Maybe they won't notice us sneaking in and stealing a truck."

"Won't notice us in our Bob Mackie gowns, trudging through the desert?" asked Blondella.

"It's a plan," said Kit. "I didn't say it was a good one."

Steve spoke up next. "There's not that many of them to begin with," he informed. "Maybe fifty at most, fewer if the zombies got any of them, even fewer if they did indeed drive off into the desert looking for us. Plus, we'll have the element of surprise on our side."

"How's that?" asked Kit.

Steve held out his hand again. "Steve Maddox," he said. "Expert electrician at your service, um, *ma'am*."

She placed her thick hand in his, her face lighting up as sure as if someone had handed her a case of Milky Ways. "Pleasure, Steve Maddox," she practically purred. "Did you like our act, by the way?"

He nodded, vigorously. "Especially that Aretha Franklin number you did."

Blondella groaned. Heck, even Creature groaned at that one. Kit, however, continued to purr. "Pleasure indeed, Steve Maddox. Pleasure indeed."

\* \* \* \*

We found the dirt road after that, but not before we created a makeshift sled out of the dresses so that we could tow Creature. So, no, they didn't exactly die in vain. Not exactly. Though we said a silent prayer for them just the same.

The night was dark, though thankfully cool. Blondella stood to my left, Max to my right, Kit and Steve taking up the rear. "Creature killed someone," whispered Blondella.

"I know," I whispered back, trying and pretty much failing to wipe the bloody image out of my head.

"She must know," added Max.

I sighed and stopped the caravan in place, wind suddenly whipping across my skin, sending a chill up my spine. "Creature," I said, staring down at her, her skin pale in the moonlight. She blinked once my way. "You... you know what you did back there?" She blinked again, slower this time. "You know what you are, then?" The blink was joined by a moan and a rising of her arm, a rigid finger pointed my way, then to Blondella.

"You know we love you," said Blondella. Creature blinked, once, twice. Blondella laughed, though I could hear the sob just the same. "I know, I know; I don't usually say it, but you know it anyway, right?" The slow blink returned. "Right."

Kit spoke from behind her. "We all love you, Creature. No matter... no matter what you are. Inside, you're still Creature Comfort, diva!"

Again Creature blinked, once, twice. And I knew what she meant without hearing the words. She wasn't who she was, not inside, not out, and would probably never be again. She must've known it, felt it, even without killing the guy back on the bus. Still, she was one of us just the same.

"You look beautiful in that gown, too," said Max while I patted his arm, glad he was standing by my side through all this.

"Cher never looked so good," Steve piped in with. I shot him a nod and a smile, a silent thanks sent his way.

Creature groaned and shut her eyes completely. Her lips quivered. We all stared in silence, waiting to see what she'd do next, the only sound that of the wind and then, jarringly, of Creature herself. "Zzz…" she managed. "Aah…" She popped her eyes open. "Mmm…" And we knew what she'd eventually say, but let her finish it just the same, the effort obvious, palpable. "Bee."

"It doesn't matter," I said, again squelching back tears. She couldn't walk, much, or talk, much, and she was obviously hungry for humans of the living variety, but we loved her. We loved her for who she was. Or at least once was. "It doesn't matter," I repeated, turning so that she couldn't see the tears that managed their way up and out before Max and I were again yanking the dresses, heading back to the makeshift base farther out in the desert.

"But it does matter," whispered Max. "It does."

* * * *

Luckily, we hadn't driven all that far into the desert before we were evicted from the bus, and we had some water, albeit in the two guns we still carried, which, of course, left us defenseless if not hydrated. Still, it took the rest of the night to haul Creature over the sand, which was easier, at the very least, than doing so down the road.

All that being said, by daybreak, we were hot, sweaty, drag messes. But at least we could see the camp now as we lay hidden behind a sandy inclined hill. The fence had been fixed, a pile of incinerated corpses rising outside of it. I was sure it was the best they could do, but it was still horrific to witness.

"Plans?" I asked, sucking down the last of the water, the sun already sweltering despite the early hour.

Steve raised his hand. In the light of day, he looked like Leonard, the short roommate on *The Big Bang Theory*: cute and nerdy. "They rebuilt the inner fence, too, so they must be planning on filling it up again. If such is the case, let's assume they're still out searching for the bus."

"Or expecting additional prisoners," said Max. "What if more military is coming? The closest base probably got here first, set up camp, and then waited for reinforcements." He turned to Steve. "If one base knew of the solar flares, stands to reason so did more of them, or all of them. Heck, the President himself could show up at any moment."

Steve scratched his chin and wiped the sweat off his brow. "I don't think so," he replied. "Back when we were all rounded up, it seemed very last minute, like they were taken by surprise by all of this. Plus, it was a huge base, but only a handful of the military survived, and not even the big brass at that."

"But more than one base made it to the temporary camp," I told him. "They did come together, but from different directions; that much we know, even if they came only in small numbers. Maybe they're just the scouting party, and the larger group is headed this way."

"And," tossed in Blondella, "we still don't know why they took you as prisoners in the first place. With most of the world, as far as we know, dead, why capture the few lone survivors and lock them up?"

"For their own protection?" offered Kit.

Steve shook his head. "It didn't seem like that. They certainly didn't make us feel like we were being protected. We were, as it looked like, prisoners, just like Blondella said." He sighed and frowned, shaking his head all the while. "None of it makes sense."

Max pointed to the camp below. It was being guarded again, and by well over a dozen armed guards. "It is weird, though, that the top brass didn't make it out alive; I'll give Steve that much. Orders would've come down from them, right?"

Steve nodded. "Always," he said. "Unless, like I said, there just wasn't time. One minute all was normal, the next they were rounding up as many civilians as they could find and then rushing us underground. They barely closed the doors before we felt the blast. Next day, they gathered their equipment; soon thereafter the camp was up and running. Tents and simple fences. Simple enough to keep the zombies out, that is, because what else could attack them?"

Kit snickered. "Apart from a handful of drag queens."

It was my turn to raise my hand. "All this speculation is great, but we're melting out here." I turned to Steve. "What was your idea?"

"To knock out their electricity and steal a truck in the dark of night," he said with a groan.

"Only," said Max, "it's the light of day and the fence has been rebuilt. We have no zombies as bait and no truck for ramming said fence with. Though it's that melting thing that has me the most worried right about now. We have to get out of this sun, and soon."

None of us replied. In words, that is. Because suddenly Creature was blinking and then pointing, as best she could, at herself.

*Bait*, Max had said. "No," I told her. "Too dangerous." Though even as I said it, I knew we had no other options. If we stayed out there any longer, we'd all be dead. I turned and whispered in his ear, "I'm not going to watch them gun her down, Max."

He put his hand on my shoulder as if to say, *she's already dead*. "We just need the bait, Destiny. We'll try and not let the fish eat the worm."

"Fishing analogy," said Blondella, with a frown. "Too butch."

Max thought it over and replied, "The worm at the bottom of the tequila bottle, then."

Blondella nodded. "Better," she allowed. "But what do you have in mind?"

"If they think there are more zombies out here, they won't wait until they make it down to the camp this time, not after what happened last time," he said. "Instead, they'll come out here and take care of things."

I put my hand on his arm. "But we aren't more zombies," I told him. "We're... we're only *one*."

He jumped up and walked away from the hill and away from the camp. "One is plenty."

And amen to that.

* * * *

Once we realized what he had in mind, we all joined him. Creature would be the bait, but she'd have backup. Sort of. Though more like Bob-up, really.

See, even beaten up as they were, sequined Bob Mackie gowns are real eye catchers, shimmering like mirages in the desert. All we had to do was spread them out a bit and adorn the odd shrub and stick, and hope that that would get the military's attention. Then, just before we set out the bait, namely Creature, we dug with the last vestiges of strength we had at the back of the hill we'd been hiding behind, dug and dug and dug until we were soaked through with sweat.

"Ready?" asked Max.

We all nodded, the group of us a few feet back as Max placed Creature at the top of the hill. She shimmered brightly, the hot desert wind whipping her gown this way and that.

Max ducked behind what was left of the hill and peeked over as best he could. "Well?" I whisper-shouted from behind.

"They're pointing up our way," he replied. "They spotted Creature and the dresses. Looks like they have binoculars on her now." He waited and watched. "They're sending a Jeep up. Get ready." My heart beat furiously within my chest as we waited. A couple of minutes later, Max pulled at Creature's dress, toppling her over backward.

That was our cue. We raced in, grabbed her, and yanked her back another ten feet, all of us turning around just as the Jeep hit the sandy hill, or what was left of it, before crashing headfirst into the desert below and seemingly out of sight of the camp. The driver was thrown up and out, landing a few feet away from us, his rifle quickly grabbed by Steve. The passenger was still in the Jeep, but he'd hit his head on the dashboard and was knocked out cold, a trickle of blood zigzagging across his stubbled cheek.

"Freeze," shouted Steve as the driver began to scramble to his feet. Our newfound friend looked at us, grinning all the while. "I always wanted to say that."

"Sugar," said Kit, nervously, "do you even know how to fire that thing?"

He nodded and gulped as he stared down at the frozen man in olive green. "Sure as hell do."

Kit grinned. "Better listen to him, then," she said to the soldier on the ground.

"Yeah," said Steve. "Better listen to me." He aimed for the man's head. "Now then, what is that camp down there? Why did you have prisoners?"

The man brushed the sand from his face and glanced up, blocking the sun as best he could with his downturned palm. "Jackson Staub. Private. 643657290."

Blondella silently pointed to Kit and me and then, lastly, to Creature. Knowing how her mind worked, namely twistedly, I knew what she was getting at. So we righted Creature and placed her in front of Private Staub. Makeup now smudged and smeared off, there was now no mistaking what she was. "Name, rank, and serial number ain't gonna cut it with our friend here, Private," said Blondella, holding Creature by the shoulder as she tilted her head down a bit. "And this bitch is hungrier than Karen Carpenter on a liquid diet."

Kit snorted. "You're showing your age, girlfriend. No way is he gonna get that reference."

Blondella frowned, wig and tits surprisingly still in place. She must've Superglued them on, I figured. "Talk or the zombie chows down, Private."

"Better listen to her," added Kit.

Creature moaned and bared her teeth as best as she could. She blinked once, letting us know that she was in on the game. Or maybe she really was Karen-Carpenter-hungry. Hard to tell, what with her limited vocabulary and blinking repertoire. In any case, Private Staub looked duly terrified, and rightly so.

"I… I don't know," stammered our prisoner, who looked barely eighteen, dressed all in green, a few badges across his chest the only color. "I'm only two months out of basic training. All I know is that I was told to guard the camp."

Steve was still aiming the gun his way. "What unit were you in, Private?"

"Science unit," came the barked reply.

"What kind of science?" I asked, curiosity now tugging my cat by its tail.

"Weather forecasting, mostly. Testing, too. Global warming stuff and how it affects our worldwide bases."

We all nodded knowingly. "That's how they knew, then," said Max as he jumped over to the Jeep. "Help me, Kit. We gotta get out of here before they come looking for these two."

So while Kit and Max tried to right the Jeep, I crouched down next to the private. "You knew about the solar flares?"

He gulped and wiped the river of sweat off his face. "Only that there would be some. Everyone knew that. It was on TV, in the papers."

"But not their severity," I added. "Not until just before they hit, right?"

He clamped his mouth shut, and again we leaned Creature down his way. "I don't know!" he shouted, covering his face with his hands. "My unit and the civilians were all taken below ground. We ended up here. Now I'm guarding the camp. They didn't tell us any more than that." He raised his hand and pointed to the suddenly righted Jeep. "Ask him; he's a captain."

Unfortunately, the him in question was still out cold.

Drenched in sweat, which, not surprisingly, looked awfully sexy on him, Max waved our way. "Everyone in. We're heading back to the convenience store. But blindfold these two first."

I saluted him before helping Private Staub to his feet, the gun and Creature still aimed his way. "Aye, aye, sir," I said with a wink.

"*Hmm*," said Max. "A guy could learn to like that. Keep it up."

"Oh," I replied. "I'll keep it *up* alright."

Blondella lumbered forward and hopped inside the Jeep. "Really? You think *now* is the time for that shit?"

I nodded as I tied a scrap of a nearby dress around Staub's face. As to time and how much we had of it, Lord only knew.

In other words, now was the perfect time for that shit.

# CHAPTER NINE
## WHAT-IFS AND MAYBES

We knew where the convenience store was and hoped, prayed really, that they didn't think to go looking for us there. Though we knew, prayed really, again, that with everything knocked out by the flares, they were riding blind. Meaning, no radar, no way to track us, not if they were using any sort of GPS, because, best guess, no way were the satellites up in space still working. Hence the cell phones not working. Hence no Internet, no TV.

We made it to the store a while later and tied the still-blindfolded prisoners together in the storage room before parking the Jeep behind the building.

"I vote we leave them here," said Blondella. "Take the Jeep and continue on to New York, then find another car or two somewhere along the way. There's gotta be more of them once we get out of this desert. Then we forget this whole fucking mess."

"What if they find Cher's bus?" asked Max. "What if they find the bus and then find out about us? Or what if they don't find the bus, but go looking for the two in the basement instead and then find out about us. With no more prisoners, maybe they'll come looking for us to fill that area behind the inside fence."

"That's a hell of a lot of *what-ifs*, sugar," said Kit. "Perhaps we should just take our chances and skedaddle. We have the Jeep. We have water again." She lifted up a newly purloined, half-eaten Ding Dong. "And we have food." She pointed to the two rifles next. "Heck, we even have real weapons now."

Steve stood and paced the aisle. "At least two bases clearly knew something about those flares, albeit mostly too late. So there's still something I haven't heard you consider yet."

Max groaned. "They might know about more solar flares coming? And if we're on the road when they hit…"

He didn't finish his train of thought. He didn't have to; we were all staring at Creature as he said it, after all. And we knew all too well what the initial solar flare had wrought.

In any case, Steve nodded. "They obviously left the San Diego base because of its too-close proximity to millions of zombies. They obviously came out to the desert because of its lack of any. They brought building materials. I saw them. Maybe they're just waiting for more."

"All they need is some steel walls, and they'd be safe," I said. "But even if your base has weather experts, there's no way to know when the next flares will hit, right?"

"Right," he agreed. "Not anymore. Unless they already knew before they left San Diego. And maybe all they needed was a handful of civilians to help with the building. Maybe they just needed to swell their ranks and didn't want to take any chances that we wouldn't help."

Kit grimaced and finished her Ding Dong. "So we went with *what-ifs* to *maybes*. So what? What do you think we should do about it?"

He nodded. "We have a base of operations here. We have ample food and water. The camp isn't all that far away, and there are no zombies anywhere in sight."

"So you're saying we should sit tight?" asked Max. "See what they're up to? Make sure we're safe from any more flares before continuing on to New York?"

Steve again nodded. "Like I said before, there aren't all that many of them. And from what I've seen, it's mostly two groups, one of which is a science unit, which isn't especially adept at fighting, I'd think. Maybe the other group is the same, which is how they also knew about the flares and knew where to head. Could be that they had just enough time before the flares hit to communicate with one another, to pick a spot to meet up."

I grabbed a Coke from the fridge and turned his way. "So you're saying what? That we should infiltrate them? See what they're up to? Make sure there aren't any more flares heading our way?" I stared at him as I downed my Coke. "We're a bunch of drag queens, plus a mortician, and now an electrician. They might be science geeks, but they're still militarily trained."

"But they won't be expecting us," he interjected.

I couldn't help but laugh. "Who in the world would expect anything like us? I wouldn't even expect us, and I *am* us." I sighed. "No way is this going to work."

He put his hand on my shoulder. "What choice do we have? And what if they are looking for us? Wouldn't it be better to have the upper hand?"

Blondella also walked to the fridge, a beer quickly in her grip. "I vote we take our chances and head to New York. All those in favor?" Her hand was up, then way up, but it was the lone one there. She grumbled and finished her beer, followed by a loud very unladylike belch. "Fuckers."

I closed the gap between us and placed my hand on her shoulder. "I promise, Blondella, as soon as we figure out what's going on, find out if it's safe to leave, that we'll head out to New York as planned." I gave her shoulder a squeeze. "If we're still alive—and that alone is a miracle—then I'm sure Johnny is also still alive."

Her grumble repeated, but, gratefully, was joined by a reluctant-looking nod of her head. "At least they sell nail polish and lipstick here." Her nod went to a miserable shake. "Or sold, that is."

Kit walked over and lifted a tube off a shelf. "It's from Britney's line!" she squealed.

"Which explains why they sell it in a convenience store on the edge of a desert," said Blondella with a heavy sigh. "But hand it over; we could all use a fresh coat."

Well, at least we had a consensus on one thing.

\* \* \* \*

After we ate and coated, and drank, of course, not to mention scrubbed layers of Mojave off us, we headed back down to the basement with refreshments for our guests.

"I have to pee," immediately informed the private.

"You're fucking dead if you don't cut me loose," added the captain, who had obviously gained consciousness.

"Pee on *him*," said Kit to the first man, setting their food and drinks down as she glared their way.

Their hands and feet were bound, and they were tied together around a post. We untied their hands and removed the blindfolds. The captain blinked and stared up at us, clearly surprised at what he saw. "You're fucking kidding me, right?"

"No joke," said Blondella. "Now tell us why you were able to escape the flares."

"And why you took prisoners," added Max.

The captain sneered. "Len Price. Captain First Class. 569234042."

"Not that again," griped Blondella. "Look, tell and us and eat. Don't tell us and starve."

"And get peed on," tossed in Kit. "Some people like that." She shrugged. "Not me, of course, just some people." Again she shrugged. "Okay, sometimes me." She kicked the microwaved Hot Pockets and Gatorade their way. "Your choice."

Jackson, the private, raised his hand. "I already told you what I know," he said. "How about letting me pee and then eat something?"

Kit leaned down and emptied one of the Gatorade bottles. "Fine, pee." She handed him the bottle.

He pointed to Blondella. "In front of the lady?"

We all snorted, Blondella included. "Not even close," she said. "But we'll all turn around just the same." Which we did, all very Geneva-Convention-like. Though I wasn't even sure they had drag queens and Gatorade in Geneva back in the day. In any case, we heard the zipper and the stream and then the sigh. When we turned back around, he was already capping the bottle.

"That a ham or a turkey Hot Pocket?" he asked.

"What's the difference?" I replied.

"I'm Jewish."

I grinned. "Lucky day then. Turkey, it is." I handed him the remaining bottle and the food. "Dig in. And the captain gets some once he talks."

Jackson munched and chomped and slurped. "Better talk, Captain," he warned. "They have a secret weapon you really don't want to see."

"Trust me," he replied, sneering all the while, "*they* have a lot of things I don't want to see."

Blondella bent down and tickled his chin. "Now then, how do you know unless you try?" Then she grabbed his chin in her daintily painted, though still strong, man-hands. "In any case, listen to the private. Or else."

He smirked up at her. "Len Price. Captain First Class. 569234042."

She released his chin. "Fine, have it your way," she said, gazing down at her recent manicure job. "Max, go get Creature."

"With pleasure," said Max, bounding up the steps two at a time. When he returned, he was carrying our friend in front of him. He set her down and aimed her toward the post. "Go say hi to the nice captain, Creature."

Creature moaned and ambled forward, while the captain's eyes went wide. "I'll talk!" he shrieked. "I'll talk! Call it off."

"*Her*," I informed tersely. "Um, mostly her. Sort of her."

She continued moving forward, moan notched up, mouth gaping open, fingernails also newly painted; though on her it looked kind of like blood.

"Call her off! Please!"

I grabbed Creature by the forearm. She stopped dead in her tracks, what with her being dead and all. "Well, since you said please." Then I turned his way. "The solar flares, how did your unit know about them?"

Again he sneered my way, but Creature groaned, and his sneer turned snivel. "It was in the news."

"World destruction was so *not* in the news, Captain," said Steve. "Lindsay Lohan was in the news and, while certainly destructive, clearly not at this level."

He nodded. "We were monitoring them. When we saw the spike, we knew we had to act quickly. It came as a surprise, but we figured we'd be safe below ground in a bomb shelter from the Cold War days."

"And yet," I continued, "no big brass was with you."

He shrugged. "There was only so much room in the shelter. Besides, we had no idea that the spike would amount to what it amounted to."

Steve again spoke up. "We were gathered up like prisoners," he said. "Even after the blast, we were kept at gunpoint in the trucks and then locked away in the camp. If you didn't have room for your own people, why did you have room for us?"

He didn't answer right away. When he did, he said, "I'm not sure."

"You're the captain," I reminded him. "How were you not sure?"

Again he paused, but it was then that a new thought popped into my head. "There was big brass, though, wasn't there?"

"No," said Steve. "I saw everyone who was gathered from our base. There was this guy, the captain, a sergeant or two, but no colonels or generals. No one with any real power."

I shook my head. "No, Steve. There was another unit, the one that met you at the makeshift camp. Ten to one there was someone who was giving the orders, someone who told your unit to gather the civilians but not the people in power." Again I stared down at the captain, who was now eyeing me nervously. "I'm right, aren't I?"

The pause was there, but so was Creature, so it didn't last all that long. Besides, I figured, why be loyal to a government that, by all accounts, didn't still exist?

Perhaps he had the same thought because he replied, "There was a general in the other unit. They came from a base in Arizona."

"What kind of unit?" asked Max. "Science, like the other one?" The captain nodded. "So they also knew about the flares just in the nick of time? Enough so that they could arrange to meet you if need be?"

Again he nodded. "How do you know all that?"

Max didn't answer, especially since, really, we were only guessing all that. Guessing correctly, but still. "So why the civilians. Why prisoners?"

"For their own protection," he said. "If they left, they would've been killed."

"Yes," I said, sarcasm dripping off my tongue. "The military is often known for its altruism, Captain."

"Believe it or not," he said. "But you know as well I do, now especially, that if the civilians hadn't come with us, especially since they were in a major metropolitan area, then they'd surely all be dead by now."

Blondella laughed. "We came all the way from San Francisco, unscathed I might add." She pointed at Kit. "Well-fed even."

"Hey!" objected Kit, who was sucking on a frozen ice cream bar at the time, chocolate dripping down her chin. Or make that chins, plural.

"In any case," said Steve. "Once you got us out of San Diego, you still held us captive in that camp."

"Temporarily," said the captain. "Until we figured out what was happening."

"As to that," I said, remembering the last question we needed answered, "what is happening? Was that solar flare an anomaly, or will there be more of them?"

He shrugged. "Beats me. It's the sun. It does what it wants to do when it wants to do it."

"But the prediction?" I amended with.

The shrug remained. "In all of human history, we have no evidence that such a flare ever occurred before; why should a second one follow the first?"

"But it could?" asked Kit, the bar finished, stick thrown to the ground.

He nodded. "It could, of course. A second, a third, a fifth, or none at all, or none for countless millennia. Like I said, impossible to tell."

I sighed and turned to Creature. "Watch them. If they try anything…" I grinned and stared their way. "Then enjoy your lunch." And with that, I gathered my troops and marched us all back upstairs.

"Well?" said Max, once we were again in the store. "Show of hands. Who believes Captain Price?" Not one of us raised our hands. "Me neither. All too easy. Pat answers."

Steve lifted his index finger in the air. "One thing was true, though," he said. "They were taken unaware. They gathered themselves and us all without a minute to spare. If they knew about the severity of the flare beforehand, then they wouldn't have waited so long."

"Perhaps," said Blondella. "But they sure managed to be in touch with the other base fast enough. Fast enough, that is, to get orders to capture civilians and to meet up in the Mojave."

I snapped my fingers. "But why there?"

Kit turned my way. "Like we said before, to elude the zombies."

"Ah," I ahed. "But they couldn't have known about the zombies before the flare hit. No one could have known that."

"Then after the flares, they communicated," said Steve.

"But how?" I replied. "The satellites went down almost immediately."

To which Blondella said, "Johnny got a message to me in that time, so they could've also."

"Maybe," I allowed. "But something had to be arranged

beforehand. They couldn't have come up with an entire plan in just under a minute. So they might not have known about the severity of the flare for certain, but they knew there was a chance for it. This is a top science unit after all."

"And if they acted any sooner than they did, they would've shown their hands, alerted the big brass on the San Diego base," said Max.

"And there wasn't enough room in the bomb shelter for any more military," Steve again informed. "If any more of them thought they'd be in danger, there would have been chaos down there."

"So they saved themselves," said Blondella. "That I get. Survival at all costs. Fine. So no Nobel Peace Prizes for them. But why save Steve and the others and then hold them captive? That's what's not making any sense."

"Plus," I couldn't help but add, "we still don't know if they're looking for us or if there are more military on their way. And I wouldn't hazard to guess that the good captain is going to tell us the truth beyond what he's already told us in regards to the latter question."

"So what should we do?" asked Kit. "New York is out for the time being, in case they're looking for us. And here is safe, but only temporarily, because for sure they're looking for those two down in the basement by now. So either way we're screwed."

"Unless we find out what they're up to," said Max. "Maybe there will be a solution if we know the proper questions to ask. Because clearly, we don't. At least not yet."

Blondella suddenly smiled, which, all in all, scared the hell out of me. "But what if those two aren't missing?"

"But they are," I told her. "And if we let them go, the rest of them will find us. Not like there are a lot of ways out of this desert."

She turned to Steve. "Not if it's too dark to see."

And yes, I knew what she was getting it, but no, I wasn't the least bit thrilled about it.

\* \* \* \*

We waited until it was dark out, the sun replaced by a silver moon in the cloudless sky, heat swapped for a desert chill. Back to the basement we went, rifles in hand, Creature still standing guard.

"We're going to untie you now," I told them.

The captain looked my way. "'Bout time."

I grinned. "And then you're going to strip."

Kit covered her mouth to hide her smile and, it seemed, prevent a snort from spewing out. Blondella, however, covered her crotch, to prevent... well, that was pretty obvious, seeing as I was telling two young, straight (presumably) military men to strip at both gunpoint and at zombiepoint. I'll freely admit, despite the circumstances, which were dire at best, it was a pretty hot command, all things considered.

"No fucking way," barked the captain. Creature blinked, then moaned loudly. The captain grimaced in return. "Fine, but no funny stuff."

I nodded. "Funny stuff is what we do best, but like you said, *fine*."

So we untied them, they stripped, we watched inappropriately, which we also did best, and then left them down there in their skivvies, tied up yet again, Creature on guard.

"That was... *fun*," said Steve, a crooked smile on his adorable face.

"That was fucking awesome," said Blondella. "But we have work to do." She looked around at all of us. "Now then, who will the *we* be?"

Kit, who was devouring a Mounds Bar at the time, replied, "All we need to do is drive the Jeep back in so that they don't go looking for those two down there," she said. "While at the same time, Steve will turn off the juice, so that they don't see that two of us replaced the two captives. And while they're trying to fix the electrical problem, the two of us will do some snooping."

I raised my hand. "Which two of us? And how do we get back here if we're returning the Jeep to the camp?"

"Fuck," cursed Kit, Mounds consumed, wrapper wafting to the linoleum.

"Not exactly the reply I was looking for," said I glumly. Guess it was too much to hope for that a three hundred pound, sugar-infused drag queen would be our savior.

"Well," said Steve. "It is half a plan, at any rate. And getting inside the camp might be all we need. Get some information, steal the Jeep again, and head to New York."

"And if we don't get any information?" asked Blondella.

Steve shrugged. "Then we probably never will," he replied. "In which case, we come back here, free the two guys downstairs, and head to New York, just like you planned. Still, it's best if we at least try, figure out what they're up to, find out what they know, and see if they'll come looking for us on our way out East or if we'll be running into any more military while we're trying."

I sighed. "All those in favor?" Seemed to be our standard question as of late. Yippy for democracy.

Reluctantly, it seemed, everyone lifted his or her hand. "Great," said Max. "So how about Destiny and I pretend to be those two soldiers while Kit and Steve figure out a way to cut the power?"

"And what about me?" asked Blondella.

It was now Max's turn to sigh. "If we don't make it back here—"

"You will," Blondella interjected.

"But if we don't," continued Max, "then someone has to let those two downstairs go."

"And then what do I do?" asked Blondella, fear replacing her usual bravado.

Max tossed her one of the rifles. "Either head to New York on foot with Creature until you can find a car, or turn yourself in to the military and join back up with us."

"If they haven't killed you first for breaking and entering," she said as she nervously eyed the weapon in her hands.

"Doubtful they'll kill just about the last surviving humans," I replied, wondering if I was trying to convince her or myself, though probably the latter.

She nodded. "Just be careful." She stared down at her feet. "These heels weren't exactly made for cross-country walking." She then smiled. "Funny, I always wanted to walk a mile in Cher's shoes; now it doesn't seem like so much fun after all."

# CHAPTER TEN
# BREAKING AND ENTERING

We drove back to the camp in silence after that, in the dark of night, me and Max in front, dressed in the stolen military garb, Steve and Kit in back, along with a bag full of as many tools as we could scrounge up from the convenience store. All the while, my heart was pounding like a bass drum, nervous sweat soaking through my uniform.

"What if this doesn't work?" I asked, nearly in a whisper. "What if we get caught, or worse?"

He patted my hand and then took it in his own, heart thumping in double-time when flesh met flesh. "It'll work," he whispered back. "And like we said, it's in our own best interests to find out what they know. If there are more flares coming, we need to prepare. If there are military following us, we need to know, so we can keep a look out. Or maybe there's news of other survivors, some sort of safe haven they're aware of. If we run now, we're running into a great unknown. This way, perhaps we have some options."

I nodded. "Or we're running straight into a trap."

Kit poked my shoulder. "Girl, I don't do nothing straight."

My chuckle echoed in the darkness. "Amen to that." I reached behind with my free hand and patted her knee. "Good luck," I told her. "Been a pleasure working with you."

She shrugged. "Well, the drinks were strong anyway." She placed her hand over mine, so that both were now held in support, then she nodded. "Ditto, girlfriend. Ditto."

And then we saw the camp glowing in the distance. We could see them, but they couldn't see us. Guards were clearly posted along the front gate. "Fuck," cursed Kit as she pointed to the inner fence. "They've got more prisoners."

I scanned my eyes from side to side. "I don't see Cher's bus, so those are new ones. What gives?"

"Drive wide," said Steve. "Get us as close to the rear fence as you can without being seen. The generators are out back." He held up a pair of chain cutters we'd found in the basement. "We'll cut our way in. When we see that you've made it past the gate, we'll sever the power."

"Where should we meet after that?" I asked.

"Park the Jeep like everything is normal," he replied. "They'll most likely be too worried about restoring power than about your sudden return. After that, head to the latrine in the far left corner. Generators are in the far right, so that's where they'll be headed."

"Won't they realize the generators have been sabotaged?" asked Max.

Steve chuckled. "The military hires only the most capable civilians," he replied.

I nodded my head. "In other words, they'll never know."

"Nope," he said. "It'll look like a short. And these guys are from a science unit, so more than likely, they'll be in the dark for a good long time. Enough time, that is, for us to snoop and then escape."

Max did as Steve had said, driving wide around the camp, hidden in the shadows, moving slowly so that they could neither hear nor see us. "There," whispered Steve, pointing to a spot about two hundred yards from the fence. "We'll walk the rest of the way and then cut our way in, a bit down from the generator."

"What if they see the hole?" I asked, turning to look at him.

I saw the glint in his eye, in his smile, and then along the blade of the pliers he was holding up. "I'll break in and seal it shut before they can spot it," he replied. "In any case, by then it'll be so dark that they won't be able to see much of anything, let alone a small hole in the fence."

Instinctively, I pointed to Kit. "Small?"

"Hey!" she whisper-shouted.

I shrugged as Max pulled to a stop. "Good luck, you two."

"You as well," said Steve as they began their walk to the fence.

We turned the Jeep around, heading in a wide arc so that it would eventually look like we were driving directly for the gate. I reached for Max's hand. "If we get caught…"

He gave my hand a squeeze. "You always worry this much?"

I turned and grinned. "Only when I'm not in heels and a dress. Got any on you by chance?"

He patted his stolen outfit. "Fresh out," he replied, turning to stare at the gate in front of us. He waved and nodded at the guard on the other side, while I did the same. "Private Staub and Captain Price returning to base," he announced, without so much a quiver to his voice. "Though sadly empty-handed."

The guard nodded, the gate clicking open before sliding right. In seconds, we were in like Flynn, my heart galloping through a furlong as it tore around the track, sweat trickling down my forehead despite the cool desert breeze rushing over us. The Jeep rolled forward, and the gate closed behind us. *Click*, it went again, my heart *kerthumping* in reply.

Two guards moved in on either side of us, rifles held at the ready. "What took you so long?" asked the one closest to us.

"Got lost out there," said Max. "Kind of all looks the same once you're off the road."

"Yup," agreed the other, also moving in, rifle up, not a smile or a friendly nod for the Prodigal sons' return. Closer he moved, closer still, the first one doing the same, closing in as my chest squeezed tight around that galloping heart of mine. Fortunately, the next comment we heard from him was "What the fuck?" when, all at once, every light in the camp went out, leaving nothing but a quarter moon to light the area around us.

"Get to the generators," shouted Max.

"Um, aye, Captain," I replied, drilling the point home that they were being given a direct order by a superior officer.

"Aye, Captain," shouted the other two, dashing to the rear of the base, as was, it sounded like, a great deal of the rest of them.

I turned to Max in disbelief. "I can't believe that worked."

He shrugged and leaned across for a quick kiss. "They're scared, Destiny. Probably don't even know what they're doing out here, let alone what's happening with the rest of the world, with their families."

I nodded and hopped out of the Jeep. "So they're not exactly at their best. Got it." And then we were rushing to the latrine, in the opposite direction of everyone else. Straight ahead of us was the enclosure, the prisoners milling about. And then an all-too-familiar sound quickly reached our ears.

Max pointed slightly to the left as he spotted Steve and Kit. "They made it," he whispered, with a relieved sigh. "Run. Quickly."

So run I did, both of us reaching the latrine a minute later, our friends waiting for us inside. Kit gave me a hug. Steve shook Max's hand.

"I can't believe that worked," said Kit.

I shot her a grin. "Been there. Done that." And then my smile vanished altogether. "You just ran by the inner fence, right?"

She nodded, as did Steve. "You heard it, too?"

"Moaning," I replied. "And lots of it."

Steve moved to the side of the latrine and lifted up a flap. He pointed to the enclosure on our right. "The cage is halved now," he told us. "See for yourselves."

I squinted into the darkness, but it was obvious that there were humans milling about, still-breathing ones on the left, moaning and lifeless ones on the right. "They captured more survivors," I made note. "The zombies probably came from our raid." I turned away. "But why capture them and not just kill them?"

They all shrugged. "Let's see if we can find out," said Max. Then he turned to Steve. "Any ideas where we should look?"

He nodded. "The tents that run along the left side of the fence are sleeping quarters, mess hall in the center. There's a large tent to the right of that. I haven't a clue what's in there. Then there's another tent just to the right of that one. If what we learned before was true, that would be the general's. He wouldn't be bunking near the rest of them."

"We'll take the general's tent," I said. "You two take the other one." I looked at my watch. "Ten minutes, then head back to the Jeep." I looked at their non-military garb. "Keep to the shadows."

"Only ten?" asked Kit. "Think that's enough time?"

I shrugged. "Let's hope so. Better to get out of here in one piece before someone figures out how to flick the lights back on."

Steve grinned, which was almost impossible to see in that dark latrine we were huddled in. "Doubtful," he told us. "I shorted the system and then rewired it a bit. So not only won't they be able to find anything loose, but they also won't realize that it's been wired incorrectly. Plus, it's dark outside, and I'm sure it'll take them some time to find a flashlight. In other words, ten minutes should be plenty."

I patted his shoulder. "Good job. Still, let's hurry; they might not know how to fix a generator, but every last one of them knows how to fire those rifles they're all carrying."

Kit groaned. "Good point."

And then we were off again, Max and me heading for one tent, Steve and Kit to the other. We could hear the men all around us, most of them rushing to secure the perimeters, a fair share of them arguing over by the generator. And above all that, the moans, the constant moans. *What are these guys up to?* I thought. *Why not incinerate the zombies like they did the others?*

We watched Kit and Steve enter their tent while we stood outside of ours. "General?" whispered Max, mouth to the flap. "General?" Louder this time.

"No answer," I told him, slipping inside, Max right behind me.

The tent was small: a cot, a desk, a backpack, a trash can. Max stood in front of the desk. Suffice it to say, it was almost impossible to see in there, aside from whatever light filtered through. "Just grab all the papers you can find," he told me. "We'll sort it out later."

And so grab I did, rummaging around the desk, the cot, any spare inch of space he might have hidden anything. "Pistol," I soon whispered, cold metal suddenly in my grip.

"Take it," Max whispered back. "Might need it. Hope not."

Which made two of us. In any case, between the time we left the latrine and then finished rummaging around, our ten minutes were almost up. I lifted the flap, checked to make sure that the coast was clear, and slipped out, Max again right behind me. To our sides, I saw two people coming out of the other tent, both of them in some sort of surgery scrubs. I froze, until I recognized the wide expanse of ass on one of them.

"Closest you could come to a gown?" I whispered.

I heard the familiar chuckle. "Will explain. Head to Jeep."

Off we walked, speedily, until all four of us were again safely inside the vehicle and driving to the gate.

"Halt!" shouted the guard.

"Zombies on the hill," said Max as he pointed into the blackened distance. "General told us to investigate before they get too close.

Open the gate, Private! Pronto!"

The private nodded and slid the gate open. "Good luck, sir," he said in reply, saluting as we sped out.

I held my breath, expecting a volley of bullets at any moment, a posse of Jeeps on our tails, though there was nothing but the sound of the gate closing behind us, a distant moaning growing more distant as we sped into the desert.

"Go right," said Steve, his hand on Max's shoulder.

"But the store is to the left," replied Max.

"Exactly. So head right over the sand for a mile or two, then head left once you hit the road. Hopefully, once they realize we weren't who they thought we were, they'll try to follow us in the wrong direction."

At last I exhaled. "Good thinking." Then I turned around and managed a smile. "Girl, drab blue is so not your color."

Kit plucked at the thin material. "Tell me about it," she said, with a smirk. "But at least it was a disguise."

"So," said Max, figuring where they got said disguises from. "That other tent was a makeshift hospital?"

I was still staring at Kit and Steve. They both shook their heads in sync. "Nope, not a hospital."

"Then why the scrubs?" asked Max.

Kit's previous smirk turned sour. "Both the units that built the camp were science units. So, like I said, it wasn't a hospital." She cringed, seemingly remembering what they'd found. "Lab," she then informed. "Hence the dreary outfits."

"Lab outfits, not scrubs?" asked Max. "What kind of lab was it?" I could hear the sound of dread in his voice and could see it on both Kit and Steve's faces as well.

"The zombies?" I said, putting two and two together as I remembered the drone emanating from the enclosure. "They're experimenting on them?" She nodded, eyes wide, the white of them glowing in the moonlight. And still the grimace remained, my belly suddenly tying up in knots, strong enough to dock an ocean liner with. "*No,*" I managed, the word laced with shock and disgust.

She nodded, as did Steve. "Yes," she said.

"Humans," added Steve. "Both on gurneys inside. Sliced open. And there was as much lab equipment as they could obviously carry with them scattered all around, piled high."

Silence enveloped us as we drove through the desert. Oh how I wished to hear a cricket, a coyote, anything but the sound of my heart beating from within my chest. "Thoughts?" I managed, the word rising from my throat right along with my acidic bile.

Steve handed me a few papers that he had hidden within his scrubs. It was dark, but I could at least make out the bold print on top. "I don't get it," I said. "This is from a science lab in Arizona." I looked over at Max and informed, "The title of the paper is: 'Corn Genetics: How to Grow a Better Crop'."

Max stared into the rearview mirror. "The Army does crop research?"

I turned around again as Steve shrugged. "Beats me," he replied. "Stands to reason, though. The Army does research on just about everything."

And, apparently, everyone.

I nodded. "So the other unit, the one that rendezvoused with your San Diego one, they were a science unit, like we said before. But genetics? So how did they know about the flares? Why the connection between the two bases?"

Max spoke up next after thinking about it for a couple of minutes. "If they were studying crops, they needed to know weather conditions. The two groups had probably been in touch." He fingered the papers that sat between us. "Hopefully, we'll find something in these that will expand upon that."

"Or upon the research they're doing now," said Steve. "That, I fear, is more important."

It was the way he said it that made my blood curdle. "*Fear?*"

He frowned. "Dead humans and dead zombies in the lab," he said. "Live humans and, uh, well, undead zombies in the holding pens. I'm no rocket scientist, but it stands to reason that the two are somehow related." He gulped. "In other words, it could've been me sliced open on that table had events unfolded differently."

"Saved by the grace of drag queens," offered Kit.

"And Cher," I couldn't help but add.

"What's the difference?"

And amen to that.

\* \* \* \*

We arrived back at the store a good while later. The lights were out, the place seemingly deserted and eerily quiet.

Almost.

"Halt, mother fuckers!"

My heart leapt to my throat as I jumped in place. Slowly I turned, staring into the eye of a rifle, with two more eyes right behind it, both bloodshot, obviously soaked in a great deal of purloined malt liquor.

"Girl, you better put that thing down before someone gets hurt," said Kit, thick finger wagging. "Namely you, you crazy-ass bitch."

Blondella hiccupped and lowered her weapon, and dress, which had ridden up in all the excitement, tight as it was and all. "Sorry," she said. "You were gone a long time. Everything okay?"

I lifted up the stack of papers we'd stolen. "We'll know soon enough," I told her. "Hopefully." Then we parked the Jeep around back and entered the store through the rear door, locking the place up good and tight before heading back down to the storage basement—well, after we grabbed whatever malt beverages that Blondella had somehow missed.

"So," I began, once we were all downstairs again, the private and the captain only marginally happy to see us. Minisculely, really.

"Fuckers, let us go," said Len, the captain, sneering our way as he sat on the cement floor in his skivvies.

"We will. Eventually," I told him. "But first, please explain the connection between your two units. One was studying weather patterns, the other crop genetics, right?"

The captain smirked. "Len Price. Captain First Class. 569234042."

Kit trudged over and crouched, as best she could, down to face level with him. "Do you know what they're doing in that large tent dead center to your camp, sugar?" She poked his chest. Barely leaving a dent, by the way. Hard to scratch steel, I figured. "Well, I know. I've seen it with my own two eyes."

Blondella hiccupped. "Beady. Beady two eyes."

Kit sighed, but continued. "Ain't no ears of corn they're operating on in there."

The private, Jackson, turned his head her way as best he could. "Operating? That's not a medical tent. We didn't have any doctors in our unit, and it's doubtful the other unit did either."

The captain elbowed him in the ribs. "Quiet down, Private."

"No," said Kit. "He's right. Science units, like ones that study weather or plant genetics, they wouldn't have medical doctors. Least not the healing kind."

"What's that supposed to mean?" added Jackson.

Kit crab-walked—again, as best she could—over to the private. "They're experimenting in there," she said. "Slicing them open."

"Which them?" asked Jackson. "The zombies? Guess that makes sense. See what makes them tick. Figure out a way to stop them." He stared up, Creature still there, on guard. "Or cure them."

Kit poked him now. I assumed, knowing her, it was more because it was hard to resist such a perfect chest. "Oh, they're cutting up the zombies all right." She moved her face in closer to his. Again, hard to resist such a perfect face. "Right alongside people. Humans. Non-zombies." She paused for effect. And Kit always got effect. "Get the picture, sugar?"

His eyes grew wide. "No way," he said. "You saw it wrong."

She shook her head. "Wish I did, sugar. Really, I wish I did." Her head kept shaking as she stood up. "But that's what we saw. Humans and zombies sliced open." She shivered, obviously remembering the scene in her head.

Max moved in. "And there are more prisoners now. More humans and zombies. Why? Why the prisoners if not for experimentation?"

"They're lying," barked the captain. "These guys have *us* as prisoners, remember?"

The private squinted his eyes shut. I remembered that he was fresh out of boot camp, meaning he couldn't have been more than eighteen or nineteen. The world had ended, and he was in a basement nearly naked and held captive by a bunch of drag queens. Poor guy.

"You're only prisoners," I told him, "because if we let you go now, then they'd find us and also lock us up."

"For your own protection," he replied, barely above a whisper.

"No," I said. "You don't lock up innocent people in order to protect them." I let that sink in for a minute. "Why do you think that your unit gathered up civilians and not more Army men and women?"

His head sunk to his chest. "I… I don't know." He looked up at me, hurt in his eyes, a wounded pride of sorts. "I was just following orders at the time. There was no way to know that it was all going to turn out this way."

"No way for *you* to know," slurred Blondella.

"What's that supposed to mean?" asked the captain.

"The flares," replied Kit. "The Army knew about them. Maybe, just maybe, seeing as one of the units studies the weather, they had a contingency plan. And maybe, just maybe, since they were working with the genetics guys in the other unit at the time, they included them in on the plan."

"Doesn't make sense," said the captain. "Why not save everyone, then? Or at least more people?"

"How?" I asked. "How do you save more people without causing mass pandemonium? And where would everyone go? The private here already told us that they maxed out the shelter as it was." I sighed. "No. I think they had a contingency plan, just in case the flares were worse than they thought, and they acted on that plan at the very last moment so as not to alarm everyone else in the camp." Sounded reasonable enough.

"But what about the civilians?" asked Jackson.

That, of course, was the part I was having problems with. Why not save more of their own kind? Plus, they couldn't have known about the zombie uprising, couldn't have planned on whatever experiments they were doing now. Could they have?

"Piece of the puzzle still missing," I replied, holding up the stack of papers we'd gathered from the general's tent. "Hopefully, that piece is in here somewhere."

"And if it's not?" asked Len, the captain, the sneer still evident on his handsome face.

Oh how I wish I had an answer to that one.

That among many, but that one was the most troubling.

For the time being.

# CHAPTER ELEVEN
## SMALL MIRACLES

With the rifles aimed their way, we untied our prisoners and allowed them a quick potty and meal break. Then we dressed them in the stolen scrubs and tied them back up. The uniforms, for now, we kept. Just in case. And since it was late, we shut the lights off down there and wished them a pleasant nighty-night—with Creature standing guard, of course.

"Max and I will take aisle one and the general's papers," I announced once we were back upstairs. "Steve and Kit take aisle two along with the papers they grabbed."

"What about me?" asked Blondella as she teetered from side to side.

I smiled and patted her shoulder. "Girl, you've done enough already."

"Tell me about it," she said, wobbling toward aisle three.

Then we found two flashlights and some batteries and got to work. Um, mostly. Because, come on, it had been a stressful day, and it was late, and even a bitchy drag queen needs a little bit of T.L.C. when the world has ended and there's a zombie invasion going on.

"Hi," I whispered to Max, both of us lying on our sides, the flashlight and the papers between us. "Missed you."

He nodded and leaned his face across the gap. "Missed you, too."

The kiss was very nearly perfect, warm and wet and wonderful.

Just like Max. Minus the wet. Unless he was leaking like I was right about then, at crotch-level I mean—then go ahead and include the wet. In any case, his tongue ran rings around my tongue, his hand inside my shirt pinching a tender nipple as a shiver ran up and down my spine, eyelids fluttering all the while. My hand followed suit, running through his dense matting of chest hair before landing on his thick nub.

We heard the gripe all too soon from two aisles over. "What's with the moaning?" shouted Blondella.

"Must be Creature," I shouted back.

"She's in the basement," Kit volleyed back. "Working. Just like you two should be."

I giggled and removed my hand. Max did the same, though the kiss was repeated and repeated again. "Shame on us," he chided with a heavy exhale down my throat.

"Yeah, shame on us," I echoed, swapping him breath for breath. "But maybe we should just read these and then get some sleep."

He sighed and reluctantly pulled away. "Agreed." He lifted the papers. "How should we proceed? Split them up?"

I shook my head. "I'll read straight through and hand them off one by one. That way we won't miss anything."

"Good idea," he said, then kissed me. Again. And again.

We heard Kit grunt from the other aisle. "Then fucking get to it already!"

Max chuckled. "You heard the lady."

"Cleveland heard the lady," I retorted. In any case, I started to work, taking a paper, reading it through, and then handing it off to Max.

They weren't in any particular order, nor were they numbered, and since we just grabbed and dashed, they weren't even grouped together properly. In other words, the job, already difficult enough, was now doubly so. Still, I slogged through, page after page after friggin' page.

When I was done and he was done, I looked up and over his way. "Well?"

He grimaced. "Bastards."

And I nodded. "And that's putting it nicely." Then I yawned. "Should we tell the others?"

He shook his head. "It's late; I'm exhausted. It can wait until morning."

His head was flat on the tiled linoleum, mine on his chest, his hand rubbing the small of my back.

Shame the world was so fucked or I might've been enjoying myself a bit more instead of falling fast asleep on the floor of a convenience store on the edge of the Mojave.

* * * *

"Rise and shine, sleepyhead," I heard, some eight hours later, a kiss placed squarely on my stubbled cheek, the morning's rays making my eyes go instantly watery.

"Please tell me I was dreaming," I groaned, stretching and yawning my way into the day.

"It was just a dream, Destiny," he cooed as he stroked my hair.

"Then why are we on the floor of this shit-hole?"

His fingers moved to my neck as he repeated the kiss. "Nightmares are dreams, too."

I pushed myself up on my elbows. "Uh huh," I reluctantly agreed, the yawn repeated. "You got that right."

I hopped up and helped him to his feet before we walked to the next aisle. Kit was on her side, her head on a roll of paper towels, Steve wrapped in her arms, both of them snoring like a pair of Hoovers.

"Cute," whispered Max.

"Too early to argue," I replied. "So, fine, we'll go with cute." I moved a couple of more feet. "Wake up, you two. Time to make the donuts."

"Donuts?" she uttered, her head popping up, a line of drool connecting her mouth with the paper towels.

I turned to Max. "Always does the trick." I pointed to Steve. "Speaking of tricks."

But Kit glared my way. "Don't start, girlfriend. Not unless you really do have a box of donuts with you."

At that, a box of them came flying over. "Breakfast of fucking champions," shouted Blondella from over on aisle three. "Now someone please tell me why my head is splitting?"

Kit chuckled. "To match your face," she whispered.

A can of coffee came flying over next, landing with a dull thud on

Kit's belly before rolling off and down aisle two. "I heard that." She appeared by my side a moment later, miraculously looking as if she'd just come from the beauty parlor. "So then, what did you find out?"

I squinted her way. "How did you do"—I pointed at her face—"*that*?"

She grinned and poufed her already poufed hair. "I always wake looking like this." Kit snickered and shook her head. "You have a price tag on your face, girl," added Blondella, reaching over to pull said tag off. "Two dollars and a quarter. Sounds about right." Then she again looked my way. "And now, if the morning repartee is quite complete, again, what did you find out?"

I sighed and waved my hand in a *follow me* fashion as I led them all down the stairs to the storage basement.

"We have to pee," said the private, right off the bat.

"In a minute," I told him, squatting down next to the captain as I said it. "We know that you knew."

"Knew what?" he replied, barely glancing my way.

"Yeah, what?" said Private Staub, craning his neck my way.

I'd taken the stolen papers with me to the basement. I waved them in his face. "Tell him, Captain. Tell him how you knew about the flares, knew about what was going to happen, and then took prisoners just beforehand." I moved in closer to draw the point home. "And are now using said prisoners to experiment on."

"Nuh uh," said the private, who was tied to the other side of the beam.

"Tuh huh," said Max, who was now also crouching along with me.

Kit tried to crouch, but settled for a lean instead. "The geneticists you have with you, they're studying the zombies *and* the humans."

"Nuh uh," repeated the private.

"Tuh huh," repeated Max, his hand rifling the pages in my hand. "It's all here in black and white."

The captain sighed and squirmed against his bindings. "It's not what it seems."

Blondella was the next to crouch. "What's it seem? That the world went to pot and the Army did nothing to stop it? Or that the Army is now experimenting on the few lone survivors?"

Price's sigh repeated. "We knew about the flares, as did everyone else." He glanced my way, locking eyes for a brief second or two. "But we were a science unit, specializing in weather, so, yes, we knew that the flares could've been larger than everyone else was predicting." He shook his head. "By the time we realized what was about to happen, we had mere minutes to react, same for the other science unit in Arizona, which was working with us at the time, weather and crops intimately tied together as they are. Then we gathered as many of us that would fit in the shelter and hunkered down."

"And the prisoners?" asked Steve. "Me and my civilian coworkers?"

That I knew the answer for. I lifted the page and handed it his way. "The science units," I told him. "They had a contingency plan. Should the worst happen, they'd meet at a predetermined location midway between them, namely the Mojave, in case there was flooding."

"Which there was, up north," added Max. "Though in the middle of the desert, this time of year, that wouldn't have been an issue."

Steve moved in closer. "But you didn't answer the question. What about us, the civilians? Why were we penned in? Why are you conducting experiments on us now?"

Captain Price looked his way. "You know why we took you with us."

Steve nodded, apparently figuring it out at just that moment. "What would a unit of weather experts and plant geneticists be able to accomplish in the desert without people like me? Without an electrician or two, plumbers, computer specialists, etcetera?"

The captain nodded. "Besides, you weren't prisoners." Then he paused. "At least, not at first."

My over-the-head light bulb pulsed. "When you realized that the worst, as you put it, was even more worse than ever imaginable, that everyone was now zombies, the undead, then you had little choice but to turn civilians into prisoners."

"For their own protection," he justified.

"Without giving us a say in the matter," Steve amended, scowling now.

"What say?" said the captain. "What choice did you have? Where would you have gone to? We were your only hope for survival."

Steve pushed in between me and Max and bent down so that he and the captain were eye to eye. "No, *we* were your only hope for survival. You could build the camp, get the basics together, but then you'd need us to keep it running, to fix things, wire things properly. Slaves, that's all that we were to you."

"And science experiments," I chimed in with.

"Nuh uh," said the private, sounding much like a broken record now. "Can't be."

"It isn't," said Captain Price.

"We saw the bodies," said Kit. "We have the paperwork with us. The Army is now experimenting on both humans and zombies."

"Not what it looks like," he protested. "The humans you saw, they were... ours."

And then the scenes from the last few days flashed before my eyes, spliced together inside my head. "When the zombies attacked your camp, there were casualties?"

He nodded. "It was dark. There was gunfire. People... got in the way. And those zombies that weren't killed—or re-killed, that is to say—were captured." Again he looked my way. "Look, I'm not saying it's ideal, but we have to see if there's a possibility for a cure or if we can even figure out how the zombies came to be in the first place. We presume it's some sort of genetic mutation brought about by the sudden radiation. We have geneticists with us, plant geneticists, yes, but still, experts in the field and probably the only hope of unlocking all this, perhaps of finding said cure."

By then, my knees were aching, so I righted myself and retrieved the rifles. "Here," I told Blondella and Kit. "Take them to the bathroom one at a time, then tie them back up and give them some food and water." I turned to Creature and smiled. "You did an excellent job guarding them," I told her. "*And* not eating them."

She groaned, and the prisoners shuddered. The comment was meant to scare them. Evidently, it worked.

Then I left, Max and Steve right behind me, Blondella and Kit, for once, not arguing with me and doing as was told. Thank heavens for small miracles.

The three of us then went outside for some fresh air and away from prying military ears.

"Huh," immediately said Max as he stared out at the desert all around us.

"Huh what?" said Steve. "Huh that he was lying?"

I turned to him, bottom jaw dangling. "Lying? How do you know he was lying?"

He looked at me and then at Max. "Wait, it's cooler out here all of a sudden, isn't it?"

Max nodded. "Hence my *huh*." He squinted up at the sun, which was making its way skyward. "The flare effects must be wearing off. Maybe the sun has settled back down to normal."

And maybe my small miracles had turned large. Still, Steve's initial comment hung in the air. "That's great, but please go back to the lying bit. What makes you think he was lying?"

"Not think," he replied. "Know."

"Know *how*?" I asked.

He sat down on the step in front of the store. We joined him there, all of us breathing in the air that was merely hot and not the recently standard sweltering. "He said that the dead humans were theirs, military."

"And?" Max asked.

"There were a couple of battery-powered lanterns in that tent Kit and I were in," he replied. "It was dark, but we could see the bodies, the faces uncovered." He turned his head left and looked at me, then right and looked at Max. "I noticed two guys, one with a faux-hawk, the other with long hair, ponytailed."

"So you saw two guys with unfortunate hair styles," I said. "So what?"

Steve shook his head. "Guys in the military have neither faux-hawks nor ponytails, Destiny. And the zombies, their faces look different, sort of twisted, out of whack. These two were never zombies. Which means that the captain was lying. Intentionally."

"Still, that doesn't answer the question as to why he was lying," Max said. "Unless it was to trick us into thinking that the Army is on our side. All of our sides. Everyone that's still alive, I mean. Maybe he thinks we'll let them go, then."

By then, my head was hurting and the sun was making my skin itch. I stood and wiped the dust off my ass. "In any case, we do know two things."

Max also stood. "Which are?"

"One, they have innocent prisoners again, which we saw in the holding pens," I replied. "And, two, they know they were robbed and that we're all still missing, as are the private and the captain."

Steve hopped up and groaned. "And the Army doesn't just let things like that fall by the wayside. If they weren't out looking for us before, they certainly are now."

"Fuck," I cursed, heading back inside, cold air an instant relief. At least from the heat. As to the other things, the possibility of getting found, then getting penned in, and—*gulp*—potentially getting experimented on, for that there seemed to be no relief in sight.

* * * *

A few moments later, our group had rejoined and were sitting down to breakfast, repackaged though it was. Still, at least the coffee could be made fresh, and there was juice and bananas and a few oranges. Meaning, at least we didn't have to worry about scurvy. Small miracle again, but I was taking them where I could get them.

It was after we filled Blondella and Kit in that yet another of those miracles fell into our laps.

The ring was barely audible, a Lady Gaga snippet chiming, muffled. "My phone!" shouted Blondella, her beehive of a wig suddenly a blur as she took off for aisle three, the rest of us right behind her, breakfast toppled and strewn. "Hello?!" she shouted into it. "Hello?! Johnny, is that you?!"

She listened, eyes so wide it was a wonder they didn't pop out of her head. Then she clicked the phone shut.

"Well?!" we all shouted in unison.

She jumped. "Dead."

My heart tore in two. "Johnny's dead?" I yelped.

She shook her head. "No, idiot. *Phone* is dead." Her head kept on shaking. "How could he call me if he was dead?"

She had me there. Then again, maybe the zombies could make phone calls, old habits dying, pardon the expression, hard. "Was it Johnny? What did he say?"

She smiled, then frowned. "It was Johnny, but it didn't seem like he could hear me, and the connection was bad, crackling."

"The sun," said Max. "Maybe now that it's settling down some the phones will come back, maybe the Internet as well, the satellites."

"But what did he say?" asked Kit.

Blondella smiled, then frowned, again. "I... I'm not sure. Sounded like Perry Ellis Land... totally safe." The smile quivered back in place. "But at least I heard the *safe* part for sure. He's safe. And alive!" She looked at us each in turn. "We have to leave and go to

New York. Now."

And it was then that my heart plummeted from within my chest, landing in my gurgling belly with a dull *splat*. "You know we can't, Blondella." I placed my hand on her shoulder. "They're looking for us now. And they're taking prisoners. And experimenting on them. It's just… just not safe."

She pushed my hand away. "It's safe in New York. He said so himself."

Kit parted the ranks. "He said that *he* was safe, sugar. He didn't say that *it* was safe, did he?"

She paused, the frown again returning, no smile to take its place. "No," she barely whispered. "Not exactly."

Kit's frown mirrored Blondella's "And what does Perry Ellis Land mean, anyway? Maybe he's not even in New York anymore. Maybe that's a city or a town someplace else."

Max reached inside his back pocket and retrieved his iPhone. "Bars, but no Internet." He scrolled through his contacts and dialed. And dialed. And dialed. "No connections."

Blondella did the same. "Nope, but if it happened once, it'll happen again." She looked up, hopeful. "Right?"

I nodded. "Definitely, hon. But we have to wait it out just a bit longer. If we get on the road now, they'll find us for sure. Plus…"

She sighed. "Plus, they have prisoners. Got it. But when did we get to be so noble? Last I checked, we were a bunch of snotty, belligerent drag queens."

"With hearts of gold," I amended with.

Kit snickered. "Girl, I think you've been out in the sun for too long," she said, three fingers held up in a W, the universal sign for *whatever*. "In any case, I'll agree with you on one thing: the roads, right now at least, are dangerous. As to those prisoners, well now, maybe that captain was telling the truth. Maybe they're being held for their own protection. How are we to know?"

I slunk back to our now-cold breakfast, and it was then that I had an idea. "Maybe we can't, but I think I know someone who might be able to find out." And then I prayed for yet another of those small miracles. Then again, if He was listening to any of my prayers, He had a funny way of showing it.

\* \* \* \*

Aside from Max, I had the others wait as we made our way downstairs. He held the rifle while I untied Private Staub. Gun aimed his way, we led him back upstairs.

"Where are you taking him?" shouted the still-tied-up captain.

I turned and replied, "We need an extra set of hands to help us lift some things. He'll be right back."

That was that. We kept walking. Then I grabbed a couple of pairs of cheap sunglasses and two cold Cokes before walking just me and him outside.

"Not me?" asked Max as he stood by the door.

I glanced behind me. "The private and I are just going to talk. No guns needed, Max." He nodded and backed into the store again until Staub and I were alone.

"Not lifting?" he asked, blinking into the harsh sunlight just before the sunglasses were slipped on.

I sat on the cement steps and patted the space next to me. "No lifting; just talking, Jackson." I adjusted my sunglasses and glanced up at him. "Can I call you Jackson?"

He shrugged, then unscrewed his bottle of Coke and sat down. "That's my name, so, sure."

Then we were sitting side by side, cold sodas gliding down our throats. "Do you know what's going on, Jackson?" I asked.

He sighed as he flipped the bottle cap between his fingers, rolling it around and around. "Not a clue."

I placed the cold bottle against my hot cheek. "And remind me how long you've been in the Army?"

He glanced my way. "Two months out of basic training." He stared at the cap. "And guess what?"

I nodded. "They didn't train you for this shit?"

And he nodded. "Exactly. Not even close." Then he paused before asking, "They're all dead, aren't they? Everyone? My family, friends?"

And still my head kept nodding, slowly, ruefully, my heart suddenly pounding. Head, too. I'd been thinking the same thing, of course, but hadn't said it out loud just yet, figuring that if I didn't say it, it couldn't be true.

But it was true; I knew it was.

"I'm sorry, Jackson. For all of us."

"You have a family…"

"Destiny. My friends call me Destiny. And, yes, Jackson. A mom, a dad, two older brothers, cousins, the whole shebang. You?"

"Same, but with two younger sisters." He squelched back a sob. Truth be told, so did I.

I let our words hang there, thick like the air around us and just as painful to take in. I took another swig of my Coke, as did he. "The captain," I said. "He's lying. We're pretty sure of it."

He sighed. "And?"

I gave him a roundabout answer. "The Army you joined, it's not there anymore. This country, our country, our world, it's all gone now. All that's left, I'd imagine, are a few lucky ones."

"Lucky?" He chuckled, but it was the least mirthful chuckle I'd ever heard.

"Point taken," I said. "Anyway, we are alive and trying to stay that way, me, my friends back there, *you* I hope."

"Sir," he said. "*Destiny*. I got it, you want something from me. Just tell me what it is, okay?"

Another chug and my Coke was done. "If what's left of the Army finds us, they'll lock us up, just like they're doing now to the other captives. There can't be all that many of us, Jackson, survivors I mean. What if they're experimenting on the remaining few, which is what it looks like? And, even if they're not, shouldn't we be allowed to find our families? Find out if they're really all—"

"Zombies," he said, finishing my sentence as he also finished his soda.

"Zombies, right," I said. "And maybe the captain does know more than he's letting on. Maybe what he knows can help save me and my friends and those people in the holding pen back at that makeshift camp of yours."

"So you want me to find out? Find out what he knows and help you rather than him, rather than the Army I enlisted in, which may or may not still exist? That about right?"

Again I nodded and turned his way. "Yep, that's about right."

His back went in reverse until it was flat on the cement, face pointed skyward as he inhaled deeply. "My sisters, one just turned ten. Back in Kansas." His head turned my way. "Tornado country."

I understood what he was getting at. "Storm shelters?"

He again stared up. "Storm shelters. Thick concrete. Think that would do it?"

Honestly, I hadn't a clue. Our shelter was steel, same for Johnny's, same for the Army's, I'd imagine. Still, it was a possibility. The flares were brief, after all. Maybe thick concrete, below ground, was enough to block the heat and the subsequent radiation spike. "She plays down there? This sister who just turned ten?"

Again he sighed and then nodded, strumming his chest with his fingertips. "Yup."

I hoped she had made it to that shelter. God, I hoped so. "My friend inside, the blonde one, her boyfriend is alive. We know this for sure. He's alive in New York and, as far as we know, safe. We're trying to get to him, but—"

"But the Army is trying to get to you," he said. "Got it. And, um, okay."

I smiled finally. "Okay, you'll help us? Find out what the captain knows and tell us?"

He sat back up. "I'll find out, and if what he knows doesn't sit well with me, then I'll tell you." He held his hand out my way. "Deal?"

I grabbed it and shook. "Deal."

He held my hand tightly in his. "Kansas is three states over. On the way to New York. I help you—"

"That's part of the deal. If we can, we'll take you there. Promise."

He let go of my hand. "You're all gay, aren't you? That friend inside, the blonde one, is a man?"

I gulped. Was this a deal breaker? "All gay, yes."

He smiled. "My uncle is gay. Or, um, was." He paused. "Maybe still is. Has a shelter of his own. A boyfriend of his own, too. Funny guy. You'd like him."

I exhaled, relieved. "I'm sure I would, Jackson. I'm sure I would."

And with that, we returned him to his prison and tied him back up.

Then I prayed again, not for another small miracle or even a large one, but for my family and his, for his sisters and his uncle and his uncle's funny boyfriend. For all of them and all of us.

And then I prayed again, just in case.

# CHAPTER TWELVE
# WHERE THERE'S SMOKE

"We have to get out of this store, off this main road," Steve said once we'd all amassed again. "The Army is going to come looking this way, probably sooner than later. There aren't, after all, that many directions we could've gone in."

"Suggestions?" asked Blondella.

Kit raised her hand. "The guy we Wicked-Witch-melted," she said. "The one who used to work here. Best bet, he didn't live all that far away." She pointed to a rack of maps by the register. "We get his wallet, check his driver's license, take his keys, his car out back, then find his house using one of those maps."

"What about the zombies?" asked Max. "One house probably means many, and once they smell us, they'll surround said house for sure."

She shrugged. "Look, it's them or the Army; the zombies we can handle, but the Army I'm not so sure about. Besides, they're less likely to go house to house; there just aren't all that many of them to be able to do such a thing. Plus, we still have our secret weapon, the private in the basement. Maybe he'll find out what we need to know, and then we can go from there. But here in this store, we're sitting ducks."

Each of us nodded. "Not it!" I then immediately shouted, Blondella and Steve and Max quickly following suit.

Kit sighed. "Fine, I'll go dig around the dead guy's pants." She glared at us. "Chickenshits."

Which was fine by me, because melting a zombie was one thing, but rifling around in his pants, nuh uh, no thanks. In any case, she grabbed a Milky Way before heading out back, downing it in barely two hearty chomps.

Then we watched as she retched and rifled, then retched again before dangling the dead guy's wallet and keys our way. After that, she popped the trunk of his car open.

"Load her up and let's get a move on!" she shouted.

We nodded and loaded, filling the trunk with the essentials. In other words, it was laden with booze, water, water guns, and candy in about three minutes flat. And then we retrieved our prisoners, tied them together, carried Creature up the stairs, and divided ourselves up between the Jeep and the newly stolen car, with me and Max and the prisoners in the former.

Easy as that.

That is until it wasn't, because nothing, I repeat, *NOTHING*, is ever that easy. Not before the world went all loopy on us and certainly not after.

In the silence of the desert, where the only living things around us for miles were in fact us, we heard them long before we saw them. Squinting into the distance, where the road wound through the barren land, a vehicle of some sort was kicking up dust as it roared our way.

"Friend or foe?" I hazarded to ask, swallowing hard as sweat stung my eyes. And then we heard another sound, their voices over the Jeep's radio as they communicated with the base camp, telling them that they were approaching a gas station/convenience store, namely ours. "How are they doing that if the satellites are down?"

Max turned my way. "Shortwave, Destiny," he informed. "Not satellite." He smiled. "Which gives me an idea."

The captain snickered from the back seat. "Pity you won't get to use it."

Max turned and glared his way, then leaned over and whispered in my ear. "Remember what you're about to hear." I nodded, though I hadn't a clue what he was getting at. Then he again turned to the back seat. "What is your mission, Captain?" he spat.

Once more the captain snickered, nodding his head as he replied, "Len Price. Captain First Class. 569234042."

Max looked at captive number two. "What is your mission, Private?"

Jackson looked at us, confused, and replied as his captain had. "Jackson Staub. Private. 643657290."

Again Max leaned over to me. "Listen for it," he whispered, covering my mouth so that I wouldn't ask the obvious out loud. Namely, *listen for what?* But before I could even blink, he grabbed the rifle and was gone, all of us plus our friends in the other car watching him run around the corner of the store and out of our line of vision.

"What the fuck?" whisper-shouted Blondella through the open window.

"Listen for it," I whisper-shouted back.

"Listen for what?" came the terse reply.

But all she got in return was a nervous shrug, my head tilted up, listening for it. Whatever *it* was.

And yet all I heard, all we heard, was the sound of the enemy fast approaching, engine loud in the all-enveloping quiet. I wiped the sweat off my forehead. I knew we couldn't drive away, leave Max, or let them know we were there, hidden behind the store. All I could do was wait, my rifle aimed at the prisoners.

"Trust me, Captain, I'd have no problem shooting this if you try anything." Which was mostly true, especially with Max out there doing Lord knew what.

He grinned. "They'll find you, *us*. If not them, then the next Jeep or the one after that one. After all, where there's smoke, there's fire."

Little did I know, however, just how prophetic his words would soon be.

Still, I couldn't risk him shouting our whereabouts, so, instead of shooting him, I merely slammed the butt of the gun into his face. "Pleasant dreams, asshole." Then I stared at the private.

He smiled nervously, then pointed to the conked-out captain. "Asshole." Then he pointed back to himself. "Not asshole."

I gave him the thumbs-up and again listened for whatever it was I was listening for, but all I heard was their Jeep pull up in front of the store, then two doors opening and slamming, even their footsteps as their boots crunched on the hard asphalt. And all the while, my heart sped like a bunny on meth as the sweat waterfalled down my face.

Then through the silence cut the noise: *rat-a-tat, rat-a-tat, rat-a-tat-tat.*

"Gunfire," I squeaked out. *But whose?* I thought. *And is this what I was listening for? Now what?*

Only, that was just the coming attraction; the main event came a split second behind it. And like the captain had said, where there's smoke, there's fire—though the inferno that erupted was no mere fire.

And *that* was what I realized I was listening for.

I slid over and gunned the engine, the Jeep squealing out of the rear parking lot and away from the blast that kept right on blasting, a fireball shooting into the sky, that aforementioned smoke billowing up in a cloud of noxious black as we sped into the desert, my friends right on our tail.

I zoomed the Jeep into a wide arc, though I was mostly driving in the dark until I got far enough away from the thick blanket of smoke. We were now a quarter of a mile or so in front of the store, the group of us staring ahead. It looked like a war zone, though we all realized right away that what we were looking at were the exploded gas tanks and the equally exploded Jeep parked just to their side.

Again there was a boom that shook the earth beneath us, another ball of fire shooting skyward, followed closely by yet another cloud of smoke. We all coughed and covered our faces from the fumes as best we could. Still, I didn't budge as I scanned the area for Max.

"There!" shouted Kit, thick finger pointing about five hundred feet to our left.

At last I exhaled, allowing for a brief smile as I spotted him running, legs and arms pumping as he raced to keep ahead of the black cloud of dust and ash and smoke.

"Drive!" I shouted in return, speeding his way.

An agonizing minute later, we pulled alongside of him and he hopped in. Then we took off through the scrub and away from the stench and the fiery sight behind us.

"Thanks," he said, wiping the sweat and dust and grime off his face as best he could. He turned around and spotted the zonked-out captain. "What gives?"

Jackson pointed at me. "Butch dude conked him one."

Max giggled. "Who, *him*?"

I punched him playfully in the arm. "The gene is merely dormant, not missing altogether. Just needed a little boost to kick-start it." I pointed behind me at the raging fire. "*That* was kick-start enough, thank you kindly." It came out very Scarlett O'Hara-like. So much for that butch thing. "Now then, what and why?"

He paused, seemingly to catch his breath, then lifted up the radio transmitter. "Do you remember what these two said just before I took off?"

I nodded. After all, a good drag queen has to have an excellent memory. I mean, you try learning all the words to the Barbra Streisand catalog of songs without a few able-bodied brain cells. "Got it," I replied.

He then he pressed a button and began speaking. "This is Captain Price, serial number 569234042."

I leaned over and added, "And Private Staub, serial number 643657290."

He patted my shoulder and continued. "Following escaped civilians approximately ten miles due west from base, over."

There was a crackle on the other end, then, "Captain Price, we just heard an explosion coming from that direction, over."

"Roger that. Civilians blew up gas station. Two casualties. Ours, I'm afraid. We're giving chase now, over."

"Your coordinates, please, Captain?"

Max grinned and squeezed my arm as I continued speeding south, now following a barely there road that I'd remembered from the map. "Heading due north through the desert. No roads. Will try and herd them your way. Try to intersect, over."

"Roger that, Captain. Will attempt to intersect, over."

He powered down the transmitter and turned my way. "That should buy us some time."

I smiled, but said smile quickly vanished. "You said two casualties?"

His smile disappeared as well. "The store was still standing, so presumably they're fine. Still, I didn't want the Army to come looking for them just yet. In any case, it was them or us, Destiny." Again he squeezed my arm. "And I went with us." He turned to Jackson. "Sorry about that."

The private nodded. "In war there are always casualties. And trust me, if you guys hadn't declared war before, you certainly have now."

Max's hand gave mine another squeeze as the Jeep and the car behind us continued speeding south, heading toward the dead convenience store clerk's house. "Well," Max soon said, "at least they'll be fighting said war nowhere near where we'll actually be. And doubtful they'll go looking for us, or the captain and private here, south of the base."

I looked at the private in the rearview mirror. "And like Max here just said, we just bought us some time, too."

Jackson knew what I was getting at and nodded. "Fingers crossed the captain will be even more pissed at you and will confide in me."

"Throw in a few crossed toes," I replied, yanking the Jeep west now. "On second thought, better make it all of them."

\* \* \* \*

We arrived at a small desert town about twenty minutes later. Though *town* might've been a bit of an exaggeration. Basically it was a handful of small homes, a few trailers, a bar (yippy!), a tiny grocery store, and a rusted water tower towering above everything. The road through it all was cracked and dusty, which were the two most appropriate adjectives for the town itself.

This being the desert, most everyone had obviously been indoors when the flare hit, we presumed, so as to any errant zombies, we thought we'd have few to contend with. Still, better to dispatch all of them before we got settled, we figured, rather than waking up in the morning surrounded by a horde.

"You take the west side," said Max to Blondella, Jeep and car now parallel, "and we'll take the east. Water guns only. Let's preserve the bullet ammo as best we can."

She nodded and drove off. The captain was still out cold, so I handed Jackson a water gun and told him to consider it target practice. He took it, smiled, suddenly frowned, and then promptly dropped it to the seat. "Um," he croaked out as he pointed dead ahead—all in all, a fitting phrase, as phrases went—and added, "there must've been a funeral happening when the solar flare hit."

Max and I turned to where his finger was pointing. At the edge of town were at least three dozen zombies, all in their black finery, their groans all of a sudden evident as they spotted us spotting them. I looked at my measly water gun and matched Jackson's frown with one of my own.

And then to make matters worse—as if things weren't worse enough as it was—just at that moment, Blondella came screeching back our way, window down, her frown twice as hang-dog as my own. Though, yes, she had somehow managed to reapply her makeup and reposition her wig into an upsweep.

"Not good," she said.

I pointed at the funeral procession headed our way. "Gee, ya think?"

While she pointed behind us. "Not them. *Them!*"

I turned from the nightmare in front to the nightmare in the rear. "School children," I coughed out. "There had to have been some sort of recess happening when the sun went berserk." There were at least fifty of them, all ages. "School must've been kindergarten through twelve by the looks of them."

So, to recap, we had a throng of groaning undead adults in front of us, a throng of moaning undead children behind us, one thin stretch of cracked road to drive along in either direction, and a bar to our side, so tantalizingly close that I could almost taste the gin.

"You thinking what I'm thinking?" asked Max, revving the engine.

I nodded. "Happy hour. Minus the happy."

Blondella yelled from her side of things. "And we don't have an hour either!"

Max sighed and pointed to our left. "Head between those two houses."

"Too narrow!" shouted Kit. Blondella said something snarky that I couldn't quite make out and got a slap on the arm for her troubles.

"Just drive!" shouted Max, turning the Jeep, dust flying, tires squealing as he sped between the wooden buildings, my heart in my throat as we just barely cleared them, walls on either side of us so close that I could stretch out my pinky to touch the one on my right.

I watched in my side mirror as Blondella followed close behind, Steve and Kit and even Creature holding on for dear life—or in Creature's case, *afterlife*—their car much wider than the Jeep. But at least, for their sakes, it was metal versus very old wood, so the outer house walls might've had height, but the car had bulk. In other words, the screeching and slamming we soon heard quickly obliterated the sound of undead moans and groans, but at least the car was still close behind. As were the zombies, suffice it say, the lane cleared for them by first the Jeep and then the car.

Then I looked from the mirror to what lay ahead, my eyes moving up the rusted metal beams. "No way," I rasped.

"You got any better ideas?" barked Max.

"I vote for the bar," said Jackson.

"Second it," I readily agreed, hand held up.

"Third," said Max. "After we do *this*."

"Fuck!" I hollered, though it came out more like *FUUUCK!!!* as I braced myself as best I could, eyes wide as the Jeep maxed its speedometer and went tearing into the first and then second legs of the metal water tower.

Then everything went into slow motion as we shaked, rattled, and rolled but otherwise remained in one piece, more or less. Out of the corner of my eye, I saw Blondella swerve to the left as we banked to the right, the zombies rushing through the alleyway like Moses heading through the Red Sea—though Dead Sea was more like it.

The Jeep righted itself as I stared up, the steel structure crunching, bending, and twisting in a heavy metal cacophony as the tower pitched and ultimately—thank goodness—toppled and fell like King Kong, post Empire State Building air-assault.

Then *CRASH!* and *BOOM!*

My heart, sad to say, made the same noises right about then.

"You've got to fucking be kidding me!" I quickly shouted as I stared at the split-open water tower. Considering the week we'd been having, it shouldn't have surprised me that it was bone dry, not a drop in sight to melt the zombies with. I turned to Max. "Now what?"

He looked at me, I looked at the private, and the private looked at the slumping and still-comatose captain. In other words, we weren't gonna find any answers in that beat-up Jeep of ours. "Kit!" I shouted at the top of my searing lungs. "Eat a fucking candy bar!"

I leaned my head out and watched her do just that, one candy bar and then another, two certainly better than one when it came to her.

She swallowed, nodded, and replied, "You guys ever watch any zombie movies?"

They weren't high on my to-do list, but I had seen my fair share of *Day, Dawn, Night of the Living, Undead, Newly Risens*, so I nodded and shouted, "Why do you ask?" as the dense mass of zombies continued to head our way, half of them splitting off to Blondella's car, the other to our Jeep, all of them barely thirty feet away as they skirted the useless, empty water tower—or make that just tower, since Lord only knew the last time it actually held any water.

Blondella put the car in gear and drove to our side. Behind us was nothing but rocky and cacti-laden desert, in front of us, well, we've already covered that.

Kit opened the door and got out, chocolate smearing her lips.

"Why do you think the zombies always go for the humans, but despite obviously being hungry, never go for each other? I mean, it's the same meat, right? Or brains, depending on the film."

"You lost me," I freely admitted.

She sighed and then rephrased the question. "Why do gay guys go to gay bars when the booze is the same in a straight one?"

That I knew the answer to. "Like goes to like."

"Exactly," she said, pointing to the likes in question.

"You lost me," I freely admitted, yet again.

Her sigh repeated. "Like goes to like. Like sticks with like. Like *obeys* like, dimwit!"

Though my dim did, thankfully, go bright at that last remark: *obeys*. "Creature!" I shouted. "She's *like* them."

Creature moaned from the back seat of the car. Blondella had somehow found time to apply a fresh coat of lipstick and eyeshadow to our dearly departed friend, not to mention a fair share of concealer to hide all that ghastly grey, so maybe *like* was a strong word, but she was the next best thing we had. In any case, she was still predominantly zombie.

And so Kit picked her up and placed her down in the sand and dust and dirt at the edge of town, while we all hopped out, captain excluded, and stood directly behind her. The undead, for their part, continued trudging along, moans and groans reaching a fevered pitch as thirty feet became twenty and then—*gulp*—ten. By then, my heart rate was going in the exact opposite direction, ten beats per second to twenty to thirty, body drenched with sweat, Max's hand in my own as we stared our fates dead, as it were, in the face.

Blondella tapped Creature on the shoulder. "You're on, girl."

Creature managed a nod as she slowly lifted her arm, hand held at the vertical, palm out. "Stop," she grunted, rigid body swaying at the obvious exertion.

My shoulders hunched and my jaw clenched as they moved to within five feet of us, the stench of them very nearly overpowering. "Say it again. Say it again," I managed, knees fairly quaking.

"Stop!" she shouted as best she could.

And stop, lo and behold, is what they did—dead, of course, in their tracks.

"No way," I said.

Max chuckled, his grip on my hand even tighter all of a sudden.

"We keep saying that, but way keeps, well, *waying*."

"Friends," added Creature, pointing our way. "Not… lunch."

"Good one," whispered Kit, then added, loudly. "Not snack, not dinner either, folks."

"Too fatty," chimed in Blondella, Kit's elbow quickly appearing deep within her ribs.

I chuckled, more out of relief than anything else, seeing as the undead horde wasn't tearing us limb from limb as planned. And then I had a new idea. Because *like* as they were to her, they could still be, um, *liker*. "Head to the store," I said, maintaining a placating smile as I inched our group over and around them.

Just then, the captain came to. "What the fu—" And then he just as promptly passed back out.

"Don't mind him," I told them, still inching.

"Ass… hole," grunted Creature.

"Mmm," they groaned in unison, following closely behind us.

"Um," ummed Kit. "They're following, not killing, so maybe we can widen our strides just a bit, you know, before it gets dark out here."

I nodded and quickened my pace, my posse following me, secondary posse following us. Or following Creature, more than likely, but that was fine by me, so long as they were simply following and not killing, as Kit had said.

When we reached the general store, Max and I rushed in and then just as quickly rushed out, holding all the iodized salt that we could find, a half-dozen canisters' worth. "Think it's enough?" I asked Kit.

She shook her head as her eyes scanned the dense undead throng. "Too many of them, so let's do the adults first and worry about the kids later."

"Do?" Blondella asked. "How do we *do* them exactly?"

"Yeah," said Max. "Last time you tackled Creature and dumped it inside her opened mouth as she thrashed beneath you." He looked at the adult zombies that lined the first few rows. "Think you have it in you, Kit?"

And still her head shook. "Not enough candy bars in the state." Then she glanced up, and her smile somewhat righted itself. "Henson's General Store and Apothecary," she read. "Did you see any household items while you were in there?"

Max shrugged. "Tampons count?"

She sighed and pushed past us. "Never mind; I'll go see for myself."

We listened as she stomped around inside. I turned to the zombies. "You'll have to excuse her; she's usually a lot sweeter."

Blondella snickered. "Well, a little sweeter."

"Fuck off!" we heard from inside the store.

I paused and tilted my head their way. "You'll just have to excuse her, then."

And then she returned, a box held aloft as if it were the Holy Grail—or a good stiff martini.

"Funnels," said Steve, reading the box. "That should make it a little easier. Genius."

At last she smiled. "Not just another pretty face." Then she glared at Blondella. "Don't even."

Blondella hopped off the store steps and stood, for apparent protection, behind a tall zombie with a mullet, before asking, "Did you say pretty or pity?" She snorted. "Sorry, couldn't help it. Too easy."

"That's what he said," countered Kit.

"Ladies!" shouted Steve, clearly already accustomed to where these verbal matches led. "We have work to do." He then pointed to the canisters of iodized salt. "Dump the contents into the funnels, everyone, and please make it quick; they might look docile for now, but—"

"Never mind," I interjected. "At least we have a *for now*."

And so we poured the salt into the funnels, to the brims, so that everyone would get an equal dosage, then distributed the funnels between us, fingers blocking the holes. To the first line of zombies we then went, each of us with funnels held aloft.

"Heads... up!" shouted Creature, in her halting manner. "Mouths... open!"

Up the heads went, open the mouths went, in the funnels went, down the salt went, and without so much as a whimper from the undead. Then the funnels quickly got refilled, and the second line of zombies got their doses. On and on we went, until all the salt was gone.

Sweating and panting, we waited and waited and waited some more. "Maybe we didn't use enough," I lamented.

"The funnels were max-sized," said Kit. "The doses were almost exactly what we gave to Creature."

And then all of a sudden we saw it. "This one's blinking!" shouted Max.

"This one, too!" gleefully hollered Blondella.

"All of them!" shouted Kit. "All the ones we dosed!"

At last I exhaled. About two dozen of them were all closer to life than death. Or, well, as close as they were ever gonna get, but at least now cognizant. The couples paired up, strange smiles appearing on their faces, as if they'd overcome some impossible obstacle. All in all, I suppose that cheating death was the most impossible obstacle of all, so perhaps the smiles were well-deserved. Still, they weren't all that happy with their current stiff conditions or that of their children's zombified ones.

"What... can... we... do?" asked one woman as she approached her apparent son, only to have her hand nearly bitten off when she went to stroke his cheek.

We handed the funnels over. "Find more salt," instructed Kit. "It must be iodized. Fill the funnels up to the brim. That will cure them."

The man who'd been standing next to the zombie woman moved up an inch. I presumed it was her husband. "Not... cured."

My heart broke at hearing the words. And the look on my friends' faces meant that their hearts were tearing apart at that very moment as well. *Not cured*. I knew what he meant; his face said it all. "You're, um, you're alive. Together. It's more than most of the world can say." Sad, but that was the best I could do, could say; sugarcoating it seemed pointless.

He stared lifelessly at his undead wife and son. "Thank... you," he managed just the same.

Suffice it to say, it barely made me feel any better. "You're welcome. Now go and revive your boy."

He nodded, and the group dispersed, those that were still zombies staying put, standing before Creature as though she were a god—or maybe make that goddess.

I smiled. That, in fact, did make me feel strangely better.

Because diva is one thing, but come on, a goddess? No contest.

# CHAPTER THIRTEEN
## UH OH

We found the dead store clerk's house after that. It was starting to get dark, and we were all worn out, frazzled, too pooped to pop.

*Almost.*

I mean, really, how much energy does it take to pop, right?

It was a small place, just barely large enough for the group of us. By then the captain had risen, so we stashed him and the private in a smallish attic along with a couple of fans and some food and water, so at least they wouldn't melt or starve to death.

"If you're thinking about climbing out the window, don't," I told them. "The zombies are outside waiting for you. And they'll do far worse to you than we ever could." Which might or might not have been the truth, but seemed to do the trick if the look of terror on the captain's face meant anything.

After that, we ate what food the clerk had, washed the dust and grime off, and said our goodnights. Max and I then took the master bedroom, Kit and Steve the guest room, and Blondella crashed on the living room sofa. Creature stood guard—or maybe make that god; take your pick.

"How did I end up alone?" whined Blondella. "I'm the pretty one!"

"Karma, bitch," shouted Kit through the door.

I chuckled as I got undressed and then hopped into the stranger's bed, Max joining me a second later. "Man, this is so fucked," I said through a yawn and a stretch, my body, brain, and soul aching.

"Sleeping in a dead man's bed, surrounded on all sides by

supposedly friendly zombies, with the Army searching for us?" he asked, also yawning.

A sigh replaced my yawn. "When you put it like that, maybe put a royally in front of that fucked."

He reached for my hand and gave it a squeeze. "Bright sides, Destiny," he said, sidling in next to me, thigh to thigh, shoulder to shoulder. "We're all still together, all in one piece, with food in our bellies and—"

I pointed downward. "Boners that could pry open a steel safe?"

"See," he said, clutching said boners in his hands. "Bright sides."

I grinned and watched as he stroked us both, a warm rush of adrenaline rising up my spine. I rested my head against his. "I just wish we could head to New York already. I feel bad for Blondella, and I'm tired of dealing with this Army shit."

He tilted his face sideways and kissed my cheek. "Not like we have a lot of routes we can take to get us from here to New York. We'd have to make a really wide arc to go either north or south, and even then we'd never know where they might show up. Or the zombies, for that matter, because the closer we get to civilization, the harder it'll be for us to get past them. Plus, despite my better judgment, I would like to know what the Army's up to, in case, somewhere down the line, it could affect us." He spit into his mitts and continued working the come up from our balls. "But I do agree about New York. If Johnny is safe, as he said he is, then maybe we would be too. Though it strikes me as odd that he could possibly be safe in one of the most densely populated cities on the planet."

That warm spot of mine began to spread. "Right about now, Max, nothing strikes me as all that odd. I mean, what could be odder than all this?" I pointed to the dead man's bedroom, but was really pointing to everything we'd done and seen and experienced in our short time together. "I mean, I'm a drag queen and I have two prisoners held in an attic, which is being guarded by a zombie."

He chuckled, then inhaled sharply, his back suddenly arching, head tossed in reverse. I stared down in a rapturous combination of both wonder and lust. How many times had I watched him come now? A scant few? And yet how many times had our lives been in danger together, our fates united? More than a few times, that was for sure.

His cock spewed a moment later, the wide head widening all the more, first a river of pearly peter-glue gliding over, then a shot straight up, then another, like those dancing fountains I'd seen at Disneyland, only stickier and more aromatic.

At the sight of it, of him, the smell of both, my own cock erupted, my breath getting sucked in, spine as rigid as my prick as he stroked every last bead and drop out until our bellies and chests were covered in sticky sap.

He laughed as he gazed from my mess to his.

"What's so funny?" I panted.

"Another bright side," he replied, pointing at said messes. "The world is fucked, and we're still coming."

"Must've rescued a few orphans and/or kittens in a past life."

He ran his fingers through my spunk-trail. "Or an entire orphanage/pet rescue center." He turned my way, and I his. "Or maybe we just rescued each other."

I couldn't help but smile despite the awfulness that threatened to bubble up at any moment. "Glad to rescue you any time, Max." I kissed his cheek.

"Ditto, Destiny," he said, kissing mine. Then he laughed again.

"What's the chuckle for?"

He shrugged. "The weight of the world is on our shoulders, and we're covered in come."

I smiled and hopped up, heading for the bathroom, thankful, at least, that we were covered in come and not something far, far worse.

\* \* \* \*

Sometime in the middle of the night, Max shook me from my much-needed slumber. "What's that noise?" he asked, not alarmed, thank goodness, so much as curious. "Sounds like someone's singing a Neil Diamond song." He craned his ear up. "'Hello Again', if I'm not mistaken."

Neil and not Barbra? In our group? Had to have been a dream. And yet, I heard it, too. And the voice sounded strangely familiar.

We slipped into our boxers and tiptoed to the living room. Blondella was staring out the window, frowning. Oh, and she was singing, the lyrics changed but the melody unmistakable:

*Uh oh again, uh oh*

*Just thought I'd say uh oh*
*I couldn't sleep at all tonight*
*And I know it's late*
*But it couldn't wait*
*Uh oh*

*Uh oh, my friends, uh oh*
*Just thought I'd let you know*
*The army was here during the night*
*When we were here alone*
*And in this stranger's home, uh oh*

*Uh oh, my friends, uh oh*
*It's not good to surprise your foe*
*It's not good to get splattered like goo*
*And to get eaten in that way*
*When you should just say, uh oh*

*Uh oh again, uh oh*
*Just thought I'd say uh oh*
*I couldn't sleep at all tonight*
*And I know it's late*
*But it couldn't wait*
*Uh oh*

"What's she doing?" whispered Max into my ear.

"Ambien, I'm guessing," I whispered back. "She must've found some in the bathroom. Best guess, she's sort of half in and half out of sleep."

"And yet making up new lyrics to an old song?"

I shrugged. "Gotta give the old broad credit; she's nothing if not creative. Big part of her act, in fact." I moved in closer. "But what do those lyrics mean? Army and goo and eaten?" I stood beside her and also stared out, and all at once I knew where she'd come by her gruesome wording. "Uh oh," I squeaked out.

Max moved in and stood on her other side. "Uh oh," he echoed.

"*Uh oh again, uh oh,*" she sang dreamily in that way that only a good dose of Ambien can do. Right about then, I envied her not being fully awake. Odds were good she'd forget what she saw once the

140

morning came; we, however, would not be so lucky.

"We have to go check it out," said Max, about as lackluster as I'd ever heard him, like saying we had to go get a filling or two—without a shot of something numbing first.

"Too bad the bar is closed," I replied, thinking of the perfect numbing elixir right about then, something that would put a Long Island iced tea to shame.

He grabbed my hand, then found our clothes before leading us outside.

It was dark, though moonlit enough and warm but with a pleasant nip in the air; which, suffice it to say, was the only pleasantness we'd be experiencing. As it turned out, two soldiers had found the town, presumably looking for us or anyone that had recently associated with us. The Jeep's ignition was off, the men barely a few feet away. Or at least, that is to say, their bodies. Or at least what remained of their bodies.

"They probably never saw what hit them until it was too late," Max said.

I remembered Blondella's song. "Their foes, splattering them like goo and then eating them, you mean?" Goo, as it turned out, was the perfect word choice.

He touched fingertip to nose, frowning all the while. "The zombies might have human emotion again, but they also still have that undead hunger. Even Creature has it, as we've seen." He pointed to the mangled corpses, barely recognizable as human save for the tattered clothes, blood shimmering in the moonlight all around them. "Though, ironically, if it wasn't for Creature, it would've been us like that right now."

"What if their superiors send backup to look for them?" I couldn't help but ask.

He nodded and closed the gap between us and the men. I looked away as he bent down. As a mortician, he'd of course seen bodies before, but I ventured to guess that none looked quite like this. Still, he did what he had to do, and a minute later, he cranked up the Jeep and was flicking on the radio.

"This is Sergeant Bertrand and Private Green reporting, over."

"What is your location, Sergeant? Over."

"Just leaving the town of Smithville. No signs of life. Town is full of zombies, however. Unsafe to search further. Anyone who escaped here would be dead in minutes, over."

We heard a sigh from the other end. "Return to base, Sergeant. Pens are full enough as it is, over."

"Roger that, over."

*Click* went the radio. *Thump* went my heart. *Gulp* went my throat. "Pens are full enough as it is," I then repeated. "Meaning, fuller than last we saw them, and these men here were looking for either us or others like us to fill said pens." I looked to the window behind us. Blondella was no longer standing there. "To quote a certain singing someone, *uh oh*."

"Doesn't seem to cover it completely, but okay, we'll go with that." He groaned and hopped out of the Jeep. "Still, at least for the time being, they won't be looking for us down here."

"Bright side?" I asked as we stood in the dim silver glow, trying to keep our feet gooless and bloodless.

"Well, brighter, at any rate."

"Like ten watts," I allowed. "Now what?"

He shrugged. "It's late. I'm exhausted. Sleep, dear one, sleep."

I grimaced. "Perchance *not* to dream."

Though nightmares were all I'd certainly be having for the foreseeable future.

\* \* \* \*

Max and I woke late the next morning, as did our friends. We closed the curtains lest anyone decide to stare out and see the mess from the night before. As to that, and as expected, Blondella had no recall of it. Steve and Kit had heard nothing, but considering my friend's snoring abilities, that wasn't saying all that much. A Triple Seven taking off would've been drowned out by that racket.

And that left only our captives to look in on.

Did we find them up there naked and huddling together? Fetching as that image might have been, it's not even close to what we discovered. Though what we found was indeed better. Um, well, maybe not better, image-wise, but it did, at least and at long last, bode well for us.

Creature had sidled out of our way and allowed us entrance to the attic stairs. We climbed, slowly squeaked the door open, and were greeted by Jackson, frowning as he held his head in his hands.

Captain Price was still dead to the world—though, of course, not nearly as dead as the rest of said world, especially as dead as his fellow soldiers outside, so at least there was one blessing to count.

"What's wrong?" I whispered.

The private pointed to the corner of the small attic, empty bottles littering the space. "Homemade hooch. Easily ninety proof." His frown sagged farther south. "*Ouch.*" Then he gazed our way, a smile just barely managing its way up. He tiptoed toward us and leaned in next to me, breath so potent it could start a small forest fire. "He talked. Or at least, the booze did." I squelched a surprised gasp, nodding instead. Then he added, much louder this time, "I gotta take a leak."

The captain stirred, flinging his forearm over his eyes.

"Okay," I replied, also rather loudly. "Follow us."

He followed, and we closed the attic door behind us, again leaving Creature to guard it. Then we led the private to the kitchen, the rest of our ragtag group pouring in at the same time, all in search of coffee, some sweetened cereal for Kit.

"He knows something," I told the others.

"Do tell," said Blondella, opening the cupboards until she found some instant brew.

"Yes, Jackson," I said. "Please do."

He frowned. "Any aspirin in one of those cabinets?" Blondella nodded, retrieved a few, and handed them over. "Thanks, um, ma'am." She grinned. He got an A for effort on that one, I figured. Then he downed the pills and took a seat. "The captain was, it turns out, telling the truth... *to a point.*"

Max sat down across from him. "Which point?"

I handed him a cup of instant coffee and a newly toasted and jammed piece of bread. He smiled my way. "The Army, or at least the two units, knew of the solar flares and were prepared for an emergency evacuation, with a rendezvous in the desert afterward if need be. They kept this a secret between them so as not to overly alarm the masses, seeing as there was so little they could do."

"Like presumably save some lives," said Steve.

Jackson shook his head. "Or lost even more in the ensuing mayhem."

"Then what happened?" asked Kit.

He took a sip of coffee and a nibble of toast, eyelids fluttering as the first droplets of caffeine hit his system. "The zombies, the bases back in San Diego and Arizona were full of them when everyone emerged. The phone lines were dead, Internet too. The survivors knew, or at least suspected, that the entire world looked much the same as the bases, so the units set out for the desert as planned. Safety in numbers, combine their knowledge, maybe find a cure."

"Ah," I ahed.

"Yeah, ah," he replied.

"So they're looking for a cure by dissecting humans and zombies?" asked Blondella. "Killing what few remaining humans there are in order to save them? Talk about ass-backward."

He took a deep swig of his coffee before he continued. "They're dissecting the zombies to see how they've been reanimated, perhaps see if there's an easier way to *turn them off*, as the captain put it. Easier than, say, with water or guns, which we clearly don't have enough of, not in our meager numbers and their vast ones."

"How would that work?" asked Max. "What could be easier than water?"

Jackson shrugged. "Who knows? Maybe something you can pump into the air, empty an entire town of them, then, a city, or anywhere that we're left to inhabit. In any case, right now it's just preliminary research to see how they all came back, how the radiation acted and on what organs."

I sighed as I drank my own coffee, ruing the day I ever lambasted dear, old Starbucks. Oh to think how I'd never enjoy and/or not enjoy another tall, overpriced latté again.

"And the humans we saw, the non-zombie, non-military personnel? The ones in the holding pens and the ones being dissected? Are they just guinea pigs?"

His coffee and toast finished, he glumly looked my way. "You're not going to like the answer, Destiny."

"Shock," I replied. "I don't much like the questions either."

He stood and looked at each of us in turn, all our eyes glued and stapled and locked onto his. "Have you stopped to think how the radiation is affecting not only the zombies but us as well?"

The coffee cup shook in my hand. "It lingered?" I asked, voice now trembling, because, no, none of us had given that any thought, what with the zombies and the Army after us and all. We were, it seemed, alive and healthy, pickled livers excepted, so it never even came to mind.

He nodded. "It lingered, of course. It was an awfully heavy burst of it, after all, even if just a quick one. The unit has Geiger counters, so it knew about the lingering, even if you couldn't. But to what degree we're all affected, to what degree we will be affected moving forward, well now, that's a mystery."

"And the humans, they're there to help solve this mystery?" I asked.

"The Army also has radiation sickness medicine," he informed. "They knew there was a potential for the radiation, so they amassed as much as they could beforehand. It's easy enough to come by if you're a research unit."

"Ah," I ahed yet again. "So the ones in the pens are being held for their own protection, in case they get sick?"

He nodded. "In case they get sick *or worse*."

"Worse as in killed by zombies?" asked Kit.

"Yes," he replied. "For now, the Army thinks it's better to keep the survivors together as much as possible. For everyone's protection. *Theirs* as well. Like I said before, safety in numbers."

Max tapped his fingers on the table. "But that doesn't explain the two humans being dissected."

Jackson looked his way. "As far as the captain knows, one had a heart attack, the other died of unknown causes, presumably not radiation related. Their organs are being harvested as controls, to test the effects of a possible zombie cure on, and to see how the existing radiation has affected them."

"So the people in the pens," said Blondella. "They're not going to be guinea pigs as well? Just held for their own protection? But for how long?"

Jackson turned her way. "The military has the only power now. They have weapons. They have numbers on their side. There is no U.S. of A. anymore."

It was now Blondella's turn to *ah*. "Ah," she ahed. "Slaves then? Keep them healthy and alive, and then use them as needed?"

He nodded ruefully. "In times of war, there is no right or wrong, just survival of the fittest. For now, *they* are the fittest."

"And, in truth, perhaps our only chance for survival," I couldn't help but add. "Maybe they can deactivate all the zombies, or at least any that come looking for them. And maybe they can keep the survivors alive as well."

"So what are you saying, Destiny?" said Kit. "That we should turn ourselves in to them?"

I snorted derisively. "Get real, girlfriend. If Stonewall has taught us anything, it's—"

"Never fuck with a drag queen," said Blondella, finishing my train of thought to a tee.

"Exactly," said I. "In any case, what I was getting at was that they're not the only game in town. And I, for one, am feeling pretty darn *fit* myself. All we need is to even the playing field a bit and change fit to fittest." I rose from my chair and lifted my fist up high. "Seize power! Go all ape-shit on their asses!"

Kit tapped me on the shoulder. "Um, seize power with what? A couple of water guns?"

"No," I replied, mouth in a snarl as I walked to the kitchen window before parting the curtains. "With *them*!"

\* \* \* \*

Jackson was returned to the attic after that so the captain wouldn't get suspicious, while I led Creature to the master bedroom. I sat, she stood, which seemed her only real option these days. It was time for a talk, and one I'd been dreading having. Mainly because I was certain not to like the answers.

"Do you mind if I ask you a few questions, Creature?"

She blinked once, her head just barely nodding, the rest of her otherwise stock-still.

"Are you in, um, any *pain*?"

There were two blinks as I reached for her hand. Her skin was still exceedingly hot to the touch, but not nearly as bad as when we'd first found her. I knew that the heat was from the radiation, which was also what was keeping her animate.

"Are you hungry?" One blink. One blink. One blink. "Want a sandwich? A candy bar?" Two blinks followed by a gulp from yours truly. "Flesh, huh?" There was one slow blink followed by a groan. "But if you don't eat any flesh, you'll, well, *survive*?" It was the best word I could come up with. In any case, she didn't blink right away, but when she did, it was a lone one. Thank goodness.

I squeezed her hand. "Are you glad to be with us?"

"Sisters," she replied, the word forced up from her lungs, ragged, without feeling, though the meaning was felt just the same.

"Sisters," I replied with a weak smile. I felt it in my heart, in my soul, but that didn't make it any easier to look her in her deadened eye, in her face covered in makeup that barely hid the ashen pallor.

"Not... pretty," she managed next.

I shook my head. "No, the situation is pretty bleak."

"No," she replied. "*Me.*"

I chuckled, the drag queen in me coming out to play. "You were never very pretty to begin with, hon."

"Bitch." Oh how that word filled me with joy, with hope, fleeting as it might have been. See, despite how she looked, which, in all honesty, was God-awful, it really was her inside there. Tamped down, maybe, but her just the same. "What... next?"

I sighed. "Do you know why the others, the townsfolk, listened to you before? Why they didn't kill us? Why they seemed to follow you, are still following you?"

She paused, clearly thinking it over. "Common... language." The words were hard for her to get out, but I understood them just the same.

"Zombie language?" She blinked once, slowly, sadly. "That's why you don't attack each other, too, right? Why you stay together?" Another single blink followed. "And because you alone could speak, they listened?"

"Must... be," she replied. "Why?"

I nodded. She was no less smart in death. "The military, those men in that makeshift camp, they want you and others like you dead, and they want to imprison us, to enslave us. And they are all that stand in our way between here and New York." Well, besides a few hundred million zombies, but why quibble? One ferociously large obstacle at a time, I figured.

"Us... or them... then?"

And still I nodded. "Yes, Creature. It's either us or them. And I'm voting for us."

Her head barely nodded, her now-familiar groan joining in. "Us," she told me, her vote added to my own, to our friends'. Then she paused. It seemed that she understood what I'd been getting at, why we were having this little tete-a-dead-tete. "I'm... the leader?"

I nodded, smiled. "I like to think of you as more goddess-like, but if you want to go with leader…"

"No… I think… goddess… will do."

And, yes, that was the Creature I knew and loved.

Now all we needed was a plan.

And hope that the other zombies would follow said plan.

And then pray said plan worked.

And then somehow make it to New York after said plan worked.

So, in terms of those large obstacles, yes, we had more than our fair share, but at least we were on the right track.

Fingers crossed.

# CHAPTER FOURTEEN
## THE PLAN

Again we amassed in the kitchen, all of us standing around our newly elected, recently risen goddess—odd as that sounded, it didn't even crack the top ten list for that week. "So how is this going to work?" asked Steve. "Your friend here can barely get a few words out, let alone a whole list of commands."

I smiled and lifted up my phone. "There's an app for that."

Blondella coughed. "There's an app for a surprise zombie attack?"

I nodded, then typed a short sentence out, then hit play. "Follow your leader," the phone proclaimed, about as flatly as Creature could say it, though with considerably less effort.

"Amazing," she said.

"Thanks," I replied. "I like to think so."

"Not you," she sniped. "Amazing that you have enough brain cells left to even find the correct keys, let alone the app itself, let alone get the phone to turn on."

"Amazing," I responded.

"Thanks," she replied, with a self-satisfied smile. "I like to think so."

"Not you," I sniped in return. "Amazing that the world is coming to an end and you're still a dick."

"Or that she can even find her dick," added Kit, never one to be left out of a veritable snipe-fest.

Max sighed. "Ladies, and I use the term loosely, can we just get on with this, please? Before the world really does come to an end."

Kit patted his shoulder. "This *is* our world, sugar."

"Amen," said Blondella.

Steve raised his hand. "Not to bring an end to such a delightful conversation, but even if we can lead, um, *them*, out there, where are we going to lead them to? Any of you know the first thing about surprise attacks—of the non-verbal variety, I mean?" We all glumly shook our heads. "Well, the enemy does. And the enemy has weapons and training and the protection of a fortified gate. And all we have is a town full of slow- moving zombies."

"So what are you suggesting?" asked Max.

Steve nodded as he stood there, then pointed to the ceiling, eyes gazing that way as well. "The kid up there, at least he has training. At least he knows their strengths and weaknesses. And at least he has a vested interest in all of this, right?"

I nodded in return. "He wants us to take him home."

Steve's own nodding amped up a notch. "And we already have all the information that we need from the captain, so I say we release the private and have him fully join forces with us."

Blondella chimed in next. "But the private in question is nothing more than a teenager. You want him to lead an entire undead town and a ragtag, if not completely lovable, drag troop, along with their drag troop groupie men-folk?"

"Hey!" protested Max.

Steve shrugged. "Eh, I'm good with it. In any case, yes, that's what I'm saying. He's the best shot we have, unless one of you has a better idea."

"I'm tapped," I admitted. "Reached my quota with the whole app thing. Which, now that I think of it, might not work all that well, seeing as the volume on my cell isn't all that great."

Kit sighed. "I vote for the kid."

Blondella also sighed. "Fine, let's give it a try. If nothing else, at least he's cute."

"But is he willing?" I asked, already heading us up to the attic.

\* \* \* \*

I opened the door. By then, the captain was wide awake, looking completely hung over and not the least bit delighted to see me. Little did he know that people once paid a cover to do just that. The private also looked up, surprised to see me again so soon, let alone the group standing directly behind me.

"Need something?" asked Captain Price wearily.

I pointed to Jackson. "He's free to go if he wants to."

The captain appeared confused. "Just him? Why's that? I didn't win you over with my charming personality? I mean, to be honest, hard to be all that charming when the world has gone to hell in a handbasket."

Kit snickered. "I used to know a drag queen by that name: Helena Handbasket. Royal bitch, she was."

Blondella started with "Takes one to…" and got an elbow in her ribs for her troubles.

"Anyway," I said. "The private can go free if he chooses to join with us instead."

"Instead of what?" asked Price, the sneer even more evident. "Instead of the Army? Why would he do that?"

I didn't answer the question, nor did the private. Answered, no, but stated, yes. "I'll go with you guys," he quickly blurted out. "Um, I mean girls. Uh, girly guys."

Now it was Steve's turn to chuckle. "Not all of us are girly guys. Some of us are just groupie guys, or so it seems."

"Hey!" objected Max yet again, then just grumbled and shook his head in apparent defeat. "Fuck it. Never mind. Just come on already, Jackson." He cleared the way, as did the rest of us, the private walking two steps in our direction before the captain roughly grabbed his arm.

"He's not going anywhere!" barked Price.

"Yes, *he* is," replied Jackson, trying to pull his arm away.

Trying, that is, and failing, seeing as the captain was a good few years older and many pounds, not to mention muscles, heavier. Still, Jackson wasn't to be deterred; he was being given his freedom and the chance to be with his family, and commanding officer or no commanding officer, he was going to take those things. In other words, young, straight, and testosterone-filled as they were, a struggle quickly ensued.

Sort of.

See, these guys were hung over and tired and certainly not up to their usual snuff. So, while Price pulled, Staub eventually relented, and the momentum of that caused the captain to go in reverse, his hold on the private released, his body charging backward at full steam—backward, that is, and directly toward the attic window.

One moment he was up there with us; the next, he wasn't. And all that remained to point to that fact was a large, gaping hole in the pane of glass.

We all rushed over and stared down, then just as quickly looked away as the teaming horde of zombies descended onto the broken body below, their collective moan literally shaking the house to its very foundation. We covered our ears and our eyes, little good it did us.

"Why did he do that?" muttered Jackson, his body suddenly trembling, lower jaw hanging limp.

"It was an accident," I replied, my hand on his shoulder.

He turned and locked eyes with me. "Easy to say."

I shook my head. "Easy to say because that's exactly what it was."

He whimpered, blinked, and looked away. "Fine," he whispered, then added, only louder this time, "Can we just go now, please? Out of this attic, this town, this fucking state?"

My hand remained in place. "Not yet, Jackson. We can't. You know that. But I promise you that we will and soon."

* * * *

The kitchen was again full a few minutes later and considerably glummer than a mere ten minutes prior. Yes, like I said, the captain's death was an accident, but he was our prisoner, our responsibility, so, no, I didn't exactly mean what I'd said to Jackson. And yet, we needed him to be at his best, at his full mental capacity, and feeling guilty for what truly was an accident wasn't going to exactly put him in that state of mind.

"So what's the plan?" he asked, just after he took a seat at the kitchen table.

Kit snickered. "We thought we'd leave that one up to you, sugar."

Jackson stared at her incredulously. "Got any water?"

She tilted her head his way. "Yeah, why?"

"So I can do a spit-take with maximum effect," he replied, then looked at me as he pointed his thumb her way. "Is she serious?"

"Not usually," I told him, "but in this case, yes. You know the camp and have military training. You can organize us so that we can take said camp, release the prisoners, and get the hell out of Dodge without any casualties."

He laughed. "Well, if that's all…"

"We know that's a lot to ask," Max said. "We're not delusional."

Now it was Blondella's turn to snicker. "Not so much that we'd need medication for it."

Max sighed. "In any case, you're our best hope. Besides, we have backup."

He looked around and counted us all on his fingers. "Medication, maybe not, but contact lenses, most definitely."

I moved to the kitchen window and raised the blinds, zombies, many of them with blood now dripping down their purpled lips, all staring our way.

I cringed and proclaimed, "Backup." Then, suffice it to say, I quickly lowered the blinds.

"Never mind what I said," Jackson coughed out. "You *definitely* need medication."

I shook my head and pointed at Creature. "You'll lead us; she'll lead them."

His face turned to each of each of us, one by one. "You're not joking, are you?"

And then we all shook our heads in unison. "Not without the promise of ample tips, sugar," added Kit. "Got any spare fives lying around?"

Blondella patted her back. "Or in this one's case, a candy bar. Or six."

Kit nodded. "That would work."

A silence enveloped the room. And drag queens hate silence. Still, we all stared at the private and waited. Eventually, a small grin appeared on his youthful face. "Guess it beats the alternative." He pointed to where the zombies were standing, just behind the wall. "Think they're full?"

Creature groaned. "Never."

Which seemed like an awfully long time, if you ask me.

\* \* \* \*

We split up after that. The boys went off to strategize, while the, um, well, the *girls* went off to amass the undead. After we freshened up first, seeing how amassing can be lethal to the pores. Or just plain old lethal. Plus, our nail polish, by then, was so cracked that we'd practically need a spatula and some spackle to get it back into shape.

"Ready?" asked Blondella, wig readjusted and makeup very nearly perfect again.

Kit and I had settled for some lip gloss and a fresh coat on our nails. After that, I vowed to go drag shopping as soon as all this shit was over and done with. I mean, really, I could now filch with abandon at Tiffany's and Neiman Marcus, right? Fuck the credit cards and just glide on in with a shopping cart and a caffeine buzz. But, no, here I was in a dead man's bathroom in the middle of the desert with nothing but convenience-store-quality polish.

In any case, we quickly left said bathroom, carrying Creature along with us, and creaked open the front door, sunlight pouring into the living room just as a collective groan filled our ears. It was, I realized, like a cheer, a zombiesque hurrah for their apparent leader. Fuck the app idea anyway; we had the real deal.

They had to have smelled her, sensed her, because all heads turned her way—as best as said heads could. "I'm guessing they've never seen your act before, hon," whispered Blondella.

"Bitch," grunted Creature in return.

I grinned, despite the scene unfolding, the masses suddenly amassing, pouring in, or at least seeping, dozens and dozens and many more dozens of them, all of them gathering around the house, around *her*. Dead upon dead upon walking dead, many more newly iodized than before, or so it appeared, considering how tame most of them now seemed. Then my grin promptly faded, seeing as they also collectively stunk if not looked something awful.

And it was then that I realized our dilemma—one of many, yes, but this was a more pressing one—namely that, while Creature could in fact talk, it would take her hours to get it all out, one impossibly slow word at a time. Thankfully, Kit leaned into her ear just at that moment and whispered, "Tell them that I'm your mouthpiece."

Blondella snorted. "Then you better warn them to back up first; bitch hasn't brushed her teeth yet."

I elbowed my supposed friend in the side. "Please, not now."

Creature cleared her throat, which sounded much like a bulldozer running over a road scattered with broken glass. In other words, or word, *nasty*.

"Is she channeling Ann Coulter?" asked Blondella, hand covering her ears.

Fine, that one I let her have. And then prayed that aforementioned bitch somehow hadn't escaped her fate. Maybe she was locked in a room somewhere for all eternity with Fox News on auto-loop.

In any case, Creature started to haltingly speak. "Must... defeat... enemy." Another groan went up, the sound like a swarm of bees. "Listen... to the... fat... one."

"Hey!" objected Kit.

"The dead don't lie," said Blondella.

"Ladies," I interjected. "So *not* the time."

Kit nodded. "Right," she whispered, then addressed the zombies. Surprisingly, they looked more attentive than her usual audience. Or at least substantially more sober. "The nearby Army wants you dead, all of us dead. Or at least captured, enslaved. They see you as no longer human, no longer meriting a, uh, *life*, different though it might now be. They would burn you and this entire town down if they could, burn your homes and all you've accomplished here." She raised her flabby arms into the air and spoke with unexpected zeal. "We must crush them before they crush us, before they wield enough power to rule everyone and everything that remains."

"How?" asked a zombie down in the front row, voice thick and gravelly, eyes seemingly glazed over.

Kit lowered her hands and grimaced. "We're working on it."

We waited for her to say more, but she merely stood there, staring and sweating. Creature sighed, sort of. "Dismissed," she croaked out.

The communal groan again rose before, as she'd commanded, they dismissed, slowly, very slowly, like ants that had been drinking from a bourbon bottle.

Blondella turned to Kit. "What exactly are we working on?"

She shrugged. "Beats the hell out of me."

"I'd love to," Blondella muttered in return, then said, louder, "Well, at least it looks like they're following us. Or at least Creature here. That's one point in our favor, right?"

The shrug repeated. Like Kit had said, it beat the hell out of me, too.

* * * *

Again we found ourselves in the kitchen. Max and Steve and Jackson were still working on their plans, a crudely drawn map now lying before them on the table.

"Well?" I hazarded to ask.

Max looked up with a beguiling grin. He pointed to the map, to the far front right corner. "They do seem to have an apparent weakness," he informed.

"Which is?" asked Kit.

"Supplies," replied Steve. "The Army originally chose the desert because of its lack of a threat of flood and its proximity to both camps. They hadn't counted on the zombies, of course."

I managed a smile. "So they have limited supplies and difficulty in getting more, and if they wanted to pick up and move, they'd risk bringing the zombies to wherever they settled. That's an Achilles' heel if ever I heard one."

Kit nodded. "So all we have to do is attack at said heel, right?"

Jackson nodded. "Cut off their supplies and force them to capitulate. Right now, they simply have numbers on their side and a modicum of firepower, but destroy their water and food sources, and those things don't matter nearly as much, if at all."

Kit, who had found a Snickers Bar in a kitchen drawer, snapped her pudgy fingers together and proclaimed, "Then let's circle the wagons!"

"Huh?" huhed Blondella.

Kit turned and replied, "The Indians would circle the wagons, block any escape, and then fire." She waited for us to catch up, then sighed and added, "No Indians, but plenty of zombies."

I grinned. "Too bad the people at Hershey's never knew about you, girl."

Blondella shook her head. "Oh, they knew about her all right; she practically kept them out of the red all these years."

Kit faux-guffawed. "As in all that red you wear on your cheeks, sugar? The stuff that covers the dull gray and the age spots?"

I jumped between them. "Again, ladies, not the time." Then I turned to Jackson. "Even if we can circle them, they still have firepower and the protection of the fence. Won't they just gun us all down?"

Max then pointed to another small building on the map. "They keep the spare weapons here. If we can sabotage this, then that will leave them only the few weapons they carry with them."

But I wasn't so sure. "Even a few weapons can take out a great many of us. Plus, they still have prisoners, potential innocent victims, maybe even human shields."

Max shook his head. "Hopefully, they'll surrender before anyone gets hurt. I mean, without food or water and spare artillery, what choice do they have?"

I frowned and sat down, the day's events already wiping me out. And it was still early yet. "Choice? How about stay and fight until the last man is standing?" I replied. "You know, go all *military* on our asses, what with them being the military and all." I turned to Jackson again. "Which do you think it'll be?"

He scratched his head and squinted his eyes my way. "Look, these are science units, not combat ones. Best bet, they'll see what they're up against and call it quits."

"And worst bet?" asked Blondella.

His squinting stopped. "Yeah, then that other thing, the last-man-standing shit. But again, that seems unlikely. I mean, not like they risk any court-martials for quitting, right?"

He had a point. Still, it didn't make me feel all that much better about any of this. "And what about the zombies?" I asked.

They all looked at me in confusion. "What about them?" asked Max.

I turned to Creature. Though it pained me to ask it, I did just the same. "Are you more dead than alive? More zombie than human?"

Death being the ultimate poker-face, I hadn't a clue what she was thinking, if the question had hurt her or not, if anything could still hurt her. She was Creature in body, but what about soul? Who could guess how deep it went beyond that? Which is why her answer surprised me.

She slowly raised her fist and placed it over her chest. "Does not... beat... but still... feels." She slowly lifted the same fist to her head. "Still... thinks." She lowered her fist to her side. "All... human. Just... *different.*"

And though I might not have known much about her kind, I certainly knew what it was like to be different. And so I again turned to my friends. "Back to my question, then."

Max sighed. "What about the zombies?"

I nodded my head. "We need to ask them what they want to do."

Steve broke in with, "They want to follow Creature. They *are* following her."

And still I nodded. "At first, because she was the only one of them who could still communicate, could breach the gap between what they once were and what they find themselves now to be. Perhaps, like I'd joked, she was some sort of goddess to them, someone to put their hopes in. But why listen now?"

Steve rested his head in his hands. "What choice do they have?"

I turned to him. "If they blindly follow Creature to their deaths— or, well, re-deaths—then how can we live with ourselves? If this plan of ours isn't foolproof, how can we not at least give them the option to nix it, to refuse to help?" I then sighed. "Look, they know why we're fighting now. They know what's at stake. But that doesn't give us the right to lead them into a potentially worse fate. Then we wouldn't be any better than the Army."

He looked up at me and nodded. "Fine, we'll give them the option, then. But what if they decline?"

I turned away and looked between the blind slats, at so many of them still standing around, staring into oblivion. "Let's hope they don't, Steve," I said. "Let's hope they don't. For all our sakes."

\* \* \* \*

We sent Creature out a short while later. This was her show, her *people*, as it were. If it took hours to get her point across, to hear theirs, then so be it. If nothing else, we did have time to, pardon the expression, kill. The Army, as far as we knew, was searching for us elsewhere, and we still had plans to draw up, ones, we hoped, that would include the townsfolk.

I turned to Kit, her candy bar long gone, a sugary soda now in her grip. "Anything?"

She nodded as she gulped. "Back to the Indian analogy."

"The circling of the wagons?" Jackson asked.

"Right," she said with a well-placed belch. "The Indians didn't have guns, at least not at first, but they did have firepower."

I knew what she was getting at. "You mean fire power, two words, right? The wagons were made of canvas and wood, highly flammable."

She touched fingertip to nose. "And fire can also be used as a diversion, a scare tactic. That fence of theirs protects them, but it also makes them prisoners. So while they're scrambling to put out said fire, we can attack, subdue them."

We were all nodding and smiling at her plan, all that is save for Jackson.

"Why the long face?" I asked. "You don't think it'll work?"

He turned my way. "What happened to the Indians in the end?"

And suddenly my smile flattened. "Massacred, lost everything, the survivors made prisoners. Because—"

"Because," he said, finishing my train of thought, "the white men, the Army, had weapons and training and numbers on their side."

"But we have the numbers now," I reminded him. "There are way more zombies than humans."

"Slow-moving zombies." It was his turn to do the reminding. "In a confined space, fine, I'd give them the victory, but the desert is anything but confined. And you might have surprised them before with a zombie attack, but now they'll be better prepared for one. The Army at least *tries* to learn from its past mistakes. As far as we know, they might have even laid traps for them now, for us. That would be easy enough to do."

Max looked over at him. "So what are you saying, Jackson? There are too many hurdles to clear here? One mistake and we're done for?"

Though, at last, there was a twinkle in his eye. "Well now, I didn't say that. I'm just laying our cards on the table here. And from where I'm sitting, we still have the better hand. We just need an ace or two up our sleeves to take the pot, is all."

"And where do we come by these aces?" asked Kit as she busied herself making lunch for the group of us.

And his twinkle went all supernova. "I'm working on it," he replied, pointing to his forehead. "But I think I might have a few ideas."

Kit turned and clapped her hands.

"He said *think* and *might*," I reminded her. "Not already *had*."

"I heard him," she replied as she reached into a cabinet above her head. "I was clapping for these!"

And in her hands were now two bottles of vodka. And yes, Blondella and I promptly joined her in her applause. Because, while we weren't as adept in our poker analogies as was Jackson, *booze* we knew.

"Liquid lunch," sighed Blondella. "Oh how I missed it."

"Cheers to that," I said, already searching for the glasses.

"It's not even noon yet," Jackson had the nerve to remind us.

Blondella paused, but only momentarily. "Liquid *brunch* then!"

Kit set the bottles down. "And we have eggs and sandwich fixings and orange juice."

"See!" added Blondella.

I patted Jackson's hand. "Stick with us, kid," I told him. "You'll learn."

He stared at my hand on his. "That's what I'm afraid of."

Blondella was already mixing the orange juice and vodka together. "See, you're learning already."

\* \* \* \*

We ate our brunches in the living room—well, ate *and* drank, of course. Outside, we could just barely hear Creature, though the groan of the zombies came through loud and blood-curdlingly clear.

"You do realize," said Blondella, "that all our futures rest on a drag queen who has built a career on lip-synching to Britney Spears, right?"

Kit chomped on her sandwich. "Well, if it was good enough for Britney…"

I laughed, but it was either that or cry, and since I still had a bit of eyeliner on, crying didn't seem like such a swell idea. In any case, it wasn't all that long before the front door slowly opened and in Creature Comfort trudged.

We all stopped eating and looked up at her with hope in our eyes. "Well?" asked Max. "What did they say?"

"Mostly… groan," she replied.

"Yes," said Blondella. "But groan in approval or disgust?"

"Disgust?" grunted Creature.

"Yeah, for that outfit of yours. Clearly, you're not an autumn, dear one."

At that, Creature managed the slightest of grins. "Least… mine… fits… right."

"Tie!" I shouted. "Just tell us what they said and/or groaned,

160

Creature, please."

Her grin remained, but if it was locked in rigor mortis or not, well, that was hard to tell. And so I sat on pins and needles waiting for her reply, one that I knew would forever seal my fate, all our fates for that matter.

"Hard… to… say no… to such a… pretty face."

Ironically, Blondella and Kit and I all replied to that in unison. "Tell me about it." Because great drag minds do think alike, especially while they're swimming in cheap vodka.

"So they'll join with us?" asked Jackson, clearly confused at the turn in the conversation. "Of their own accords?"

She nodded, sort of, and replied, "Zombie… prisoners… in camp… are their friends… and family."

So they, like us, had a reason to win this war of ours, but that also meant that we had more people to keep alive now, whatever that word meant anymore. And a war without casualties seemed as likely as those bottles of vodka remaining full.

In other words, good luck to us.

# CHAPTER FIFTEEN
## ROSE-COLORED GLASSES

While the men worked out the plan, the queens lounged—as all great queens do—on the veranda, cocktails in hand. Though replace veranda with dirt-covered backyard and cocktails with vodka-filled mason jars, and you'd be much closer to the truth of it. Sadly, Creature remained sober and standing, the latter because she had little choice and the former because none of us had a clue as to how the radiation would mix with the booze. Though probably, we figured, it would be in a rather sizzling mess.

"So you and Max, huh?" said Blondella, turning my way.

I smartly and rather quickly changed the subject, looking to Kit instead. "So you and Steve, huh?"

Her face momentarily froze before her neck jerked Blondella's way. "So you and Johnny, huh?" To which she added, in the apparent hope of locking the conversation in, "Have you heard from him again?"

Blondella sighed and took a mighty gulp of her drink. "I can't get any signal out here. No bars." She smirked and pointed into the kitchen, to the vodka bottle on the countertop. "Well, *almost* no bars." Then she set the glass down on a plastic lawn table and looked our way. "I, um, well… *thank you*, by the way." And through the numerous layers of makeup I could just about make out the uncharacteristic look of gratitude on her face. Had it not been sweltering out there, it might've given me the chills.

"For?" I asked.

"You know what for."

I nodded and reached over to pat her hand. "Johnny?"

Her head tilted back into the lawn chair. She sighed as she said his name, the word more like a purr. "*Johnny.*" She shut her eyes and, if miracles could still possibly occur, which I had serious doubts about, she removed her wig. "Don't even think about saying anything," she cautioned, mainly because none of us had ever seen her without one on before, or her makeup for that matter. Heck, we didn't even know her boy name. So maybe this wasn't a miracle, like, say, the parting of the Red Sea, but it was something akin to it. Let's call it the parting of Blondella's hair, said part running down the center of the top of her head, thinning blond strands on either side. If it was dyed that color, I wasn't about to ask—think, yes; ask, no fucking way.

"God, it's hot out here," she added, and rightly so.

I nodded. "How did you two meet anyway?"

She chuckled as she scratched her head. "His salvage work is backed by some rich guy in Napa. Johnny was in town for a meeting with him, caught my act, and the rest is history."

"How long ago was that?" asked Kit.

Blondella's eyes popped open as she turned Kit's way. "Ten years ago." She did some counting on her still-somehow-manicured fingers. "In two months from now." She took another healthy swig of her drink and continued. "I see him every month or so, when he comes for a meeting or when we're on the road, doing the act out east." And then I stared in shock as her lower lip began to quiver. "I…" Her eyes began to water, and when you're wearing that much mascara, crying is a definite no-no. "I love him, you know." And then a tear welled up and over, a crooked black line zig-zagging down her face. "So, um, again, *thanks.*"

It was Kit's turn to lean over, Blondella's other hand patted, which was yet another miracle in less than a few minutes—which could only mean the end of the world, if the world hadn't already come to an end already, that is.

"We'll get you to him, girl."

My hand kept patting. "We will; I'm sure of it."

She wiped her eyes and managed a smile. "You are?"

I shrugged. "Well, maybe not *sure* so much as, well, *determined.*"

And it was then, during our virtual lovefest, that Creature cleared her throat and barked, "Problem."

Our hands stopped patting as the three of us slowly looked her way. "Another one?" I asked. "Haven't we already met our quota?"

She shook her head, mostly, and replied, "Medicine... wearing... off."

My heart suddenly stopped beating as a torrent of flop-sweat plunged down my face. "No," I croaked out.

"Yes," she rasped, the word tearing through me like a dagger.

Kit raised her hand. "So let me get this, for lack of a better word, *straight*," she said. "You're turning back into a zombie? Then the rest of the town will do the same? And without you to tell them not to, they're going to dig into us like a Las Vegas buffet?"

"All... you can... eat," she replied. "Yes."

"Fuck," cursed Blondella. "How long?"

Creature managed a half-shrug. "Soon."

"So we'll get you more iodized salt," I said, wiping the waterfall off my face as best I could.

"None... left."

I turned to the others. "Jackson said that there was radiation sickness medicine in the camp."

Blondella frowned. "In the camp, behind the gate, guarded, at least for now." Her frown got joined with a groan. "And not to rub, again for lack of a better word, *salt* into the wound, but what if *we* need that medicine? What if the army finds that we've all been radiated to the point of sickness?"

I finished my drink with a hardy gulp. "Then we steal all they have and hope for the best. Not like we're eating fresh food or drinking unbottled water, so at least we're not ingesting any more radiation than we've already been hit by."

"And our hair's not falling out," added Kit. "Apart from Blondella's."

"That was a wig," Blondella hissed.

Kit chuckled and pointed. "I meant *beneath* the wig, sugar." And so much for that aforementioned lovefest. Guess we also met our miracle quota.

I stood up. "In any case, Creature needs the medicine more than we do for now, as do, I'm afraid, the townsfolk, so long as we're all together like we are. As for us, let's just hope there's enough medicine to go around, or better yet, we don't even need it. For all we know, the radiation already dissipated." I looked at my recently zombified friend and grimaced. "But most of all, let's hope we get to that medicine before she, uh, *turns* again."

"Yeah," said Kit, a wagging finger aimed Creature's way. "This buffet is closed, hon."

Creature managed a chuckle. "Waste… of a… waist."

"Good one," I whispered.

Though not good for us.

No, sir, no how.

* * * *

We regrouped, no happier than before, but at least with a little buzz on. Then we filled the guys in on our latest dilemma.

Thankfully, Jackson replied with a cocky smile and a completely drawn-up plan held out for closer inspection. I grabbed it and said, "How did you manage to work it all out that quickly?"

He pointed to the empty bottle of vodka. "You finished that off and left us with nothing but this." He then pointed to the equally empty bottle of Jolt Cola.

"Ah," I ahed. "Brain lube."

He strummed his fingers on the table as his leg bounced beneath it. "Something like that. In any case, if the plan goes as planned, we'll have the radiation sickness medicine before sunrise tomorrow. Then *home*." It was another word that came out like a purr. I prayed he'd have better luck with his home than we had with ours. Then I prayed that someone was listening to all those prayers that we'd been making as of late.

"Tonight?" I thought to ask. "So soon?"

Max nodded, pupils dilated, knee also bouncing. "No time like the present. Besides, now we really are under a deadline, if you'll pardon the expression."

"*Dead*line," grunted Creature. "Funny."

She said it, not me. Guess her humor had grown darker since she, uh, died. Go figure. "So when do we start?" I asked.

Jackson rose from the table. "Now."

"Suddenly, my buzz got killed," I lamented.

"Killed," grunted Creature. "Funny."

This time when she said it, I gulped. Because it really wasn't funny. None of it. "Yup," I said. "*Now* would work." I turned to

Jackson. "What do we need to do?"

He grinned. Clearly, as a mere private, he was well-accustomed to following orders; now he was in charge. Better him than me, I figured. In any case, he handed each of us a list of our duties before we split up.

I went with Max, Kit went with Steve, and Blondella and Jackson lifted up Creature and rushed out the door, with Jackson shouting over his shoulder, "Good luck. And hurry!"

"No duh," I muttered as I stared at the list, then over to Max. "Is he kidding with this?"

"Why?" asked my overly caffeinated partner.

"Lighter fluid, fine. Gallons of it even, fine. But six bows and as many arrows as we can find? Where are we going to find six bows?" I asked. "There's one store in this town, and I doubt they even have six bows for your hair, let alone six to shoot arrows with."

He leaned in and kissed me. "You know, you're awfully cute when you're frenzied."

I grinned. "You should see me when I'm harried then. Or manic. Then I'll go all GQ on your ass." But my grin promptly faded, right along with my hope. "Anyway, cute ain't gonna cut the mustard right about now."

He kissed me again, my lips buzzing upon contact. Then he pointed down the street to a longish building across a field, then at the smaller building beyond that. "Bet that's the school and the gymnasium."

"Okay, and?"

He sighed. "Where's Kit when you need her?"

My shoulders scrunched. "Please don't say that while you're kissing me." In any case, it was then I figured out what he was getting at, without the help of the chocolate-infused Einstein I called a friend. "Gymnasium. Like where they keep the kick-balls and the gym mats and the, fingers and innumerable toes crossed, archery equipment."

"*Ding, ding, ding,*" he said. "Cute and smart and all mine."

Then, suffice to say, there was a pause. A big one. One you could drive a Mack Truck through. "That the caffeine talking?" I managed, heart suddenly pumping fast.

He grinned and stroked my cheek. "The world went berserk, and still we found each other, Destiny."

My heart rate cranked up another notch. "Pretty romantic."

He put his fingertip on my nose. "Pretty." Then he put it on his nose. "Romantic." Then he kissed me so adeptly that that pumping heart of mine literally skipped a beat. "A perfect fit."

"Perfect, except for the army, the radiation, and the zombies."

He shook his head and pulled me into him. "Nope. Still perfect," he whispered, the kiss repeated and repeated and repeated again. When he pulled way, if only by an inch, he added, "And all mine?"

Fine, so it wasn't the best timing, what with, well, *everything*, but better late than never, I figured. "All yours," I readily replied, no pause needed this time. And suddenly I felt like Cinderella. Heck, I even had the two ugly stepsisters to go along with it. Throw in a pumpkin and a couple of rats, and we'd be good to go. Though maybe subtract the few billion zombies first.

So on to the school we went, so wet with sweat that we could've formed our own collective river. Still, we didn't have far to walk, and luckily, the gym was open, as was the equipment room.

"Well, I'll be," I exhaled, a grin working its way up my face.

Then he counted our find. "Eight sets of archery equipment," he proclaimed. "Two more than we need." Max turned his head to the right, eyeing a garbage can on wheels. "And something to carry it all in. See, things are looking up, Destiny."

Not that I don't so love the color rose, but I knew better than to tint my glass in said hue. "Fine, Max, one step forward, and for now, I won't point out the obvious few hundred steps back."

He patted my sweat-covered shoulder. "That's the spirit." He started to reach for the bows and arrows. "Now start loading. All we need is the gasoline and some rags, and our list will be all checked off."

I snapped my fingers and turned. "The field between the school and the gym, it's a football field."

He also turned. "Uh huh. And?"

I crossed my arms over my chest, all proud-as-a-peacock-like. "And a football field needs to be mowed, right?"

It took him a minute, but he got where I was going with it. "And a mower needs gasoline. Brilliant! I must have the smartest girl-boyfriend on the planet."

I nodded, then shrugged. "Or possibly the only girl-boyfriend left on the planet, but I'll take what I can get."

And wouldn't you know it, but not thirty minutes later, we'd returned to town with a garbage can full of archery bows and arrows and gasoline and rags. Then all we had to do was find the others, which wasn't as hard as expected.

Steve and Kit were coming from the opposite direction, backpacks flung over their shoulders, whatever it was they were searching for also apparently found. "What's going on here?" asked Kit, the four of us closing in on the now-densely packed and groaning crowd we found upon our return.

"Prayer rally?" I guessed.

"Doubtful," said Steve, leading us through the milling zombie throng. And no, even rose-colored glasses couldn't have made that scene any prettier.

When we reached the front of the line, we found Blondella and Jackson and the leader of this odd assortment of, um, humanity, namely Creature. The first surprise, apart from having a hundred or so zombies standing directly behind us, was that Jackson had a welder's mask on and was busy blowtorching his way through the crumpled water tower. The second surprise? Well, it was more like a bombshell, as in Blondella Bombshell. Because she too had a welder's mask on and was also blowtorching. Fine, the beginning part of that word I could see, the blowing part, but the ending? Um, nuh uh. And yet, there she was, torching away, wig flowing out and around the steel mask, all Rosie the Riveter like.

"What gives?" I asked Creature.

Slowly, she turned and pointed at the tower. "Steel… is… mostly… bulletproof."

I grinned, despite the circumstances that surrounded the need for all this. It looked like there was enough brilliance to go around, after all. "But won't that take forever?"

She slowly turned back my way. "Work… in… shifts."

And my grin promptly vanished. "In this heat?"

"Better… than a… bullet… through you… right?"

She had me there.

It was then that Blondella stopped and lifted her mask, makeup even more of a fright than the horde behind us. Well, maybe not more, but pretty close to it. "Don't I butch up nicely?"

Kit leaned in. "Did you say butch or bitch, girlfriend? Because you've been bitched up nicely for years."

Blondella sighed and rose from her crouched position. She then handed Kit the torch and the mask. "Watch out for the sparks, hon. *Fat* is flammable."

Kit snatched the equipment and reluctantly took her place before the twisted mess of metal, while Max tapped Jackson on the shoulder and soon did the same.

"You're back already?" asked Jackson. "Things go well?"

I pointed to the garbage can, while Steve jiggled their purloined backpacks. "So far, so good."

Jackson nodded and pointed to the sparking steel. "And still so far to go." Then he rested his hand on Creature's shoulder. "Your turn."

"Her turn?" I asked. "What is she going to collect?"

Jackson smiled. "*Them.*" Oddly, he was pointing to the undead crowd. Not so oddly, my stomach did a series of backflips, all scoring perfect tens from the judges.

"Them?" I asked nervously.

He nodded. "Watch."

Creature moved a foot away from us and closer to the them in question. Slowly, bones creaking, she raised her arms. "We… need… all your… cars and… buses."

"Huh?" I huhed. "Why? And even if they get them, how will they drive them?"

Creature looked my way, eyes dead, face frozen, but still I saw something there, some spark. "Push… down on… my shoulders," she told me.

I shrugged and did as she asked, pushing with all my might, her body as rigid as the steel being welded by my friends. Or so it seemed. Because, given enough force, her knees began to buckle until her body appeared as if it were sitting, albeit without a handy-dandy chair beneath it. An odd look to be sure, but given how odd everything else was leading up to that, it paled in comparison.

Again she turned to the zombies. "Help… each other. Gather… anything… you can… drive… and line up… just… out of… town."

I sighed. "That will take hours to accomplish."

Jackson nodded. "So will this." He pointed to the crumpled tower. "In any case, we'll need the cover of darkness for what we're about to do, so at least we'll be killing time."

"Killing," groaned Creature.

"Killing," groaned the entire lot of them, mouths agape, jaws sagging, eyes unblinking, those backflips in my belly turning to full-on floor exercises.

"Hurry," I whispered, more for our sakes than theirs. "Before it's too late."

* * * *

The sun beat down upon us as the zombies ever so slowly dispersed, Jackson and Steve included, their remaining job probably the most difficult, even more backbreaking than our own. As for the rest of us, we toiled away, taking turns every twenty minutes with the blowtorches, our breaks indoors, air cranked up, water guzzled down, trying to replenish what we were losing through our pores at an alarming rate.

The hours ticked by, the fiery orb above us moving across the sky. Still, as slowly as it progressed, at least we were in fact progressing. The steel was giving way, forming into shields, small hand-holders welded on to each of them.

I tried to lift the first one up, which was about like lifting a car door that had managed its way off the hinges. "Um," I said to Max. "Not to rain on our pride parade or anything, but what good will they do us if we can't lift them up?"

Max grinned and pointed to Creature, who had remained with us all the while, standing there like a statue. "Super human."

I tilted my head sideways as I gave her the onceover. Was she even human, let alone super? And, if she was indeed human, for how much longer? "You lost me," I told him.

He bent down to the first shield. "Help me lift it, Destiny." I bent down on the right side, him on the left, and then we held it in front of her before she gradually managed to take a grip of the holder. When we let go, lo and behold, it remained, held up as if it were no more than a shield made of plastic.

"Too heavy?" I asked her.

She groaned. "I do… not feel, Destiny. It… just… *is*."

Max nodded. "I thought as much. And with her steely grip and fairly locked limbs, she and her friends can hold these shields up for as long as we need them to, for our protection and theirs."

"Brilliant!" I yipped.

"Must be contagious!" he replied.

"Like… herpes," tossed in Creature, that dark humor of hers growing all the more creepy as she slowly, ever so slowly, reverted back to her zombiehood.

"Um, yeah," said Max, prying her fingers off the shield before we set it back down and relieved our friends on the torch line.

This, of course, went on and on, twenty minutes at a time, over and over and over again, until our backs and hands were sore, the sun long gone, the stars twinkling overhead as the shields lay in a neat row on the ground.

"Are we done yet?" griped Blondella, looking about as exhausted as I felt.

By then, Jackson had returned, the zombies nowhere in sight. "Done," he replied with a barely stifled yawn. "Just finished loading the trucks. Now let's relax for an hour or so and put this plan of ours into action."

At hearing him say it, my belly once again tied up in knots, tight enough that I'd need a team of Boy Scouts to untie it all. "You, uh, really think it'll work?" I couldn't help but ask, staring down at all the work we'd done to ensure just that.

"It'll work," he replied with a nod. "It's late; we'll catch most of them unaware. We outnumber them now and have enough protection to guard against whatever they manage to throw our way. Plus, it's dark out, and all they'll know is that they're under attack by an unseen enemy."

Knowing the zombies like I now did, they might not have been seen, but I knew they'd be heard. That alone would give the Army pause, I figured. "But what if they're expecting us?" I asked just the same.

His smile grew brighter than the moon. "Oh, trust me, no way are they expecting us. Not all of us, at any rate. Not all of… *them*." He pointed out of town, finger aimed into the deathly silence of the night.

I knew the zombies were out there, waiting for the plan to unfold, but still my stomach remained tangled, twisted, and tied.

Because what if the salt wore off before the plan started?

What if it wore off and all that separated them from us was, well… *nothing*?

# CHAPTER SIXTEEN
# CIRCLING THE WAGONS

"Okay, then," said Jackson, clapping his hands together, the sound jolting me out of my groggy stupor. "Time to end this war."

We all looked from him to one another, none of us saying a word. After all, what was left to say? A prayer? Trust me, that's all I'd been doing as of late. Instead, we followed as he led, the line of us heading the way we'd originally come, down the center of town and then right on out.

And there, we found, is where they stood, an endless line of cars and trucks and vans and tractors and anything with an engine and some wheels, the metal on each dully gleaming beneath the overhead stars and moon. It was a caravan of both death and hope. Such a strange dichotomy, I realized.

Jackson again placed his hand on Creature's shoulder. "Ready," he whispered in her ear.

"Ready," she echoed in return, the word seemingly harder than ever to push beyond her purpled lips. Still, she rallied. "Go," she then grunted as loudly as she could, one groan after the next suddenly rising up, trailing on down the line, the desert fairly erupting in it, the night wind carrying it along, until it was all I could hear, piercing through my very soul.

One by one the cars started, headlights purposely kept off. Then again, we knew where we were headed. All it would take would be a few turns, so that even in their stiff states the zombies could make it, could adequately both steer and drive with the help of whoever was in the passenger seat. Slow going, yes, but we still had plenty of time.

Or so we hoped.

As for us, we piled into a school bus, Jackson at the wheel as he zoomed through the desert, passing the zombies and taking his rightful place in the lead. I turned and watched the line that trailed behind us, the cars as lifeless looking as their drivers. Still, it was a formidable sight to see, this town on wheels, moving with purpose.

Max stared, too, his hand in mine. "It'll all be over soon."

I grimaced. "Any way to sugarcoat that remark?"

He nodded and chuckled. "It'll all be over soon… with us as the victors."

I gripped his hand harder. "Better." If only by a hair.

* * * *

It took us a good hour to get where we were going, to circle the wagons, as we'd put it; though, suffice it to say, we circled from a rather distant outer orbit. After all, there were still guards, and there was no sense alerting them to us. At least not yet.

The idling cars and trucks and vans and our one lone bus made a ring far out into the flat desert, the halo of light from the camp just barely visible in the distance. Could they hear us? It seemed doubtful. More than likely, we probably sounded like the desert wind to them, if anything at all.

"Ready?" asked Jackson, yet again.

"Ready," we all replied, my gulp repeating on down the line, hopping from one throat to the next.

"March," he then commanded.

We hopped out of the bus and scattered. There was, after all, still much work to be done, the zombies needing help to extricate themselves from their cars. After all, bending down was one thing for them, but straightening back up, well now, that wasn't nearly as easy. Though for that, we'd only need to right about a dozen of them, the ones we'd help in turn helping their neighbors, until all the vehicles were finally emptied.

That was the easy part. And, trust me, it wasn't all that easy. Talk about *dead weight*. In any case, we then ran back to the bus, which in turn drove us down to the flatbed trucks, each of them preloaded with cinderblocks. That was what Jackson and Steve had been doing while we were making the shields, their hands even more dried and cracked and shredded than our own.

I drove one truck, Blondella the second, Kit the third. Slowly, we made our way around the circle with Max and Steve and Jackson dispersing the blocks, one per vehicle placed in a zombie's outstretched hands. I stared at the clock on the dashboard; it was just barely four in the morning, still pitch black outside, the desert otherwise silent save for the hum of the endless array of engines.

An hour later, cinderblocks distributed, we'd returned to our starting point, to Creature, who'd been standing out in the desert, watching, waiting for her cue. "You're on, girl," I said. But she didn't move, didn't react, though her body seemed to be vibrating, like she was fighting something—or holding something back. I gently placed my hand over hers. "Almost there, old friend. Just this last thing. Tell them. Tell them now."

Her mouth at last pried open, that groan of hers revving up before going full throttle, sending a shiver up my spine as the word slowly formed. "*Go!*"

We knew what was happening without having to see it. One after the next, the zombies were dumping their cinderblocks onto the gas pedals, and then, again one after the next, each vehicle slowly began to accelerate forward, a steady stream of them, all pointed in one direction, to the bull's-eye, to the camp.

Could the Army hear what was coming? Probably, at least soon enough. But by then, they would be surrounded, not to mention mostly all in bed and asleep. As to the wakeup call they were soon to get, that we heard about ten minutes later.

*BOOM!*

It shook the desert, quaked the very ground beneath us—certainly my heart as it furiously pounded within my chest.

"So they did lay booby traps," said Blondella as we watched the fireball heave its way heavenward, illuminating the sky all around it.

*BOOM! BOOM! BOOM!* came next, spread apart, a siren suddenly roaring to life from deep within the camp, drowned out by the next *BOOM!* and the next and the next. Which meant that it was our turn to move, all of our turns.

The zombies were on foot, side by side behind their shields, while we drove the bus eastward. There was one gap we'd purposely left in our vast vehicle onslaught. After all, we couldn't risk hurting the prisoners, human and zombie alike. Plus, there would need to be an escape route.

"Look!" I soon shouted, jumping up and down as I witnessed the steely attack. "It's working!"

Though, again, I didn't have to see it since the evidence was quickly reaching my ears, loud and crystal clear. The cars and trucks and vans that didn't go up in booby-trapped infernos smashed into the gate before coming to screeching halts, metal twisting with metal as the gunfire got added to the aural assault. *Pop, pop. Pop, pop, pop.*

But what were they shooting at? Their wheels were spinning as much as the embedded cars'. After all, when one car hit, so did another and another, until a barricade was formed, and beyond all that were the zombies, their shields held up in case any errant bullets made their way through, unlikely as that now seemed. But as loud as the slamming cars and the siren and the bullets were, they were no match for the united groan that echoed throughout the desert: music, at long last, to my ears.

"They're trapped!" shouted Blondella above the din.

The bus zoomed through the gap and drove in parallel to the gate, just outside the holding pen, the one area where bullets weren't coming from. The human throng inside had grown since last we'd been there, the prison now full of solar-flare survivors, all of them just as confused as to what was going on as the Army was. As to the zombies held separately, their moans and groans joined with their brethrens' on the outside. They too wanted out—but to feed, of course. Of that, I was certain.

The Army was now running around, panicked, caught off guard, firing into the darkness, wasting valuable ammunition.

"Quickly!" shouted Jackson, pointing to a wooden building in the center of the camp. "Fire your arrows at that!"

We all had our bows in hand, six of us, arrows at our feet, all of them wrapped in gas-soaked rags. All it took was a match and, *poof*, flaming weapons. It was equally beautiful and terrifying to watch them as they streaked through the air, rising up before raining down, lighting the sky up as they began to hit their mark. One by one, those that didn't miss slammed into the wood, until, all too soon, the building was engulfed by flames.

We dropped the bows and emptied the backpacks that Kit and Steve had stolen. Inside were the four wire cutters they'd found. We tossed half of them inside the pens; the other half we used to begin their rescue, just before the armory promptly exploded.

In barely a minute, they came rushing out, at least the humans did, for now. "Behind the bus!" I shouted. "Run!"

They hurried past, all of us ducking and covering just before the loudest *BOOM!* yet. It knocked us off our feet, the blast like a massive bomb had gone off, which, all in all, wasn't too far off the mark.

Max turned my way, a smile widening on his face. "They're powerless now, surrounded, no weapons."

We could hear the shouts from within the camp as men and women ducked for cover, the bullets no longer firing, the groan of the zombies growing louder as they made their way between the vehicles, closing in, squeezing the Army into submission, a veritable tourniquet of corpses.

The last thing Kit and Steve had located earlier was lifted off the desert floor. It was a megaphone. Jackson held it up, flicked it on. "You have three minutes to surrender! We can hold the zombies off only for that long." He paused for effect, which I'm sure he achieved. "They're awfully hungry, by the way."

I turned to Creature, who was now hobbling our way. "Hungry," she moaned. "So… hungry."

I grabbed Max's hand. "Uh oh." His eyes met mine. "If she turns back now, she could set the others on us. She still controls them more than likely, even if their salt cures are still in effect."

We hadn't thought of that. Given everything else that had happened, it was a wonder we'd managed to get that far. I grabbed the megaphone. "One minute! You have one minute to surrender!"

I flicked it off and raised my ear up, listening for the surrender, gripping Max's hand as I listened and waited, holding my breath all the while.

"Hurry," whispered Max.

"Hurry," echoed Kit and Blondella.

"Please," I added, staring at Creature as she in turn stared into the oblivion. "Creature," I then said. "Creature, can you hear me?"

Her jaw slackened further, her groan the most terrifying one yet. I stood there, ready to run, when my ears were finally greeted by the Army's reply: "We surrender! Call them off!"

Oh, were it that easy.

"Run!" I shouted to the human crowd around us. "Back inside the camp! Now!" I took one last look at Creature. She, or at least the she that I knew, had in fact known for so many years now, was no longer there; in her place was the monster we'd found roaming the streets of San Francisco, her mouth agape, teeth exposed, the groan telltale.

And it spread like a command, like a… a… a *dinner bell.*

And guess who the main course was?

Not too surprisingly, the humans we'd just rescued were none too eager to return. Then again, they hadn't a clue that they'd just gone from the frying pan to the fire. All they saw was a means of escape, open desert as opposed to the confines of a holding pen. In other words, many of them went in the opposite direction, tearing off into the darkness—and straight into their bloody fates.

Those of us that raced forward, back inside the camp, into the pen, heard the screeching shouts and wretched screams a mere moment later. It was then I truly understood the phrase *blood-curdling.* Mine, in fact, curdled like so much cottage cheese as the shrieking quickly pierced my ears.

By then, my group was joined by at least thirty others, all of us huffing and puffing, eyes wide, covered in sweat and choking from smoke. I turned to Max as he turned to me.

"What do we do now?" I managed. "There are dozens and dozens of them now, all moving in and all obeying Creature."

As for her, she hadn't followed the escapees who had turned to appetizers. In fact, she was slowly making her way toward us, toward the apparent entrées.

"Girlfriend looks hungry," croaked out Kit, now by my side.

"Gross understatement," added Blondella from behind us. "Emphasis on the gross. And to echo Destiny's question, what do we do now?"

Jackson pushed his way through the newly rescued, newly screwed humans and pointed to a tent about thirty feet away. "The radiation sickness medicine is in there. We get to that, we can turn Creature back. In, um, theory."

I groaned almost as loudly as the zombies that were, even as we spoke, closing in. Because in order to get to *that,* we first had to get through the metal barrier holding us there, then past the military men and women who hadn't a clue what we were up to and who were still well-armed, and then hope beyond hope that the armory, which was still belching heavy amounts of fire and smoke into the air, wouldn't set us and the *that* in question ablaze, seeing as the two structures were barely fifty yards apart. The tent wasn't yet on fire owing solely to the fact that there was a slight breeze blowing in the opposite direction, at least for the time being.

"Find the wire cutters!" shouted Max. "Find them and start cutting!"

Seeing as those cutters were the only things standing in the way between us and the amassing horde, that's just what we did, the two we'd thrown inside the pen quickly located and passed along to Jackson and Max, who then promptly began to cut away. All the while, my heart raced as sweat stung my eyes. I turned, Creature now barely a couple of car length's away, dozens and dozens like her trailing just beyond, all moaning up a storm.

"Hurry," I whispered as I again turned to watch their progress. "Hurry up and cut."

The stench of the smoke and fire and undead made me retch, but at least my friends were making progress, both of them frantically cutting away until a small gate started to appear, a tiny doorway to safety.

"Done!" shouted Max as he scooted through. "Hurry, everyone!"

Which was about as smart as yelling *fire* in a crowded theater. Or *zombie* in a crowded holding pen. Either/or. Mostly the or. Because suddenly everyone was pushing forward, screaming as the zombies groaned even louder, their heavily veined hands now held up as they slowly teetered forward.

Max kept cutting from one side, Jackson on the other, both trying to widen the gap as the human side of things tried to escape. Sadly, all they managed to do was cause a logjam. No one was crossing the threshold, try as we all might.

That's when we heard the first God-awful shriek as Creature sank her teeth into flesh, whoever she'd caught quickly surrounded by more and more zombies, all of them chomping and groaning, with more of them filing into the pen every second.

Pandemonium naturally ensued, fingers ripping at the exposed metal ends, everyone trying to tear at the fence. Though, that's all we needed. The door widened, two feet becoming three, humans scampering inside, making room for more to exit as Max promptly yanked them out of the way.

I clawed and pushed and elbowed with the rest of them, figuring that it was every drag queen for herself. I was moving on pure adrenalin now as I spotted Max on the other side, though my vision was blurry with sweat. He was yelling for me to hurry, yelling for all of them to hurry. We, on the other hand, were just yelling, especially when more and more of us were falling prey to the eternally hungry undead crowd, blood now pooling on the dusty ground all around us.

Finally, I made it through, Max grabbing for me and pulling me into his arms. At last I exhaled, if only for a moment. "Where's Kit? Blondella?" Frantically, I turned this way and that, catching sight of Steve to my left, of Jackson as he finally made it through, then Blondella. "Where is she?" I shouted, panicking as the pen emptied out of humans and filled in with zombies, the latter pounding away at the fence, their purpled hands punching at the metal, clearly hungry for more and more flesh and blood.

"There!" shouted Blondella. "There she is!"

I stared, aghast, jaw clenched. She was trapped inside the pen, at least five of them descending on her, all of them pawing at the air around her, while she in turn swatted them away. Big as she was, she was also mighty strong, so at least she had that going for her. Still, it was all of them against one.

Astonishingly, it wasn't Jackson or Max or even Steve that came to her rescue.

"What the hell?" I managed, just as Blondella shimmied her way back through the hole. In her hands were two beams of charred wood that must've blown off the armory and landed by the fence. Her face was black with soot, her wig dangerously askew, her mouth in a ruby-red snarl.

"Get"—*swat*—"the hell"—*swat*—"away from"—*swat*—"her!"

Wood met flesh and bone in brittle crunches as, one by one, the zombies staggered, no one more surprised by Blondella's ferocity than Kit, who'd quickly grabbed the other beam and also started swatting. Jaws came unhinged, noses flattened, eyes gauged, but still they came, drawn to the two of them, to the smell of life—or possibly Chanel.

Max went through next, chain cutter in hand, then Jackson with his. The groans were nearly deafening now, but at least the space around the four of them had grown as the zombies got beaten back, falling to the ground, creating a barrier of downed undead.

"Run!" I shouted, noticing the gap that had formed around them. "Now's your chance!"

Max nodded and tapped Jackson on the shoulder. They were the first to turn and retreat, with Blondella right behind them, Kit just after her, my heart ready to leap from my chest as they sped toward the fence. One by one they dove through the gap, one by one clearing it, all, that is, save for Kit, who was instantly stuck. Or at least her wide expanse of ass was.

She looked up at us, panting, terrified. "Where's Jenny Craig when you need her?"

I grabbed one arm, Max the other, both of us pulling from the front as the zombies approached from the rear, Creature again in the lead, her face awash in blood and gore.

"Pull!" shouted Blondella. "Hurry!"

"Yeah," screeched Kit. "Listen to the bitch!"

Sweat again stung my eyes, but still I pulled, yanking with all my might until I was certain that her arm would come right on out of the socket. Fortunately, said socket was heavily padded. Which didn't prevent her from cussing up a veritable storm at us, all followed by that one miserable word: *hurry*.

Creature was still moving in as well, three feet giving way to two then one, bloodied teeth exposed, the groan intolerable. She bent down as best she could to grab at Kit's ass, which surely would've been a meal fit for, well, a queen, but just as her hand touched tushie, the fence at last gave way, Kit landing on our side of things with a thud and a grunt.

"Took you long enough," she panted as she spit out dust and debris.

We all crouched down to help her to her feet, the zombies again pushing at the fence, none of them able to bend low enough in order to breach the gap, try as they might. Still, to be on the safe side, we closed the hole back up as best we could.

With Kit again righted—or at least as right as she was ever gonna get—I pulled her in for a tight hug. "You okay?" I asked.

She chuckled. "I've been better." She turned and stared at Creature, who was barely two feet away on the other side of the fence. "But at least I'll live."

It was then that our ranks were parted, the camp's commander, the general we knew about, pushing his way to the front. "You'll live?" he barked, eyes mean, mouth twisted in rage. "None of us will live now. We're surrounded on all sides by them, with barely enough bullets left to do the slightest bit of damage, and certainly not enough food and provisions to make it past a few days."

Kit broke our embrace, the terror returning to it. "Please tell me you have chocolate though, sugar."

He paused, clearly unaccustomed to anyone like her, or at least anyone calling him by such a term of endearment. "Are you fucking kidding me?" He then stared at her, at the smudged mascara and equally smudged lipstick. Lord only knew what was going through his head.

Though she, of course, just grinned back in return. "Hon, I never kid when it comes to chocolate."

Blondella snickered. "Nope. Never."

The general sighed and pointed to the dense throng of undead pawing their way at the gaps in the fence. "Never, huh?" he said. "Well, never is coming all too soon, folks. Forever never, in fact."

I tapped him on the shoulder. "Um, excuse me, sir, but, well, maybe not."

He turned and gave me the onceover. "*Maybe* not?"

I nodded. "Like we said over the megaphone, we had control of them." I pointed at Creature, her hands through the fence, fingers twisting, desperate to reach us. "Or at least that one did. Or still does, by the looks of things."

At last, a smile broke free on his face. Not a pretty smile, mind you, but still. "Ah," he ahed. "So we kill that one and the rest will leave?" He pulled a pistol out of his waist holster.

"*NO!*" we all shouted in unison.

He fired. His hand jerked at our outcry. He missed. *Phew.* "Why no? You just said that that one was the leader."

I reached my hand down and lowered his gun with it. "Um, yes, well, *that* one is. But there's a chance that we in turn can control her. And if we control her…"

He nodded. "Got it. Then we control them."

I nodded, but then shook my head, realizing the implication. "Not we," I said. "Us. Me and my friends here."

Blondella tapped him on the shoulder. "Meaning, excluding you."

To which Kit couldn't help but add, "Hon."

Not too surprisingly, he didn't look at all happy at what we were implying. Then again, he was surrounded by the us in question, plus all the survivors from the pen, plus a surrounding horde of undead who were all clamoring to get to him.

"We're your best chance for survival, you know," he tried.

I shrugged. "Um, right about now, sir, I think we're *your* best chance for survival."

He holstered his gun and sighed. "Fine, then. What do you need?"

We all pointed at the nearby tent.

Just as the wind changed.

Just as the first spark from the still-fire-belching armory wafted through the air and promptly lit the fabric.

"Oh fuck me," I said, shoulders sagging, jaw quick to follow.

"I think you just were, sugar," said Kit. "And royally so."

## CHAPTER SEVENTEEN
## THE CURE FOR WHAT AILS YOU

"Water!" I shouted, my feet rooted to the ground as I watched the tent go up in flames, its contents presumably quick to follow.

Max put his arm around me. "It's too late, Destiny. It's gone."

Too late indeed, I figured sadly watching as the flames licked the sky. I turned frantically to the general. "You were doing research here, trying to find a cure. Did you find anything?"

"How did you know that?" It was then he spotted Jackson amongst us, anger again washing across his face. "You'll be court-martialed, Private."

Jackson couldn't help but snicker. "By whom, sir?"

I put my hand on the general's. He flinched. "Just answer the question, please, sir."

His eyes locked with mine. "We, um… we think so."

"Think?" asked Max. "Why think?"

"It's just a theory thus far," he replied. "We haven't had a chance to test it out yet." He turned and pointed to the holding pen that was still full of the zombies they'd previously captured. "On them, I mean."

Kit moved in a couple of feet closer. "All you had to do was give them the radiation sickness medicine," she said. "Barring that, some iodized salt."

He nodded. "We already tried both those things. They worked, but only for a short time. The salt has all been used up now."

I pointed to the wall of flames that was once the tent. "And so is the radiation sickness medicine."

He shrugged. "All gone, yes. Not that it would've mattered."

My heart literally stopped beating. "What... what does that mean? Why wouldn't it have mattered? Are we all going to die of radiation sickness anyway?"

He recognized the terror in my voice and, gratefully, mellowed down a notch. "No, not what you're thinking. Luckily, if that's what you can call it, all things considered, the flare lasted only a few seconds. The instantaneous heat killed every living soul on the planet that wasn't fully protected at the time, and then the just-as-instantaneous radiation burst somehow reanimated them."

"And that luckily part you mentioned, sir?" I asked.

He nodded. "It was over in barely a few seconds. Plus, our ozone layer buffered the radiation. It was just enough to trigger something in the dead, to bring them back, but it didn't linger in the atmosphere beyond that. So long as we don't drink water that's not in a bottle or eat any unpackaged foods, we should be okay; hence the radiation sickness medicine not mattering. We're, for all intents and purposes, fine." He grimaced as the roar of the undead crescendoed yet again. "Apart from them, that is to say."

Blondella tapped him on the shoulder. "But you said that you thought you found a cure."

He turned, his grimace widening upon seeing her smudged makeup and slanted wig. Had it not been such a lousy moment, I might've grinned—well, okay, so I grinned. But just a little. So sue me. If, in fact, you can still find a lawyer. In any case, he replied, "The radiation, it fried them, blasted them like a microwave would a Hot Pocket. But it also kick-started them and now seems to keep them animated, like a fuel source of some kind, a nuclear power plant on a human scale."

"So the radiation was like a switch," said Max. "Do you think the switch can go in reverse, from on to off?"

"Probably not," he replied. "The radiation will keep them alive, for lack of a better word, until it naturally runs out. The radiation sickness medicine and, to a lesser degree, the iodized salt, only temporarily thins out their energy source, thereby dezombifying them, turning them back into *almost* what they were before."

"Though not curing them from death," Steve added.

"No, of course not," said the general, with a heavy sigh. "It just makes them as human as they could ever hope to be again."

I nodded. "So this untested cure then, what is it?"

"Apart from water," he replied. "How do you stop a fire from spreading?"

Blondella raised her manicured hand up. "With more fire, sir?"

He managed a slight smile. "Exactly. Start a controlled fire and the raging one will stop when it encounters the former."

At last, the light bulb flickered above my head. "So you radiate them again? What if it just makes them even stronger?" I frowned as I stared at the teaming zombie horde, all of them pushing at the barely holding fence. "And stronger would definitely not be good."

His head shook in reply. "The radiation doesn't make them stronger, just undead. But another blast of it might short-circuit the first one and, maybe like with fire, keep it in check. In fact, we tested just such a thing in the lab and found that a second radiation burst did seem to slow down the first one, to rein it in."

"But you haven't tested it on a zombie yet?" I asked. "On one like... *her*." I then pointed at Creature, who groaned even louder when we all turned her way.

Again the general sighed. "No. Not yet. Only on zombie organs."

Jackson now chimed in. "But how do we radiate her, sir? I mean, safely, as in also not radiating us?"

"The control fire, you mean," he replied as he started to walk away from us, motioning with his index finger that we should follow, which we then did.

By then, the rest of the camp had again gathered, now that the fires had died down and the zombies were, at least for the time being, held at bay by either the fences or the stacked-up cars. They didn't look happy to see us, but also weren't firing their weapons at us, perhaps owing to the fact that both Jackson and their general seemed to now be working with us. I wasn't counting my chickens just yet in regard to the latter, but at least, the eggs were still incubating.

A couple of minutes later, we were entering the research tent en masse. The zombies and the dead humans inside were mercifully covered up. Still, my stomach grew queasy upon spotting their shrouded bodies. I looked around, wondering where this radiation source of his was, and quickly recognized it when it got wheeled our way.

"An x-ray machine?" I asked. "That's it?" I stared at it dubiously.

He nodded. "Like I said, it worked in the lab, tamped down the radiation within the organs, one wall of controlled radiation blocking an uncontrolled one."

I sighed. "Worth a shot, I suppose."

And then he sighed. "Our only shot, really. Because if those zombies breech the fence, we're all dead, and nothing is going to be bringing us back."

"Any way to sugarcoat that, sir?" I asked, which seemed to be the question of the week.

He shook his head. "All out of sugar, too."

Kit groaned and grabbed the portable x-ray machine. "Come on," she barked. "Let's get this over with. No sugar means no way in hell am I staying here any more than I have to."

"Amen," said Blondella.

"Amen," said I, but more because I'd just said a silent prayer that all of this was going to work out.

* * * *

By the time we'd wheeled the machine out, the fence was severely warped, ready to give way at any moment. I gulped and wiped the flood of sweat off my face as I scanned the undead crowd in front us, all of them pushing with the full weight of their bodies, desperate it seemed to get to us.

"The machine is battery powered," the general informed. "All you need to do is wheel it in and flick it on."

I coughed. "All *I* need to do is wheel it in?" I turned and stared at him, arms folded over chest. "You're kidding, right? That's like telling a kid to go whack a hornet's nest with a stick and promising him he won't get stung. And I ain't no kid, and they're certainly a lot more dangerous than a bunch of hornets."

"I'll do it," said Kit.

Blondella nodded. "Yeah, you go, girl."

Kit smiled. "Ah, bravery, my dear, is thy middle name."

Blondella was still nodding. "She who turns and runs away lives to drink another day."

And then I was nodding. "She has a point."

But Kit was already wheeling the machine toward the fence.

"Never mind," she said with a heavy sigh. "Here goes nothing."

We watched as she slowly made her way in, the zombies groaning louder and louder the closer she got to them, the closer her scent got to them. All the while, the fence creaked and rocked and shook and threatened to give way at any moment. When she was a few feet away, all the hands within reached out for her, hundreds of crooked and bent fingers swiping through the air.

She ducked behind the machine and pushed it the rest of the way until it was just in front of both Creature and the fence; then she flicked the device on. "Now what?" she hollered over her shoulder.

We all turned to the general. "Now we wait," he told us.

"Wait?" I managed. "Um, in case you didn't realize it, we're quickly running out of time here."

"Crank it to ten!" he shouted her way.

She cranked it and waddled in reverse, leaving the machine where it was. "I don't think it's working," she said, once back by our sides. "She still looks the same, sounds the same." She waved her hand in front of her face. "And damn if she don't smell the same."

We all turned and stared at our undead friend, watching and waiting with bated breath. And then, at last, the fence gave, teetering as the posts buckled and yanked free from the earth before falling over completely. The zombies trampled over it as best they could, pushing their way toward us, the communal groan nearly deafening now, the stench worse than a mile-high heap of garbage.

We started to retreat when all of a sudden Max shouted, "Look!"

I looked but saw nothing except the advancing undead, a teaming mass of lifeless gray and purple. "At what?" I shouted in return, legs quaking, chest rapidly expanding and contracting.

"Creature!" he shouted. "She's not moving! She's still in front of the machine."

He was right. The zombies were pouring in all around her, the fence leaning against the machine, but she merely stood there, stock-still. "Creature!" I hollered. "Wake up!"

All of us began to shout it, to yell it from the top of our lungs, us and all those standing around us. "Creature, wake up! Creature, wake up! Creature, wake up!"

The seconds ticked by like hours as we stood there, eager to turn and run but realizing that we'd in fact be running into the barricade that we ourselves created. Ironic, yes. So instead we kept shouting, hoping beyond hope that she could hear us, that she was fighting to come back to us.

In mere moments, the zombies were ten feet away, the throng tight, dozens and dozens of outstretched arms and hands reaching for us, teeth bared, the groan like that of a revving machine.

By then, we could no longer see the x-ray machine or Creature, the zombies now our entire field of vision, a grizzled wall of them—and a wall that was closing in all too fast.

"WAKE THE FUCK UP, CREATURE!" I shouted so loud that my lungs burned.

I fought to catch my breath, to shout it again, when, all of a sudden, the zombies stopped. It was as if a line of robots had all lost power at the exact same moment. Their arms remained outstretched, but their fingers were now still, as lifeless as their eyes.

And in the deafening silence that quickly pervaded the camp we finally heard it: "Stop."

"Creature?" shouted Kit. "That you, girl?"

We all craned our heads up, listening for a response. There was a pause, and then we heard her say, "Mouth… tastes… funny."

Blondella chuckled. "That's because you just ate some Chinese dude."

The pause repeated. "Hopefully… not hungry… in an hour… then."

Gross but funny. Very Creature. Thank God. "Call them off, please!" I yelled her way.

"Off!" she shouted.

The undead crowd shuffled left and right, a path forming between them, Creature dead-center, no pun intended. Her hands were wrapped around the x-ray machine as she slowly moved our way.

"Welcome back," I told her, keeping my distance lest the machine zap all of us as well. I looked at the general. "Can she flick it off?"

He nodded. "I believe so. The effect should last a few hours or so."

"There's a knob in front. Turn it to zero," said Kit.

She did as was told, and then we all circled her, all patting her back and shoulders. "You tried to eat Kit's ass," I told her.

Hard as it was to apparently pull off, she grinned. "Just lost… my appetite."

"Bitch," cooed Kit.

"Hell… yeah," grunted our long-lost friend. "Hell… the fuck… yeah."

* * * *

After that, we gathered the entirety of the camp, the humans all huddled together, none of them all too eager to mix with the zombies, who, for their parts, hung at the periphery. We released the ones in the pen as well once Creature informed them to lay off the grub, namely us.

Then it was show time.

And you know how much we love a good show. Especially when we're the stars.

By then, Blondella had located the megaphone and was standing center-stage with it. She flicked it on, lifted it up, and cackled, "Surrender, Dorothy." Then she giggled. "Sorry, always wanted to do that."

Kit sighed and grabbed the megaphone away; then it was her turn. "There is no Army, no President, no U.S. of A anymore. Just us, plus whoever else has survived, them and a few billion zombies. We're heading to New York, where we've been told it's safe." The men and women surrounding us frowned, clearly skeptical, and with good reason. "In any case, it's your choice: stay here and blindly follow or throw your fates in with ours and control your own destinies."

I grinned and turned to Max. "She never fails to amaze me," I whispered his way.

He nodded. "But will they listen? That's the question."

I moved and quickly stood by her side, Max next, Steve and Jackson and Blondella directly behind her a second later: a motley crew, to be certain, but a resolute one just the same. Plus, we had a not-so-secret weapon. "And wherever we go, *that one* follows," added Kit, pointing at Creature.

Not all that surprisingly, the entirety of the camp quickly took sides. Namely ours. Still, the general wasn't done just yet.

He grabbed the megaphone for a last-ditch effort. "We can still find a cure for this." And then he too was pointing at Creature. "When we do, we can wipe them out, start this country up again, unite as one."

"At what cost?" I shouted. "Will you risk more human lives? Kill endless zombies?"

He shook his head and wiped the sweat off his face. "They're already dead."

And I shook mine. "No, they are alive. Different than before, yes, but alive. They have the capacity for emotion, for intelligence. You don't want to cure them; you want to annihilate them."

"Before they annihilate us," he retorted.

The Army men and women grumbled, many of them nodding now. We were losing them. And so I asked for the megaphone. Reluctantly, it was handed over, and then I held it up in front of the one person who could best speak for the zombies.

"We wish… to live… in peace," she proclaimed. "Apart… from you."

My lips pursed. I flicked off the megaphone. "I don't think you said that correctly, Creature," I whispered to her.

She nodded ever so slightly. "Zombies will… always hunger… for humans. For… *life*. It is…what we are."

My hand trembled. "But you can change."

Her eyes locked on to mine, hers unblinking. Of course, it was something I'd been told before, her as well, so many of us in fact. "Do not… want to… change. Want… to… just be."

I moved in even closer to her. "But you're one of us, Creature. You're our friend. We love you."

"Then let… me go," she replied, her standard groan quick to follow.

My lip quivered, but I nodded just the same. After all, our ragtag group knew what it meant to be different, that following our own paths in life, however unlike everyone else's paths, was all that mattered to us, was in fact *us*.

"We'll miss you, girl," I managed.

"Duh," came her reply. "Lost… without… me."

I grinned and laughed. "But where will you go? And when?"

"Hold up… megaphone," she replied, and I did. "Follow us… to safety." Her voice boomed in all directions, monotone as it was. And I knew that her last word was the most important one of all, safety being the one thing the Army could no longer provide.

"How?" I whispered to her.

The slightest of smiles wormed its way up her otherwise stony face. "Have… an idea." Again her eyes locked on to mine. "For *all…*

of us."

* * * *

We—and by we, I mean every last one of us, humans and zombies alike, the general included, decommissioned though he now was—boarded our bus and their vehicles and any other cars that were still in working order, loaded them with as many provisions that we could lay our hands on, and set out, Creature now leading both the living and the dead.

Guess the meek really did inherit the earth after all.

Still, we had to move fast, seeing as the salt solution in the zombies would be wearing off in no time, just like it had done in Creature. Then there was no way of telling if they'd still follow or simply kill us. And, yes, that second thing seemed highly likely.

As for Creature's condition, we pulled over every few hours for a radiation burst, which seemed to nicely do the trick. That is to say, she didn't try to eat Kit's ass again, tempting as I'm sure it was to do so. Or, um, not.

Still, we were glad that we didn't have all that far to travel: just a little bit north and a little bit east really.

When the roads past the Mojave became car-laden again, we simply drove in the emergency lane or weaved our way on through. But it was the towns that were the worst. No, not from a danger standpoint, because all it took was a collective groan to go up on our zombie friends' parts, and the undead inhabitants would simply stay put. But it was still gut-wrenching just the same. See, it was then that we'd be forced to remember what had happened, that we had miraculously survived when countless others had not, that we still had futures, uncertain though they were, while all those that we zoomed past had none to look forward to; all that they had was death, in endless supply.

After the first few towns, the hordes like herds of cattle lined up along the sides of the road, their groans rising and falling as we sped past, I simply stopped looking. Instead, I moved to the back of the bus and rested my head on Max's sturdy shoulder.

"How long will they live like that?" I asked him, out of earshot of Creature. Though I was certain that she'd had the same thought. I mean, how could she not have?

He reached his hand up and stroked my cheek. "They'll go on until the radiation wears off."

My eyes gazed up at his. "How long will that be?"

He sighed, his hand now patting my knee. "Far past our lifetimes, Destiny. Far past our generation and many of the ones to hopefully follow."

I stared at Creature as she in turn stared out the front window. "You think that's why she wants to separate from us? So that she won't have to watch us all, well…"

He gave my knee a squeeze. "Or to simply not be reminded that she won't. At least not again for a very long time."

I sighed and closed my eyes, drifting off into silent slumber as the miles ticked by.

* * * *

When I awoke, the sky had turned a dusky pink, the caravan still rolling along behind us, a new state in front. "Welcome… to… Utah," Creature announced. "Hopefully… Mormons… all gone."

I grinned, that is until I remembered what she had up her sleeve. That is until I saw the signs leading us to her destination, hers and her people, with our own destination still vastly uncertain and such a long, long ways away.

After that, it didn't take us all that long to find what we were looking for. Turned out, Salt Lake City held for us what it had held for those aforementioned Mormons, namely salvation.

We kept on the back roads as much as possible, pushing our way through traffic when needed, thousands upon thousands of lifeless eyes watching us as we drove by. And then, as we neared the Great Salt Lake, we spotted what we'd come to find.

Creature slowly lifted up her arm and pointed. "There."

It loomed in the distance, concrete rising above the flat terrain, the massive structure growing ever larger the closer we go to it. When the road forked, we turned, speeding toward it now, rushing before the zombies once again turned against us.

We braced ourselves as the bus crashed through the gate and then skidded to a stop in front of a giant warehouse, the plant behind it stone-cold silent, barely a zombie to be seen. "They must've all been at work when the flare hit," I said, pointing ahead. "The plant must be full of them."

Max stood and walked to the front of the bus. "Then thankfully that's not where we're headed."

We exited the bus, the heat still strong but gratefully diminished. I squinted at the building in front of us as we made our way toward it. It was exceedingly long and unassuming, holding, we hoped beyond hope, the plant's lone product.

There was a set of double doors to the side. Creature took the lead, just in case. The zombies inside were ready to attack, until she raised her hand and commanded, "Stop." They did, we didn't, not until we were all inside, our troupe, with the rest of the town amassing outside, zombies and humans, all watching, all waiting.

I walked to the nearest crate, one of thousands upon thousands, and read the sticker plastered along the side. I allowed myself the slightest of grins as I exhaled before I turned and gave them all a thumbs-up.

"Iodized."

Kit placed her hand over her chest. "Thank God."

Still, my grin disappeared when my eyes again landed on Creature. I lifted my hand and made a huge sweeping gesture past it all. "Think this should do the trick?"

A hoarse chuckle escaped from between her purple lips. "Doing tricks… is my specialty."

Blondella and Kit snickered. Me, my heart was breaking. Though it was Max who quickly realized what the three of us had not. "Wait," he said. "Without Creature, we can't drive to New York; there's millions upon millions of zombies between here and there. Doubtful we'd even make it to Colorado."

But, as per usual, Creature was one step ahead of us. "Not… drive," she said, sidling over to Jackson, her bony finger lifted up to his dusty green shirt, to the splay of color across his chest, to one badge in particular. "Fly."

My jaw dropped. "Fly? What, a kite?" Again Kit and Blondella snickered.

Jackson crossed his arms over his chest and nodded proudly our way. "First in my class, *ladies*. Ace pilot, at your service."

Blondella tapped him on the shoulder. "*When* exactly did you earn that badge of yours, Private?"

His smile promptly faltered. "Um, about a month ago." He

dropped his hands to his sides. "But I've been flying that whole time. Weather test missions. And through storms, no less. And you can say what you want about the Army, but it does train us well."

I didn't have the heart to remind him that the Army had just been defeated by a bunch of drag queens, but he did have a point. "So you think you can fly us to New York?"

"No," he quickly replied.

"No?" Blondella whined, hand to chest.

His grin made a triumphant reappearance. "Well, yes. I know I can. But we're not going to New York just yet, remember?"

I nodded. "Kansas."

"Kansas," he echoed. "*Then* New York."

We made our way outside, heading for the bus and then the airport, which we'd seen signs for before we took the fork in the road. The humans were waiting for us. Again my heart stopped. Even if we could fit them all in one plane, I knew that Jackson's training couldn't have been in commercial aviation. No way could he fly a jet big enough to fit us all.

I started to explain the dilemma, to promise that we'd come back for them, but they beat me to the punch.

"We're not going with you," said a woman in the front of the crowd, their obvious spokesperson.

"I know, sorry," I said. "We can't fly everyone out of here all at once."

"No," she started to reiterate. "I mean, we're not going with you. At all."

I scratched my head. "I don't understand."

"You said there's safety in New York. For your sakes, we hope so." She then pointed at Creature. "But we know for certain that there's safety with your friend here. Safety for all of us. Albeit if we smartly keep a bit of distance." She then pointed to the massive building behind us. "And, for now, there's safety from the elements, stores nearby that we can raid for food and water, a start at a new life, a chance to perhaps find more survivors." She put her hand in mine. "Thank you for all you've done, but…"

I nodded. "I get it. And I understand." I turned to Creature. "Think you're ready for all this, Madam President?"

She smirked. "Not President. *Queen*. Besides… survived… you three. How bad… can… they be?"

I looked at Kit, her face smudged with a chocolate bar that she'd obviously found inside, and then at Blondella, wig righted but with a face only a raccoon could love.

"Good point, Queen Creature. Good point."

# CHAPTER EIGHTEEN
## ACROSS THE GREAT DIVIDE

The surviving humans were instructed to administer iodized salt to the undead townsfolk, pronto. Then the rest of us hopped on board the bus, the general to be our driver because we'd still needed Creature until we were safely aboard a plane. After that, well, fingers crossed. Because, as we'd been told, Creature really was the only sure bet these days. Odd, but true. Then again, pretty much everything was odd now, so why not that as well? Par for the fucking course, I say.

An hour later, we found the airport. We bypassed the terminals and opted for the smaller private jet area. It took us a while to find a way onto the field, but eventually, we found an open gate—that and a few hundred roaming zombies, all of them groaning up a storm when they smelled us approaching.

"Stop!" barked Creature when we opened the door a few feet away from a plane that looked promising, small, but big enough for five passengers and a pilot. When we debarked, she added, "Let... them... pass."

The zombies, like all the ones before, stopped dead in their tracks. Which was pretty much the only way for the dead to actually stop, we found.

"Please be a better Queen than you were a lip-syncher," said Blondella, hugging our friend goodbye.

Kit made it a threesome. "Couldn't be a worse one."

Creature grunted. "Bitches."

And then I joined the fray, tears streaming down my face. "We'll miss you, you know."

"I know. Take... care of... each other." Then she pushed us away. "Go now."

We nodded in reply, all of us wiping the tears away as Jackson ran up the stairs and poked his head inside the already opened door. He turned and smiled. "All clear. A six-seater. Looks like it was ready for take off before the flare hit."

I breathed a sigh of relief, however temporary it would be, then moved with our group to the plane and up the stairs, all our worldly possessions fitting into a few backpacks. With the other trio of men already inside, the three of us turned and saluted our friend on the ground.

"Long may you reign!" shouted Blondella.

"Check... mirror... Blondella!" Creature shouted in return. "You look... like... crap!"

Kit and I laughed. Blondella frowned, wiping the tears from here face. "I always hated her, you know."

We patted her back. "We know, girl," I said. "We know."

I waved and blew her a kiss, then we turned and boarded, Jackson closing and latching the door behind us. I spotted Max, smiling as he stood in the rear of the plane.

"Full bar," he announced. "What'll you have?"

Blondella plopped her ass down in the nearest seat, her finger held up. "One of everything," she replied. "And make it snappy."

I turned to Jackson. "Can you really fly this thing?"

He nodded. "It's not all that different from what I've been flying."

Steve popped his head up from another nearby seat. "Not *all* that different?" He quickly turned to Max. "Make that *two* of everything."

"Three!" shouted Kit, already locking her seatbelt good and tight.

Max nodded. "Coming right up."

Again I looked at Jackson. "You sure, kid?"

He put his hand on mine and smiled. "I'm sure, Destiny. Just relax and have a drink."

"Or three," I amended, doing as he said, staring out at the window as Creature stared back in return. *I love you,* I mouthed.

She nodded. *I know.* We both turned away at the same time, her to her future, me to mine. I prayed they'd both be good ones.

"Here you go," said Max soon enough, his voice soft, reassuring, as he handed me my drink before sitting down across from me, seatbelt fastened as we heard the plane roar to life, my heart right along with it.

I turned to him and forced a smile. "Thank you."

He nodded, knowing that I meant *thank you* for more than just the drink. "Thank *you*," he echoed, the plane suddenly jerking forward as it headed for the runway. He held his free hand in mine, both reaching across the narrow aisle, as we each took healthy chugs of our cocktails. "Think he can really fly this thing?"

I shook my head, the drink promptly finished. "Nope."

He finished his as well. "Me neither." He laughed and blew me a kiss. "Nice knowing you, Destiny."

"Ditto, Max."

And then, *ZOOOM*, we hit the skies.

\* \* \* \*

By the time the plane leveled off, we were all on our second round. I unbuckled my seatbelt and headed for the cockpit. "You doing okay?" I asked.

Jackson nodded. "The tank is full, and this thing practically flies itself."

I gulped. "Nice, but I'd rather you flew it."

He grinned and gave me the thumbs-up, while I sat in the co-pilot's seat and stared down. Too bad I didn't exactly like what I saw. The world, it appeared, had stopped. No cars moving, no animals, no life. Though plenty of death, of course. Death everywhere, in fact. The suburbs were teaming with it, zombies like swarms of ants, massing together as they apparently sought out my kind, all while the sky grew inky blue around us, the last vestiges of pink dwindling fast.

"You okay flying in the dark?" I hazarded to ask.

He chuckled and pointed to the vast array of buttons and dials and monitors. "Doesn't matter. I found the coordinates for a private field near my house. All I have to do is land it when we get there. Easy as one, two, three."

I grunted. "Then let's hope you land as good as you count. In fact, let's take out the three and stick with one and two, just to hedge our bets."

\* \* \* \*

Though, in fact, the landing turned out to be the only thing easy.

Because, without Creature, we had no protection save for the few water guns we had in our backpacks. And, yes, we probably could've turned another zombie, like we'd turned Creature, seeing as we'd brought plenty of iodized salt, but how cruel would that have been to turn someone just so they could slowly unturn after we left them there? Besides, we figured, one Queen Bitch was all the world could handle right about then. So that was a Plan B, held for a just in case.

Anyway, all we had to do was go the ten miles to his house and then the ten miles back before heading to New York.

Not like there were all that many people in the boonies of Kansas, right?

Um, we'll go with right on that one.

At first, that is.

In any case, just a few of them were ambling about once we landed. They were easy enough to dispatch, sending them to their maker with barely a few squirts. Then all we had to do was steal an SUV that seated six, also easy enough, and drive through the black of night down a few basically barren roads, the cars we passed all stalled, zombies forever trapped inside.

Max sat in front with Jackson. "You doing okay?" he asked our pilot friend.

We all tensed, waiting for an answer. "I know what I'm going to find," he replied, quietly. "But I have to see it for myself just the same. Closure."

I nodded, remembering the promise that I'd made him, the reason we were there. "We're just glad we can be here for you, Jackson," I told him, patting him on the shoulder. Then I turned to Blondella. "Have you tried to reach Johnny again?"

She frowned. "There's no connection anymore."

My frown mirrored hers. "So you just need to recharge your phone then."

She turned her head and stared out the window. "No, my phone's fine. It powers up and I can still see everything stored on it. Just no connection. Meaning…"

Kit finished her train of thought. "The phone company went offline."

Blondella grunted. "Has to be. Maybe there was some sort of glitch, and without any humans around, there was no way to fix it."

"So we try a different phone," I suggested.

Again she turned her head my way. "I tried using the general's back on the bus. It was working, but it wouldn't connect to Johnny. Then I remembered that we use the same company. If I'm dead, so is he." Her frown sunk farther. "Sorry, bad choice of words."

Jackson spoke up from the front seat. "The GPS worked on the plane, so at least some of the satellites must be back up and running. Try to email him. Or check your email."

Steve reached into his front pocket and retrieved his cell phone. "Worth a shot." He handed it to her. "Check your email."

Which she did, and her Facebook, and her Twitter. But there was nothing, nothing past the second the flare hit. Still, she sent him an email telling him that we were coming, that we'd be there within a day, that we'd meet him at Perry Ellis Land, whatever or wherever that was.

"Fingers crossed," she said, handing Steve back his phone.

Though I knew we'd need a hell of a lot more luck than a measly couple of crossed fingers could offer. Heck, an entire field of four-leaf clovers wouldn't have been much of a help right about then.

And then, before we knew it, we spotted his house, the lights on, beacons in the night.

To be on the safe side, we pulled up about a couple of hundred yards away, so as not to alert anyone or anything to our presence. When we exited the SUV, the silence was oppressive, as was the stench of death, the animals in the surrounding fields still rotting away.

"Cows and pigs and goats," explained Jackson. "There are hundreds of them." He sighed. "Or at least were."

"Any neighbors?" I asked.

He shook his head. "Not for miles around."

"Thank God," I whispered.

Slowly, we made our way to the house, the six of us crammed tightly together, guns at the ready, eyes peering into the darkness as we listened for the telltale groan. And yet all we heard was the silence, deafening in its completeness.

We crept toward the house, the stairs creaking as we climbed them, causing the hairs on the back of neck to stand on end. Max took a window on the right, Steve one on the left.

"Nothing," they both whispered in unison as they stared inside.

Max turned. "But if the lights are on, they must've been home when the flare hit."

"Or survived and turned them on afterward," said Jackson, in a voice so quiet it was almost impossible to hear him. Though of course I did, my heart pounding in double time as Max tried the front door. It opened, another creak reaching our ears, breath catching in my throat.

We barely made it a few feet inside when Jackson's mom rounded the corner.

Or at least what once was his mom.

"No," yelped our young friend, hand trembling as he held the gun out.

A second groan started up, a man this time, obviously Jackson's father, then a third, a girl. She looked like Jackson only younger, and, well, sadly, deader. The three of them advanced on us, not a clue who we were, who Jackson was.

We turned, quickly, heading back to the front porch before slamming the door behind us, the sound of their fingers raking across wood breaking the stillness of the night.

Jackson was sobbing now, Blondella patting his back. "Fuck," he cried out. "We, we can't leave them like... like *that*."

I nodded. Apart from the fact that we were surrounded on every side by millions upon millions of undead, what was worse was that such a great many of them would forever be trapped in their cars and homes and offices until the radiation that flowed through them one day petered out. And what about their souls, if you believed in such things? Were those trapped as well?

And so I turned to Max and whispered in his ear, "We have to do this for him."

He sighed, turning his head my way, his hand suddenly in mine. "Take him back to the SUV. It'll just take me a minute."

"I... I can help," I told him. "If you need me."

He gripped my hand harder. "I'll always need you, Destiny." He managed a weak smile. "But Jackson needs you more right now."

My nod repeated as I herded the group off the porch, all of us trying to console our comrade as best we could. I turned just as Max raised one of the living room windows from the outside. He then quickly disappeared from sight, the groans soon reaching my ears, then not even that. Jackson's sobs grew louder and then abruptly stopped.

"Penny!" he suddenly shouted.

"Who…" I started to say, then remembered that he'd told me that he had two sisters, and the one we saw inside was several years older than ten.

He took off in a flash, disappearing around the side of the house, all of us following right behind him and, I was certain, praying. We stopped a few feet away, watching him as he miserably pounded on the storm shelter door that rose a few feet above the ground. Tears streamed down his face as the metal clanged beneath his fists.

But apart from that, there were no other sounds, the door remaining locked.

"Penny!" he shouted, over and over and over again, louder each time, until it felt like he was literally pounding on my chest instead of the door.

And then, in between one of the pounds, we heard it.

*Click.*

Time froze in that instant, none of us breathing or moving, the pounding ceasing as he backed away from the door, which all of a sudden flew up and open, light pouring out.

And then a girl.

Alive. Pink and perfect in every way.

"Penny," Jackson exhaled, his body now trembling, the look on his face like nothing I'd ever seen before, like a thousand emotions were all welling up in that one instant.

"Jackie?" cried the girl as she rushed into her brother's open arms. "But… but how?"

He grabbed her and pulled her in. "Doesn't matter, sis."

"Mom, Dad…"

He hugged her even tighter. "I know." He rubbed her back, just like Max, who had finished inside, was suddenly doing to mine. "But I'm here now, and nothing is going to hurt you."

He cried, she cried, we all cried, every last one of us.

That is, until we heard the familiar sound, the groan loud and getting louder, echoing out into the otherwise still night.

"Hurry!" shouted Max. "Back to the car!"

Jackson scooped Penny up before we all took off. But they were already past the SUV, already heading our way, fewer than a hundred of them it looked like, but not a lot fewer. I realized that they must've smelled us, that they'd been coming for us as soon as we'd got there. It would always be that way. Always.

"What do we do now?" asked Blondella. "Run around them and circle back?"

Jackson shouted, "Too risky! Follow me!"

Again we took off, not to the house, thank goodness, but behind it. And I knew in an instant what he was thinking, the lake shimmering before us, an oasis of water. It wasn't very big or all that deep, but, I figured, it would be enough. And so we all waded in, until all of us were chest deep, Penny still held tightly in her brother's arms.

She screamed as the zombies reached the edge, the shrillness of it piercing my heart. Still they kept coming, unaware of what the water would do to them. And then, one by one, they went down, steam rising off them as a pile of death soon ringed the water's edge.

Then there was silence once again, save for Penny's sobs and our own heavy breathing.

"It's okay. It's okay. It's okay," soothed Jackson.

But I was beginning to have my doubts.

* * * *

An hour later, our group having grown by one, plus some of that one's belongings, we were again seated aboard the plane. It was late, we were all exhausted, and with good reason, so we had a quick bite and decided that it was best to finish our journey in the light of day.

Sleep came easy, suffice it say, but not without consequences. First were the nightmares, unseeing eyes piercing the blackness, the stench everywhere, groans at the periphery of it all. In truth, I thought it was my mind playing tricks on me. That is until the sun's morning rays filled the cabin, waking us from our slumber.

"What's that humming noise?" asked Kit, yawning and stretching from the seat behind me.

Steve jumped up and looked out the window. "Not humming," he said, head pressed to the glass.

I too jumped up and looked out. What we were hearing were their groans through the thick window and metal, an ocean of them in all directions, the hum like thousands of waves crashing at the exact same time.

"Fuck," cursed Blondella, also now at a window.

"Language," I reminded her, pointing at Penny, who was also staring out the window, eyes wide.

"Fuck," said Penny. "Not allowed to say it, but now seems a good time."

Smart kid. But had we merely taken her from one lion's den and into another? I turned to Jackson. "Well?"

He gulped and nodded. "At least the runway is clear."

Again, I looked out the window. He was right; the runway was fine. But there were hundreds of them between us and it. "So you're going to…"

"It's the only way," he interrupted, running to the cockpit as we all quickly took our seats and belted up. And by belted up, I mean, of course, we quickly fixed us some mimosas. Extra strong.

The plane roared to life, though it was completely surrounded by death. Gratefully, it momentarily drowned out the groans. I shut my window shade and downed my drink. Penny was sitting across from me. I reached over and patted her knee. That's when we heard the first clunking noises as metal met flesh and bone. *Clunk, clunk. Clunk, clunk, clunk.* Over and over again we heard it, the plane rocking as it steadily moved forward, my heart pounding louder with every body we hit, every life we re-snuffed out. I knew you couldn't kill what was already dead, but it didn't make me feel any better.

"Sing!" I shouted.

Not surprisingly, considering that the legend had already saved us once before, Kit belted out a lovely Cher tune at full voice, the rest of us joining in, trying as best we could to forget the noises outside, to not think of what would happen if the plane suddenly stalled.

And then, at last, we heard it, the engine revving, the wheels speeding ahead, zooming across the concrete. *WHOOSH!* And my head was thrown back, as was the remainder of my drink.

I opened the shade and stared outside as the ground below grew farther and farther away from us, the hundreds of zombies all lifting their hands up to the sky as if to say goodbye, farewell, *auf wiedersehen*, goodnight.

Blondella clapped. "Good job!" she shouted to Jackson.

But it was hard to feel happy as I looked out and down. Seemed like the dead liked to amass. We were flying low, so either all we saw were farms or hordes of them, tiny armies with no goal except to march, to seek out life—to seek out *us*.

I shut the shade and turned around to talk to Penny. "Your brother is a hero, you know."

She smiled back at me and nodded. "Funny, he crashed all his cars in high school."

My own smiled promptly faded, a gulp quick to follow. Figures we rescued the only ten-year-old left on the planet with a good sense of irony.

I held my index finger against my lips. "Maybe let's just keep that secret between you and me, kid," I whispered. "At least until the plane lands."

She giggled, retrieved an iPod from her front pocket, and handed me one of the earbuds as I leaned over and she leaned over. "Lady Gaga okay?" she asked.

Like I said before, smart kid. "A-okay, Penny," I replied, with a smile. "A-okay."

## CHAPTER NINETEEN
## HUDDLED MASSES

Hours later, we arrived, the plane starting a gradual descent. Once again, I made the mistake of looking out my window. Kansas was one thing—and one bad thing at that—but it was nothing compared to Manhattan. Cars were at a standstill everywhere, but now thousands upon thousands upon thousands of zombies were milling about as far as the eye could see.

*How can this be safe?* I thought to myself, certain that the others were thinking the exact same thing as they too stared out. The zombies, it seemed, were like circling sharks, and I, for one, was in no mood to be the bait.

"Hands up if you think we should go back?" I suggested, despite knowing how Blondella would feel about it. Not that her wrath wasn't something to be scared of, no, but at least she could be placated with just the right amount booze and pills; such could not be said for the undead.

Blondella started to reply when Jackson hollered from the front, "We had enough fuel to go from Utah to New York. Best we can do now is reroute to Boston or Philly, but what good would that do us? It's six of one, half a dozen of the other."

"So what do you suggest?" yelled Steve in return.

He paused before replying. "Find a small, regional airport and hope for the best. Find this Perry Ellis Land and this Johnny dude and start new, zombie-free lives."

Penny reached over and tapped me on the arm. "Perry Ellis Land? Never heard of it. And I got an A in geography."

I shrugged and turned back her way. "A friend of ours was able to get a message through to us that said that it was safe there; that's why we traveled all this way." To which I added, "At least, that's what we *think* he said."

She scrunched up her face, obviously in deep, ten-year-old thought. I stared at her as she stared at her iPod. Lady Gaga had given way to Miley Cyrus, and I, suffice it to say, had handed back the earbuds.

A minute later, she glanced back up at me. "Safe?"

I nodded. "That's what he said. That much we know for sure."

She smiled, radiantly, angelic in every way. "Um, I got an A in American History, too."

I hadn't a clue where she was going with this, if anywhere, but I humored her just the same. "That's, um, great for you, kid." Too bad there was no America left, though. In fact, all that remained was history.

She sighed. Clearly I was missing something. "Before, when Jackson led us to the lake, why did he do that?"

"Because the zombies are fueled by radiation," I explained. "And radiation and water don't mix all that well."

"No," she said. "I mean, *why* did he take us to the lake?"

I scratched my head. She'd lost me. Still, I replied, "Well, because it was safe."

The smile rose northward on her face. "And where did the immigrants go when they were looking for safety?" She leaned her face against the glass window and pointed straight down below us.

I followed her point with my eyes. Lady Liberty was standing in the middle of the harbor, almost directly below us, resplendent in the light of day. It sent a chill up my spine to see her there like that, a constant among the ruin. She was surrounded by water. She was... *safe*.

And it was then that my heart literally stopped beating, my brain suddenly tingling, every nerve ending in my body shooting off Fourth of July fireworks. "Ellis Island!" I shouted, jumping out of my seat. "Ellis Island! Ellis Island! Ellis Island!"

Kit looked up at me warily. "She's finally lost it."

Blondella yawned. "It was just a matter of time."

I unbuckled, jumped up, and punched her in the arm. "He didn't saying *Perry Ellis Land*!" I shouted, everyone looking at me now. "He said *ferry to Ellis Island*! The one place in New York that would be safe from zombies and large enough to house survivors!"

Blondella's jaw dropped. "How did you come up with that? You can't possibly have but two brain cells left, and one of them is dangerously close to flicking out."

Again, I socked her on the arm. Then I pointed across the aisle to the still-smiling Penny. "I didn't come up with it; *she* did!"

Blondella nodded knowingly, as did Kit. "Figures," they both said in unison.

I turned and hollered, "Circle back, Jackson! Go wide around Liberty Island, which you just passed, and circle over Ellis Island this time!"

The plane banked, as did my stomach. We all ran to one side of the plane, all of us staring down, first at the water, then at the green-tinted diva herself, then soon enough to the backside of Ellis Island. After that, the plane flew over the front side. And there, lo and behold, they were, a whole crowd of them, all shouting and waving and jumping up and down. And, no, zombies don't do any of those things. Thank goodness.

I turned to Penny. "You did it, kid!"

She smiled, looking at me with a big *like-duh* grin on her face. "Guess heroes run in the family."

Jackson hollered up from the front, "And so do smart-asses! But we still have a problem."

Kit put her hand up against the glass. "How do we get from here to there?"

"Bingo!" yelled Jackson.

Penny again stared out her window and pointed. "See that bridge?"

I nodded. "Looks closed."

She also nodded. "It is. We learned about it in school. It was built to carry stuff when they were doing work on the island."

I gulped. I knew what she was getting at, but didn't like it, not one bit. "It's long enough, but it's pretty narrow."

Penny shrugged. "Looks like a runway to me. And it's blocked off, so the zombies can't get on it."

I ran to the cockpit. "That's some sister you have there."

He grinned and turned my way. "And she's still alive and back together with me, thanks to you all."

"Yeah, we can do the whole mutual fan-club shtick later," I told him. "But she seems to think that that bridge down there would make a good-enough runway."

He stood and squinted out the window. "Huh."

I stood and squinted as well. "That a good huh or a no-fucking-way huh?"

He sat back down and shrugged. "That's a maybe-it'd-work kind of huh."

"Maybe?"

Again he turned and looked my way. "This is a narrow plane; that's a narrow bridge. But it is long enough for a runway. And it is empty." His grin looked remarkably similar to his sister's. "Besides, what choice do we have?"

I shut my eyes and counted to ten, then left the cockpit and joined my friends. "He said no problem. Now strap yourselves in and get ready to land."

I bent down to Penny and put my mouth up to her ear. "Did he really crash all his cars when he was in high school?"

She nodded and put her mouth up to my ear. "Yup. But if I had been in them at the time, it never would've happened."

I grinned.

Last time: smart kid.

And then I strapped myself in, good and friggin' tight, and shut my window shade. No way was I going to watch this landing of ours. I'd tempted fate enough over the past week, and I was pretty sure that it was mighty pissed off.

Seconds later, I heard the wheels go down and my heart rate ramp up. The air was blowing cold on me, but I was sweating up a storm. And then rubber met road. And I do mean that quite literally. Because though it might've looked like a runway, it was in fact just a road—and one with barriers on either side and deep, cold water just beyond that.

I grabbed onto the armrest, teeth gnashed together, eyes squinted tight, my foot pressed to the floor of the plane like it was pumping an imaginary brake. I counted the seconds down in my head as the plane slowed, tires squealing beneath us, wings miraculously hitting nothing but open air.

"Ladies and gentlemen," shouted our pilot. "Welcome to New York!"

"Screw that!" shouted Kit in reply. "New York, welcome us!"

\* \* \* \*

Jackson opened the door, lowered the stairs, and then turned our way, his smile so bright that I wished I had sunglasses on me. "Looks like we have company."

We all unbuckled and hopped up, seven of us craning our heads out the door, though one was craned farther than the rest.

"Johnny!" she shouted, pushing her way out.

She raced down the bridge just as a lone man broke through the dense throng of humans and raced up. I wiped a tear away from my eyes as I watched thirty feet become twenty, then ten, then nothing at all, until two men, albeit one in a fabulous wig, were holding on to each other for dear life, their lips at last desperately mashed together.

"Yep," said Kit as she walked down the steps.

"Yep?" I asked, following close behind.

She snickered. "Yep, Destiny, love really must be blind, just like they say."

I turned around and smiled at Max. "Uh huh, Kit." Then I tossed him a wink. "But ain't it grand?"

She smiled as Steve caught up to her and put his hand in hers. "It sure is, Destiny," she replied. "It sure as hell is."

\* \* \* \*

A week went by. We now had our own rooms, access to showers, to food, to shelter, and, yes, above everything else, to safety, just as Johnny had promised.

Seems like a lot of survivors, those few lucky ones, had had the same idea, to head out to sea for protection. And once all the zombies on Ellis Island had been, well, sent to their maker, there was indeed no safer place in all of New York to be than there.

We even had the use of a rather nice ferry, so raids back on the mainland were possible when we needed supplies. As for the other survivors out there, anywhere, we put the word out as best we could on Twitter and Facebook and in emails while they were all still up and running, hoping that if they could come, they would come. And on those we passed the message along: all are welcome, all will be safe!

Heck, we even had a next generation to take care of. Penny, thank goodness, wasn't alone. She had friends, other kids who'd made it through the storm, parents lost, friends lost, homes lost, but resilient in a way that only children can be—well, children and drag queens, to be precise.

As for us, I had Max, Kit had Steve, and Blondella had Johnny. Talk about your miracles. Plus, we had a captive audience. And I do mean that quite literally. Heck, we even had a stage, built right below Lady Liberty herself.

See, while the men were busy building a new runway on Ellis Island, because no way were we using that bridge ever again, especially once everyone saw that we'd cleared it by maybe a few inches on either side at best, we, um, *ladies*, were setting up camp on Liberty Island. Because the one thing everyone needed right about then was some good old-fashioned entertainment—or the next best thing, namely us.

We set up a curtain and chairs down below the stage and ferried everyone across. Penny had her iPod, and we found a docking station that could be hooked up to some speakers. And Ellis Island had a slew of display costumes that we could borrow from. In other words, that turn-of-the-century look was suddenly back in style.

Then it was just me and Kit and Blondella backstage, hand in hand, staring up at our silent greenish fourth. "She looks a bit like Creature," said Kit.

"Especially around the eyes," agreed Blondella.

"You think she's okay?" I asked. "Creature, I mean."

Kit laughed. "If I know Creature, she's probably got a similar curtain and a similar stage already built. Because she might be dead, honey, but the show *must* go on."

"Amen," said Blondella, hands held up in hallelujah praise.

"Amen," said I with a bob of my head.

Our eyes then landed on the plaque just above where we were standing. Blondella began to read from it. "Give me your tired, your poor, your huddled masses yearning to breathe *free*, the wretched refuse of your teeming shore."

Kit took the next line. "Send these, the homeless, tempest-tost to me."

And I finished it off. "I lift my lamp beside the golden door!"

"Nice," said Blondella, gripping my hand tighter in hers.

"And you can't get any more wretched than the two of you," said Kit.

"Bitch," the two in question volleyed back.

Penny started the fanfare just then, the crowd below loudly cheering, the familiar tingle rising up my spine before the curtain parted. We turned, hand in hand, we three Queens of the Apocalypse, as we now called ourselves, and out we stepped, into the limelight and into our futures.

# THE END?

If you enjoyed *Queens of the Apocalypse,* then please check out the sequel, *Creature Comfort,* or any one of my other novels:

*Sparkle: The Queerest Book You'll Ever Love*
*Divas Las Vegas*
*Hot Lava*
*Southern Fried*
*Queerwolf*
*Vamp*
And my erotica collection, *Good & Hot*

I am also the editor of the following anthologies:
*Lust in Time: Erotic Romance Through the Ages*
*Men of the Manor: Erotic Encounters between Upstairs Lords and Downstairs Lads*
*Best Gay Erotica 2015*

And feel free to visit my website for more on me, my work and my life: www.therobrosen.com

Or drop me an email at: robrosen@therobrosen.com

Much Love,

*Rob*